PETE
UNE,

REGINALD Evelyn Peter Southouse Cheyney (1896-1951) was
born in Whitechapel in the East End of London. After serving
as a lieutenant during the First World War, he worked as
a police reporter and freelance investigator until he found
success with his first Lemmy Caution novel. In his lifetime
Cheyney was a prolific and wildly successful author, selling, in
1946 alone, over 1.5 million copies of his books. His work was
also enormously popular in France, and inspired Jean-Luc
Godard's character of the same name in his dystopian sci-fi
film *Alphaville*. The master of British noir, in Lemmy Caution
Peter Cheyney created the blueprint for the tough-talking,
hard-drinking pulp fiction detective.

07299

PETER CHEYNEY

UNEASY TERMS

DEAN STREET PRESS

Published by Dean Street Press 2022

All Rights Reserved

First published in 1946

Cover by DSP

ISBN 978 1 915014 17 7

www.deanstreetpress.co.uk

CHAPTER ONE
LOVING CUP

THE wind came in from the sea, driving the rain before it. It descended in sheets beating down on the rolling Sussex Downs, forming little rivulets that ran swiftly down the gutters of the winding roads about Alfriston. The wind howled dismally through the woods that topped the long rise of downland behind the village.

Dark Spinney, the old rambling Alardyse house, stood on the hillside above the village of High and Over, commonly called Hangover. The high red lichen and moss-covered wall that surrounded the house showed dimly through the darkness; reflected fitfully the gleam of the lights of a car that came over the downs and wended its lonely way towards Alfriston. Inside, in the old oak-panelled wall, a wheezy grandfather's clock struck eight.

Viola Alardyse came down the winding stairway that led to the hall. She presented a superb picture as the light at the turn of the stairs from the shaded wall lamp fell upon her. She was tall, willowy; moved with a superb grace that caught and held the eye. Her hair was the colour of corn and the light picked out its russet tints softly.

She reached the bottom of the stairs, moved across the hallway, stood at the top of the small further flight of three open stairs which led to its continuation. Before her were the main double-doors forming the entrance to the hall. On her left the small oak wainscoted corridor leading to the garden path that led to the green door set in the wall surrounding the house, the door that looked out on to the dirt road running towards Alfriston.

She stood motionless, one hand resting on the bottom of the balustrade, the other hanging by her side. She wore a long black velvet skirt with a white georgette blouse. The ruffles about her neck and the full sleeves at her wrists were caught with black velvet ribbons. One small crêpe-de-Chine shod foot tapped impatiently on the floor. There were dark circles about her blue eyes. Her mouth – beautiful like that of all the Alardyse women – was set in a straight line, hiding the small pearly teeth.

She looked at the wrist-watch on her left wrist as if the process would stop something she desired not to happen. Then, after a moment, she turned, moved towards the corridor at the top of the hall that led to the drawing and dining-rooms. She was halfway there when she heard the door open at the end of the passage leading to the garden path. She spun round, came back. She was at the bottom of the stairs when her sister emerged from the passageway.

She said: 'Good evening, Corinne.'

Corinne Alardyse put her hands in the pockets of her wet raincoat. She stood for a moment looking at her sister through half-closed lids. Her expression might have been good-humoured or contemptuous – you never knew with Corinne. She was an inch or so shorter that Viola; dark, beautiful in an Italian way. Her grey-green eyes sparkled as if she was turning a good joke over in her mind. She began to take off her raincoat.

She said: 'It's raining damned hard outside. I almost got drowned walking from the garage. How are you, my sweet?' Her mouth twisted sarcastically.

Viola said: 'Are you being funny at my expense, Corinne? I don't think that I feel inclined for humour.'

Corinne hung up her coat. She took a cigarette case out of the pocket of her tweed jacket and a lighter. She lit a cigarette. She stood leaning up against the oak wall immediately opposite her sister. A suit of armour, worn in ancient days by one of the Alardyse ancestors, standing close beside her, added an almost grotesque touch to the picture. She drew a breath of cigarette smoke into her lungs, exuded it slowly through pursed lips.

She said: 'I don't suppose you feel particularly humorous at the moment, my sweet. But whose fault is that? Isn't there a bit somewhere about the wrongdoer always desiring sympathy?'

Viola moved a little. She said: 'I've never asked you for sympathy, Corinne.'

Her sister said: 'No? That's probably because you knew you wouldn't get any. Anyway, why the hell should *I* sympathize with you?'

Viola said wearily: 'I don't know. In any event I'm not asking you to sympathize with me. But I think you might at least tell me what's happened.'

Corinne moved away from the wall. She came closer to Viola. She stood at the bottom of the little flight of three stairs, looking up at her sister. Viola stood motionless above her like a statue.

Corinne said cynically: 'Of course, my dear, you want to know *exactly* what's happened. I bet you do.' She sank her voice. 'Well, I'll tell you. The boyfriend,' she went on regarding the glowing tip of her cigarette with equanimity, 'is just as tough as ever. In fact I would go so far as to say it looks as if he might be even more tough.'

Viola said: 'Oh, my God!'

'I don't see what good it's going to do you – calling on the Deity, I mean,' said Corinne amiably. 'Although I expect you feel like it. But there it is. There's the position in a nutshell. He says it's got to be like it was before. In other words, there's to be no reduction in the payment; otherwise –' she spread her hands. After a moment she went on: 'In any event I don't see what you've got to grumble about.' She looked sideways at her sister. 'I ought to be the one to grumble,' she said.

Viola said softly: 'Sometimes I think I'm going to end it all. It's wearing me out. Anything would be better than this. I don't see why you should object to that. It would be to your advantage, Corinne.'

'Perhaps,' said Corinne. 'But I'm not particularly keen on it being to my advantage. I'm quite satisfied with the situation as it is now. In any event, I don't see what you've got to grumble at. You're a damn sight better off than if the truth were to come out.'

Viola said: 'But he's always asking for more.'

Corinne shrugged her shoulders. She said glibly: 'Men always ask for more. They're like that. Anyway, you're a rich woman.' She looked up towards the stairway. She said: 'Oh, my God! Do you see what I see?'

Coming round the turn of the stairway was a figure. It descended the stairs slowly with mincing steps. The steps were all the shorter because the figure was wearing red-satin court shoes which were in the first place too large, and the heels thereon were at least three and a half inches high. The figure wore an extremely tight-fitting scarlet frock which was cut much too low, showing a too ample expanse of bosom. Its straw-coloured hair was hanging à la Veronica Lake about its shoulders. Its face was made up dead white, the eyes being encircled with middle blue and the lashes plentifully adorned with mascara. An almost perfect mouth had been painted in a bright shade of scarlet in a cupid's bow exaggerated to the point of burlesque.

The figure was that of Miss Patricia Alardyse, aged seventeen.

Corinne said: 'You little bitch! Go back to your room and take that frock off. So you've been going through my wardrobe again. And for God's sake go and wash that stuff off your face. You look like a tart.'

Patricia leant theatrically over the balustrade. She said in a dramatic voice: 'Corinne, haven't I read somewhere or other that in every woman there is something of the tart?'

Corinne said: 'At the present moment it looks as if there is a lot of it in you. Go and wash your face and take my frock off and put those shoes back where you found them.'

Patricia, leaning against the banisters in an attitude which she considered to be expressive of Miss Lake at her best, said: 'I'll be damned if I will.'

Corinne said angrily: 'You'll be damned if you *don't*. What do you think will happen to you if Gervase sees you like that. We shall have a lecture lasting for hours.'

Patricia said: 'I don't care. Strevens, the butcher's boy in the village, told me the other day that I was the very image of Greta Garbo.'

'Quite,' said Corinne, 'and two or three days before that the boy who delivers the newspapers told you you were like Lana Turner. Silly little fool! I'm sick of having my wardrobe raided by you.'

Patricia continued to descend the stairs with what she considered to be an air of dignity.

She said: 'Corinne, what you say leaves me quite cold. Your remarks pass off me like water from a duck's back. *I* know what the trouble is. You're jealous of course.'

She swept across the hall into the passage leading to the drawing-room.

Corinne said to Viola: 'That Patricia is a fearful little jerk. I don't know what's coming over her. She spends the whole of her life acting.'

Viola said: 'Well, she's young. It doesn't mean anything. She'll get over it.' She laughed a little bitterly. 'I think most of us spend the greater part of our lives acting.'

'You speak for yourself,' said Corinne. '*I* don't act. Sometimes I think I'm the only natural person in the family.' She looked wickedly at Viola. 'At least *I* have nothing to hide,' she said.

A gong sounded from the direction of the dining-room.

Viola said: 'Hurry, Corinne, and change. You know Gervase gets fearfully angry if you're not changed for dinner. We don't want any more scenes. It's been so unpleasant lately.'

Corinne said: 'Yes. Actually, I'm getting rather bored with stepfather and his likes and dislikes. He thinks people have nothing else to do but change their clothes all day.'

She began to walk up the stairs. Almost at the top, where the meeting of four passageways formed a well looking down into the hall, she turned.

She said over her shoulder: 'Keep your pecker up, Viola. You're all right, my dear, you know, so long' – she dropped her voice – 'as you go on paying. I'll be seeing you.' She tripped up the stairs.

Viola stood in the hallway, looking at the great oak doors in front of her. She stood there for two or three minutes; undecided, unhappy.

She thought that life was an odd and peculiar thing. It came back and hit you and it went on hitting you. Actually your motives for doing things didn't matter a great deal. Nothing mattered to life. If your motives were good or bad it was all the same.

She felt very near to tears. Then, with the sudden, illogical decision that comes to women who are in the process of feeling deeply rather than thinking calmly, she moved towards the passage that led away from the drawing-room towards the east side of the house. She moved quickly as if she were afraid that delay would alter her decision.

She stopped before the door at the end of the passageway. She knocked softly on it.

Her stepfather's voice said irascibly: 'Well . . . what is it? Can't I get a moment's peace? Who is it, and what do you want?'

Viola shrugged her shoulders, helplessly. She said: 'I'm sorry . . . it doesn't matter. I'm so sorry I disturbed you.'

She went back to the hall; began to ascend the stairs. Her eyes were filled with tears. She moved quickly up the stairs to her room on the first floor.

Inside, she threw herself face downwards on the bed. She began to sob bitterly.

Presenting Colonel Gervase Stenhurst (once – a long time ago – of the Indian Army; now, by courtesy, squire of Dark Spinney; also, by courtesy, titular head of the Clan Alardyse and the remains of the Clan Wymering – and when I say titular, I mean *titular*) who sits at the head of the long – too long for its few occupants – oak dining-table, and regards his family connections with an eye inclined to be yellow, bad-tempered and gloomy.

The Colonel is a member of the 'old school'. His manners are very good – when someone is looking. He is a great respecter of the ladies; he likes whisky and a good cigar; soft living appeals to him. Above all, he likes peace and quiet so that he may enjoy the concomitants of peace and quiet.

Underneath – and when no one is looking – he is bad-tempered to a degree entirely damnable. He still has an eye for a well-turned ankle, especially when he has imbibed more than four double whiskies and sodas. He has too an eye on the main chance and knows on which side his bread is buttered, but is disinclined to let anyone else realize the fact. That is, if they haven't already guessed it.

The Colonel is so obvious that he creaks. But he has a capacity for self-delusion without comparison. He is unique in the fact that he is conceited and sixty-two, and when a man is conceited at sixty-two it isn't so good for somebody – even if the somebody is himself.

Miss Honoria Wymering, sister of the late Mrs Stenhurst, who was mother – by her first husband Ferdinand Alardyse – of Viola, Corinne and Patricia, sits at the foot of the table and casts about her glances inclined to be apprehensive. She looks warily round the table from time to time with blue eyes – eyes that, in spite of her years, are still bright and attractive. She realizes that the air is thick with 'atmosphere' and that, on the slightest provocation, there may be one of those quarrels that have become far too numerous during the last few weeks.

Miss Wymering is plump and still beautiful. Her bleached hair is attractively dressed. Looking at her, you realize that the Wymerings are lovely women – lovely and alluring. You realize that the amazing beauty of Viola, Corinne and Patricia is a carrying on of the Wymering tradition of stateliness and beauty – so far as Viola is concerned; of beauty without stateliness where Corinne is concerned; and of beauty mixed with impishness, dramatics and what-have-you-got-today so far as Patricia is concerned.

And here a few words might adequately be devoted to Patricia, who is nobody's fool; who, in spite of her predilection for dramatics; her ability to be somebody else – somebody drawn from her wide cinema screen acquaintance – has, most of the time, her bright and observant eye on the main chance. Patricia, whose ears are attuned to whispers in case the whispers might be interesting; whose eyes can (almost) see round corners; who has contempt for her stepfather, indulgence for her Aunt; a well-concealed fear of Corinne – who, in spite of anything that Patricia might say to the contrary, possesses the ability to scare the pants off that young lady – and an almost as well-concealed love for Viola who is, let it be admitted, about the only person that Patricia admires and doesn't try to imitate.

Miss Wymering eats her soup and still manages to endow the movement of arm and finger with grace. Her eyes wander from the Colonel to Viola, from Viola to Corinne, from Corinne to Patricia. Something is wrong, she thinks, and wishes she knew what it was. Almost immediately she is glad that she doesn't. Sometimes, she considers, ignorance is really and truly bliss.

But she wonders.

She looks at Viola. She thinks that Viola is a most lovely person. She wishes that she looked less tired; that the dark circles beneath her eyes were less pronounced. She believes that something is worrying Viola. She wonders what? She remembers some of the things that used to worry her when she was nearly thirty. . . .

Miss Wymering sighs. Sometimes she wishes that she had sufficient courage to ask Viola about many things. But she hasn't sufficient courage. She is all for a quiet life. And if Viola wanted her to know she'd tell her. Wouldn't she . . .?'

And then Corinne. Miss Wymering thinks about Corinne, who is eating soup with an expression of supreme self-satisfaction tempered with disgust when her eyes fall on Patricia (who, by the way, is still wearing Corinne's red dinner frock; still wearing the terrible make-up; the film-star hair-do; an expression which she considers to be one of supreme disdain and an idea that Corinne is going to be very rude in a minute and that she – Patricia – is looking forward to the process. In fact she is, at the moment, busy rehearsing, in her mind, the 'act' with which she intends to rebut any attack from the Corinne front). Corinne, who, for some reason which Miss Wymering cannot fail to notice, looks self-compla-cent and satisfied like, Honoria thinks, 'the cat that swallowed the canary.' She wonders just *which* canary Corinne is contemplating swallowing at the moment.

And Patricia . . .! Under her breath, Miss Wymering makes a little clucking noise indicative of disapproval. Patricia is really very *naughty*. But *definitely* naughty. Miss Wymering realizes perfectly well that Patricia is wearing one of Corinne's frocks – with-out permission; that her hair is copied, probably, from the hair-do of the film star at the moment occupying prime place in Patricia's emotional being; that the make-up which the child – anyone under twenty is a child to Miss Wymering – wears is *too* terrible for words. She hopes unutterably that Gervase is not going to notice; that if he does he won't be too unpleasant.

Sallins, the butler, an aged retainer of Ferdinand Alardyse, who has been with the family, man and boy, for longer than he cares to think, white-haired, almost aristocratic in appearance, hovers about the end of the table waiting to clear the soup course. Sallins is not particularly happy. He too realizes that something is 'up'; that there is going to be a spot of bother about something.

He wonders if they are going to wait until coffee, or if they are going to start in at any moment. He doesn't know which process will give him most satisfaction – whether it is better to be present at a family schemozzle and pretend that you aren't there, or not be present and wonder what the hell it was all about.

Sallins has arrived at a state of mind and years when he is beginning to wonder what the hell everything is about.

Nothing seems to make sense to him – from the atom bomb to Colonel Stenhurst's liver attacks. He is old, and life resembles a chronic gumboil. Something that is prolonged and painful and with which no one ever sympathizes.

He moves slowly round the table, collecting soup plates, limping a little, the result of a kick from Miss Viola's pony when she was about five years of age. Those were the days, thinks Sallins . . . when Mr Alardyse was master at Dark Spinney, before Mrs Alardyse was foolish enough to marry again. Those were the days . . .

The storm broke suddenly. Sallins had served the cutlets and departed to see how the sweet was progressing. Corinne masticated a piece of mutton slowly. She put down her knife and fork.

She said coldly to Patricia: 'I thought I told you to take that frock off. Why don't you do what you're told, you fearful little thing!'

Patricia stopped eating; looked at Corinne. She said in an icy voice: 'I don't wish to talk to you, sourpuss! Before dinner you called me a bitch . . . *but* a bitch!'

The Colonel said testily: 'What the devil's all this about? What's that – called you what?'

Patricia said primly: 'A bitch, step-papa – a woman dog!'

The Colonel made a horrible noise in his throat.

Corinne said: 'Don't suffocate, Gervase. We should none of us like that.' She turned again to Patricia. She said: 'Immediately after dinner, go to your room and take that frock off, or I'll tear it off you. I suggest also that you wash your face and do your hair decently. I've already told you that you look like a tart.'

Patricia said icily: 'I'm afraid I haven't made a close study of tarts. As types they interest me only in the abstract.' She smiled wickedly at Corinne. 'You're in a pretty bad temper tonight, aren't you, *darling*?' she asked brightly. 'You know, step-papa, when Corinne loses her temper she can be a fair basket.'

The Colonel said acidly: 'I'm sick and tired of all these squabbles at the dinner table. I'm sick and tired of this shocking slang too. Young women didn't behave like you do in my days. What the devil do you mean by calling Corinne a basket? What's a basket?'

Patricia said: 'A basket is a polite expression denoting a bastard – or love-child.'

The Colonel looked at his sister-in-law. He said: 'My God, Honoria, what you do with your time I don't know. Listen to the way this child talks to me – her stepfather. Her behaviour is appalling. Everybody's behaviour is appalling. Why I stand it I don't know.' He banged his knife down on the table. His face was brick red.

Corinne said: 'Whatever do you mean, Gervase, you don't know why you stand it? Of course you do. So do we.'

Miss Wymering said: 'Corinne, please . . . that is not the way to talk to your stepfather, and I do wish you girls would not quarrel at mealtimes. It's so bad. I'm sure the servants hear.'

The Colonel laughed sarcastically. 'That's good –' he said, 'that bit about the servants hearing. Everyone hears – not only the servants but the whole village. I think it's time that somebody talked to these girls.' He glared at Patricia. 'Your sister Corinne calls you stupid,' he went on. 'You are – very, very stupid. You spend all your time going to the cinema and giving imitations of film stars. You look appalling. You haven't the remotest notion how a lady behaves. To look at you makes me feel quite ill.'

Patricia said with a wistful smile: 'I'm very sorry about that, step-papa. I reciprocate it. The colour of your face at the moment is most shocking. Do you think you are going to have a fit, step-papa?'

The Colonel's face went a shade darker. He said: 'Dammit . . . I've asked you a hundred times not to call me step-papa. Why do you do it?'

Corinne said: 'Obviously she does it because she knows it annoys you. Perhaps she thinks it would be bad for you if she called you Gervase or stepfather. You might feel too important.'

Miss Wymering said anxiously: 'Now, Corinne, you mustn't talk like that. It isn't good manners.'

There was a silence. A strained silence. You could have cut it with a knife. Then Viola said: 'Will you excuse me, Gervase? I think I'll go to my room. I really don't want any dinner.'

'No, you won't,' said the Colonel. He was very angry. His lips were set in a straight line. His eyes were gleaming almost evilly. 'No, you won't,' he repeated. 'I've got something to say to you and Corinne, and you'll be well advised to *listen* to what I have to say.'

Viola looked at him in amazement.

Corinne said impertinently: 'Really, this sounds most dramatic. I'm *fearfully* interested.'

Miss Wymering looked from one to the other. She said: 'Gervase dear, don't you think you might like to talk to the girls after we've had coffee – when there isn't a chance of Sallins coming back?'

The Colonel laughed. He said: 'I assure you it doesn't matter about Sallins, my dear Honoria. Every servant in this house, practically the whole of the village and certainly all Alfriston, know exactly what I'm going to talk about. I imagine they've known it for weeks.'

Miss Wymering said: 'Dear . . . dear . . . Whatever is it, Gervase?' There was alarm in her eyes.

Corinne said coolly: 'There's always a lot of talk in any village, you know. Usen't they to call it "throwing dung at the carriage folk?" I suppose we're the equivalent of "carriage folk" . . . or are we?'

The Colonel said: 'What I have to say I propose to say now. For a long time I have put up with the atmosphere in this house. I haven't liked it. Patricia is behaving abominably – growing up like a hoyden. Corinne' – he glowered at her – 'is probably the rudest young woman I have ever met in my life, but at least I believed that Viola had *some* good in her make-up.'

Miss Wymering said bravely: 'But Gervase, what has Viola done?'

The Colonel went on: 'What she's done or what she hasn't done is no part of this conversation. She knows what she's done, and so does Corinne – or at least they know what they're doing.'

'But,' asked Miss Wymering with raised eyebrows, 'what *are* they doing? What's the trouble, Gervase?'

The Colonel said: 'There are some very nasty rumours going about the village and Alfriston. They've even stretched as far as Eastbourne. It seems that Viola and Corinne's names are being linked with an extremely unpleasant gentleman with a rather nasty past and a bad present reputation who has something to do with one of the nastier drinking clubs on the outskirts of Brighton. Dammit,' he went on, 'I think it's pretty hard when I have to hear this from members of my club – people who tell me what they've heard – people who are beginning to get the idea in their head that two of my stepdaughters are behaving like sluts, and the third – a child of seventeen – like the village idiot.'

Patricia rose to her feet. She made a sweeping gesture. She said: 'Aunt Honoria, Corinne has called me a bitch tonight. *That* I can stand. I don't see, however, why I should be compared to the village idiot. Not,' she continued, 'that it is an adequate comparison because I don't think we *have* a village idiot' – she looked at the Colonel – 'present company always excepted of course.' She turned on an expression of extreme sadness. She said: 'I think I shall go to my room. I wish to be alone.' After which she sat down and attacked her cutlet with gusto.

Viola said to the Colonel: 'Don't you think you're being rather rude? Don't you think you ought to think before you say things like that? Really they sound rather ridiculous.'

Corinne said: 'And how! And you certainly ought to do a little thinking before you attack the family, especially Viola,' she went on, with an arch look in Viola's direction. 'After all, we all know that you only get two hundred and fifty a year as one of the trustees under mother's Will, and that the additional thousand that you receive comes from Viola, with her sanction and approval. It's rather like biting the hand that feeds you, isn't it?'

The Colonel said in a low hoarse voice: 'You . . . you . . . I think sometimes I could strangle you.'

Patricia murmured: 'Cut . . . reel two. . . .'

Miss Wymering said: 'Gervase, Sallins will be here in a minute. This conversation ought to stop. I think you've all been very foolish. If you've something against the girls, this is no place to talk about it.'

The Colonel said: 'I've been insulted. I may be the unpopular stepfather of fiction, but I'm a trustee of the Estate and whilst I am, I'm going to see that these girls behave themselves properly. Very well, Honoria, since you tell me that you do not wish me to talk about it, may I tell you ladies what I propose to do? These remarks apply to you, Viola, and you, Corinne. As for that child there' – he glared at Patricia – 'I hope that you, Honoria, will endeavour to teach her a little sense and some good manners.'

He gasped a little, seeking to regain lost breath. Then he went on: 'It is quite obvious to me that something is going on under my very nose which is bringing their reputations and this family to disrepute. Probably neither of you care for the fact that your family has lived here for hundreds of years. In order to indulge yourself in something which I imagine to be not very nice you are quite prepared to drag your family name through the dirt. I assure you that I am very glad that I am not your father. But understand this: I'm going to find out what's going on. I intend to. If I have to have you watched I'll find out what's going on. Yes, that's what I shall do, and if there is anything about which I can take definite steps you can rest assured I shall do so.'

Viola said: 'Would you excuse me, Aunt. I think I'll have my coffee in my room.' She went away.

'Life round here is going to be fearfully interesting,' Corinne said. She addressed her stepfather: 'You ought to realize that Viola is nearly thirty, and that I am twenty-eight. Don't you think we are rather old to be watched?'

The Colonel said: 'Neither of you seems old enough to have any sense. Do you think I *want* to have you watched?' He looked at her. He went on: 'If you like to tell me what's been going on – exactly what there is between this man and you and your sister . . . very well. . . . If you don't, I shall take such steps as I consider proper to find out.'

Corinne said amiably: 'So far as I'm concerned you can do what you damn well please. But I should be careful if I were you. If you begin to employ people to watch Viola and myself you'll have to pay for it out of your own pocket.' She smiled. 'You can't expect Viola to consent to it coming out of the Estate funds, can you? What an appalling dinner,' she said. 'Even Sallins seems to have missed the boat. Good night, Aunt.' She smiled cynically at her stepfather. 'And good night to you, Gervase,' she said. 'I'd take a bromide if I were you instead of your usual night-cap.'

Patricia said: 'This would seem to be my cue for exit. Anyway, it looks as if the fun's over. Good night, folks.'

Corinne moved slowly out of the room. She went out by the side door leading to the passageway that ran into the hall. She closed the door very slowly behind her; did not quite shut it. She stood there on the thick carpet. She heard Miss Wymering say: 'Aren't you making a mountain out of a molehill, Gervase? What is all this about? I can believe possibly that Corinne might have been stupid, but surely not Viola. Are you sure of your facts? If there are any facts.'

He said: 'I know what I'm talking about. And I was never more serious in my life. I tell you that it is absolutely essential that we, the trustees, should know what is going on. When I know a little more about it I'll try and tell you the whole story. In the meantime, their attitude being what it is, I propose to find out in my own way. I have got the name of some man in London. He seems to be quite a clever person – a private detective. I'm going to get in touch with him. *I'm going to find out.*'

Sallins came in, began to collect plates. Miss Wymering said: 'I don't think you need worry about the sweet, Sallins. Miss Alardyse will have coffee in her room, and I think Miss Corrine would like some in hers.'

The Colonel got up. He said: 'I don't want any. I'll have a whisky and soda in my room, Sallins. And where's the post tonight?'

'It's just come, Sir – just at this moment,' said Sallins. 'I haven't had time to sort it. It's in the hall. Shall I bring your letters in?'

The Colonel said shortly: 'No, I'll collect them on my way upstairs.'

Corinne shut the door quietly. She moved down the small passageway slowly. She heard the Colonel arrive by the main passage from the dining-room in the hallway, heard him fumbling at the brass tray which held the evening mail. She waited as she heard his staccato footsteps angrily treading the stairs. She went into the hall. She stood leaning against the dark oak wall, a little smile playing about her luscious mouth. She was watching the telephone. After a few moments it made a little noise – the almost imperceptible tinkle that a telephone makes when an extension line is being used.

Corinne felt in her pocket for her cigarette case. She lit a cigarette. She thought that her aunt would leave the dining-room by the front passage; would get to her own room, unhappily wondering what all the trouble was about. Corinne thought she was safe to stay. She imagined it would take some little time for the Colonel to get the number he wanted.

Five or six minutes passed. Again she heard the almost imperceptible tinkle. She moved swiftly to the telephone, lifted the receiver carefully. She listened. She heard the Colonel's voice:

'I've got to talk to Mr Callaghan. His name's been given to me and I am prepared to pay for his services. I'm Colonel Gervase Stenhurst of Dark Spinney, Hangover, near Alfriston, Sussex. It's most important business. I have had a letter. . . .'

A voice said: 'Yeah. . . . Well, you know what the time is? It's half-past eight and Mr Callaghan is no night worker – well not often. But if it's as bad as that, and you gotta talk to him in a hurry, maybe you could get him at the Night Light Club in half an hour's time – maybe! The number's Mayfair 43276.'

The Colonel said: 'Very well, I'll try and get him there. But I want him to come down tomorrow. I want to see him as soon as possible.'

The other voice said: 'O.K. Maybe he'll come and maybe he won't. You never know with that one. You get through and talk to him. So long.' Corinne heard the Colonel hang up.

She replaced the receiver, stood looking at it. She drew thoughtfully on her cigarette. She shrugged her shoulders; then she went to the hallstand, slipped into her raincoat. She went out of the side door into the wet garden.

Callaghan came into the Night Light Club. He looked round, put his black soft hat on a small table to the right of the door, sat down on a high stool at the bar, ordered a double whisky and soda.

He was dressed in a double-breasted blue suit, a light blue silk shirt, a dark blue tie. His thick black hair was unruly. His face was long; his chin pointed, the jaw-bone showing in a good line from the ear to the apex of the chin. His eyes were grey, and the humour lines about them were well-developed. A strong, intelligent face – impressive to men, sometimes too attractive to women.

He drank a little more whisky. He thought that he was bored.

The Night Light Club was one of those places which abound in London. Mushrooms of the war, they had provided an adequate relief from bombs, rockets and doodle-bugs. Within the narrow walls of the Night Light, uniforms of every country in the Allied Forces had met, mixed and drunk. Now only a few *habitués* of the place still came. Callaghan thought that the life of a drinking club in London was rather like life itself. It began with a fanfare, went on to excitement and finished with a flop.

Three or four people came into the bar. Now the place was beginning to fill up. A woman, wearing a heavy perfume, inserted herself on to the stool next to Callaghan. He moved his own stool a little further along to make room for her. He ordered another whisky and soda.

Outside, from the small telephone room at the end of the bar, the telephone bell began to jangle. O'Shaughnessy, the white-jacketed bar-tender, left the bar, went to answer the telephone. After a minute he came back.

He said: 'There's a call for you, Mr Callaghan. Do you want to take it?'

Callaghan said: 'Do you know who it is, Patrick?' He drank some of the whisky.

O'Shaughnessy said: 'No, the party wouldn't give his name. He said it was urgent.'

Callaghan said: 'All right.' He got off the stool, walked a little unsteadily towards the telephone room. He opened the door, stood leaning against the wall looking at the telephone receiver which hung, extended on its cord, from the wall instrument. According to Callaghan's eyes the telephone receiver was getting bigger and bigger, and the telephone room itself was beginning to revolve. A pain hit him behind the eyes. His head began to spin. Now he could not even see distinctly.

Callaghan pushed himself away from the wall towards the telephone. He fell against it. He ricochetted from the telephone to the wall, from the wall across to the door that led to the men's wash-room. He pitched forward into the wash-room, striking his shoulder against the edge of one of the wash-bowls. He lay on the floor, his eyes shut. The door closed itself slowly.

When Callaghan opened his eyes he saw the face of O'Shaughnessy, the bar-tender, bending over him. O'Shaughnessy's face looked like a full moon.

He said: 'Come on now, Mr Callaghan. Drink this. You'll feel better. What happened?' He put his arm under Callaghan's shoulders, propped him against the wall. Callaghan drank some of the mixture the bar-tender held towards him. It tasted foul. He ran his tongue over his dry lips. It felt as if it was made of yellow plush.

He said slowly: 'How long have I been in here?'

O'Shaughnessy said: 'About twenty-five minutes. Remember – you went out to answer the telephone, but didn't make it. Somebody came in here just now and found you. What's the matter?'

Callaghan said slowly: 'You ought to know. It must have been that last whisky you gave me. Where did you get it from? Did you make it in the bath-tub upstairs?'

O'Shaughnessy said: 'Have a heart, Mr Callaghan. We don't do things like that at the Night Light Club. That hooch was good. Everybody's been drinking out of that bottle.'

Callaghan said: 'Like hell it was good.' He got to his feet.

The bar-tender took a brush, began to brush Callaghan's clothes. He said: 'That's not like you, Mr Callaghan – going out like that. Maybe you ate something that disagreed with you.'

'Maybe,' said Callaghan. 'All right, O'Shaughnessy.'

The bar-tender went away. Callaghan bathed his face in cold water; took a glass, drank a little water. He lit a cigarette, went back to the bar. Only two people were there – two men who were discussing the racing news in a corner.

Callaghan said to the bar-tender: 'I'll have another double whisky, Patrick. But not out of the same bottle. Try a fresh one.'

O'Shaughnessy grinned back, opened a fresh bottle. Callaghan drank the whisky, lit a fresh cigarette, picked up his hat, went out into the street. He walked slowly towards Berkeley Square, draw-ing on his cigarette, wondering.

It was nine-thirty when he arrived at the apartment block in which his offices – with his flat above them – were situated. He said good night to Wilkie, the night porter, went up in the lift. He stopped the lift at the office floor, walked along the passage, saw the light in his room.

He went in. Nikolls, Callaghan's Canadian assistant, was sitting in Callaghan's armchair, his feet on the desk, reading *How to be a Master of Women*. The empty whisky bottle was on the floor at his side.

Callaghan said: 'Hello, Windy. Any calls?'

'Yeah,' said Nikolls. 'Tonight, some guy called Colonel Gervase Stenhurst, from some place called Dark Spinney, at Hangover, near a dump called Alfriston. This guy wanted you bad. I told him to call you at the Night Light.'

Callaghan said: 'That's a hell of a name for a house – Dark Spinney. . . . Hangover. . . .' He grinned.

'Yeah,' said Nikolls. 'It sounds like a coupla murders to me.' He looked at Callaghan. 'Whadya gonna do?' he asked. 'You gonna go down an' see this guy like he wanted?'

Callaghan got up. He lit a cigarette. He said: 'No. . . . I don't want the case.'

He went out, slammed the office door behind him.

Nikolls put on his hat. He fumbled in his pocket for a Lucky Strike, lit it; turned off the office lights. He walked slowly towards the lift.

He said: 'Aw . . . what the hell!'

CHAPTER TWO
LADIES FIRST

IT WAS three o'clock in the afternoon when Callaghan rang through from his apartment above the office, on the intercommunication telephone. Effie Thompson picked up the receiver.

She said: 'Good afternoon, Mr Callaghan. I hope you slept well.'

'Very well,' said Callaghan. 'Is anything happening, Effie?'

'No,' she answered. 'There's nothing very much in your mail.'

'No telephone calls that matter?' asked Callaghan.

She said: 'No.'

Callaghan said: 'I shall be down in half an hour. I'll sign any letters then. I may be going to the country. You might telephone to the garage and tell them to send the car round at four o'clock.'

'Very well,' said Effie. There was a pause; then she said: 'Do you, by any chance, want me to wire or telephone anybody?'

Callaghan said: 'Do I? Such as who?'

'Such as Mrs Denys,' said Effie, casually.

Callaghan said: 'You must be a thought reader. Thanks for reminding me. Yes, send a wire. The number is Waverley 78945. Tell Mrs Denys that I expect to be with her at dinner tonight.'

'Very well,' said Effie. She replaced the receiver. She said under her breath: 'Damn Mrs Denys.'

She dialled 'Telegrams'; waited; got through; began to send the telegram.

She had just finished; was about to replace the receiver, when the door opened. Viola Alardyse stood in the doorway. Effie Thompson caught her breath at the picture.

'Good afternoon. Can I help you?' she asked.

The caller said: 'Thank you. I am Miss Alardyse. I wish to see Mr Callaghan. The matter is important, and I should like to see him immediately.'

Effie smiled a little. She said pleasantly: 'I quite understand. But Mr Callaghan is a rather difficult person to see immediately. He's like that. Also he's not in at the moment. Would you like to leave a message? And he seldom sees clients without an appointment.'

'I'm not a client,' said Miss Alardyse, 'and it would be to Mr Callaghan's advantage to see me. Perhaps you would tell me when he *will* be in. I should hate to make things difficult for him without giving him the chance of talking to me first of all.'

Effie thought: So it's like that? I wonder what he's started *now*. She's beautiful and *could* be tough. Still . . . they often begin like that. She remembered other ladies. . . .

She said: 'Will you sit down, please? I'll try and get in touch with Mr Callaghan.'

Miss Alardyse said: 'Thank you.' She sat down. She crossed her legs. Effie Thompson noted, with a definite annoyance, that the Alardyse legs and ankles and shoes and stockings were quite lovely.

She said: 'Excuse me, please.' She went into Callaghan's office; closed the door behind her. She crossed to his desk; picked up the telephone; called the hall porter. She said: 'Wilkie, give me a line through to Mr Callaghan's apartment. Make it snappy.'

'O.K.,' said Wilkie.

Almost immediately Callaghan came on the line.

Effie said: 'Things are happening down here. A lady has just arrived to see you. She's inclined to be definite about life – if you get me. She says that she'd hate to make things difficult for you without giving you the chance of talking to her. She's like that.'

'No,' said Callaghan. 'Just fancy. What else?'

She went on: 'She's quite beautiful. Really lovely . . . if you know what I mean. She looks aristocratic and bad tempered. She doesn't sound as if she liked you *awfully*. She's wearing a cherry corduroy coat and skirt that were made by a real tailor, a beaver coat and toque. Her stockings are silk – *real* silk – and her shoes are hand made. She's wearing one brooch – diamonds and rubies – worth a lot of money. And driving gloves. I think she's come by car.'

Callaghan said: 'Well . . . well . . . Do we know her name?'

'She's a Miss Alardyse,' she answered.

There was a pause. Then Callaghan said: 'She sounds too good to be true. Tell her to write for an appointment.'

There was another pause. Then Effie said: 'I wish you'd see her, Mr Callaghan. She's got something on her mind. And she looks well bred enough to be dangerous.'

Callaghan said: 'Why should I worry about that?'

'I wouldn't know,' Effie replied primly. 'I thought perhaps you knew her. I said that I thought you ought to see her because I imagined she was rather your type.'

'What does that mean?' asked Callaghan.

She shrugged her shoulders. 'Whatever you want it to mean,' she said. 'But I'd see her. Even if you only took a look I think you'd say it was worth it.'

Callaghan said: 'All right. I'll come down. In five minutes. Put her in my room.'

'Very well,' said Effie. She hung up; went back to the outer office.

She said: 'Miss Alardyse, I've spoken to Mr Callaghan on the telephone. He says he'll see you in five minutes. Will you come this way, please?'

She led the way back into Callaghan's office; pushed forward the big leather armchair; opened his silver cigarette box; moved over the desk lighter.

She said brightly: 'Please smoke if you want to.'

She went out; closed the door. Seated once more at her desk, she said to herself: 'Exit Mrs Denys!'

She felt almost happy.

Viola Alardyse sat down and began to think about private detectives. Private detectives, she thought, were not very nice people. They were, she imagined, odd types who snooped about the place in divorce cases; gave evidence and were often the butt of rude remarks by counsel. Also, she considered, they were people who would scare easily. She visualized Callaghan as a rather fat man, with a beefy face, a partially bald head, and a half-smoked cigar.

He came into the office. He looked at her casually, went to his desk, sat down. He was wearing a brown tweed coat and slacks, a brown suede waistcoat, a fawn-silk shirt and collar, a madder brown tie. His thin face was freshly shaven. He looked alert and much too cheerful.

He took a cigarette from the silver box on the desk, lit it; leaned back in his chair; regarded her with equanimity.

She said: 'Mr Callaghan . . . I haven't a great deal of time, and so I'd better say what I have to say quickly.'

He nodded. 'That's always a good idea,' he said. 'Most women who come here take an awfully long time to get it off their chests. I'm so glad you're not like that.' He smiled at her benignly.

She went on: 'Last night Colonel Stenhurst, who is one of my trustees, telephoned you. I felt that I ought to see you before you decided to take any steps as a result of his call.'

Callaghan nodded. He said: 'Yes?'

'I don't know exactly what he told you,' continued Miss Alardyse, 'or what he asked you to do. But I think you ought to know that I have a decided objection to your undertaking any sort of business on his behalf to which I might object.'

Callaghan drew a long breath of tobacco smoke into his lungs. He seemed to take great pleasure in the act. Then, very slowly, he proceeded to expel the smoke through pursed lips. He blew two very good smoke rings. He watched them sail across the office.

He said: 'Aren't you getting a little mixed?' He smiled at her again, and for some reason she found the process irritating. He continued: 'You say first of all that you don't know what Colonel Stenhurst told me; that you don't know what he asked me to do, but that in any event I'm not to do it. Vaguely,' said Callaghan, 'but only very vaguely, you remind me of the late Adolf Hitler. He used to talk like that and look where it got him.'

She moved a little. She said: 'Mr Callaghan, are you trying to be rude?'

He shook his head. He said: 'I never *try* to be rude. In any event, why should I be rude to you, Miss Alardyse? I'm simply trying to project a little sense into this conversation. May I suggest,' he went on, 'that if you don't want me to do whatever it is Colonel Stenhurst wants me to do, it would be a good idea if you told me what it is he wants me to do?'

She said: 'Am I to understand, Mr Callaghan, that you have not talked to Colonel Stenhurst on the telephone? Are you telling me that he hasn't given you any instructions?'

Callaghan said warily: 'Miss Alardyse, I'm a private detective. Let us imagine, for the sake of argument, that I have had a long talk with Colonel Stenhurst, and that he has asked me to do certain things. I couldn't possibly discuss those things with you except with his permission.'

There was a silence. Callaghan inhaled some more cigarette smoke.

He went on: 'May I make a suggestion? You know, Miss Alardyse, I've always found that truth is a very potent weapon. It is quite obvious that some situation has arisen between Colonel Stenhurst and yourself that you find unpleasant. Why don't you tell me what it is? It would make things much easier in the long run.'

She raised her eyebrows. She asked: 'Would it? Perhaps I'm not inclined to agree with that, Mr Callaghan. As I told you before, I came here to stop you putting yourself into a very difficult position.'

Callaghan said: 'Thank you very much. I promise I won't put myself into a difficult position if I can help it. Of course, if you're afraid of Colonel Stenhurst –'

She asked icily: 'What do you mean?'

Callaghan continued glibly: 'Well, quite obviously, you are rather scared about something, aren't you? Let's be logical about this.' He leaned back in his chair, enjoying the situation. He went on: 'Colonel Stenhurst – and at the moment I don't quite know what the connection between this gentleman and yourself is – obviously intended to telephone me and ask me to do something. Well, if he has, I don't know anything about it. It also seems logical,' Callaghan continued, 'that you knew that he intended to telephone me and you thought you'd get here first to see that *I* didn't do whatever it was *he* wanted me to do.' Callaghan smiled beatifically. He said: 'Do you know, Miss Alardyse, I'm beginning to be awfully intrigued with Colonel Stenhurst.'

Two little red spots appeared on her cheeks. She was very angry. She said nothing.

Callaghan went on cheerfully: 'I think it would be a very good idea if I got through to Colonel Stenhurst, don't you – and heard what *he's* got to say about things? Then perhaps I should be able to discuss *your* point of view.'

She got up. She said: 'Mr Callaghan, this interview is beginning to bore me. I'll tell you exactly what was in my mind when I came here. Last night at dinner, Colonel Stenhurst – who is my stepfather and a trustee under my mother's Will – informed me that in certain circumstances he might employ a private detective for the purpose of having me watched. I do not propose to allow such a process. I don't propose to have a private detective anywhere in the vicinity of Dark Spinney, of which I am the owner. I do not propose to be spied on. Incidentally,' she went on, 'I believe there are laws in this country dealing with that sort of thing. If you intend to carry out any instructions of Colonel Stenhurst's on those lines I shall be forced to put the matter in the hands of the police.'

Callaghan nodded. He stubbed out his cigarette in the ashtray. He said: 'That, I am sure, would create a very odd, and possibly humorous, situation. By the sound of the house 'Dark Spinney' it might be somewhere in the country. If you went to the local police, Miss Alardyse, you might create all sorts of situations. People might even begin to talk. Consider,' said Callaghan whimsically, 'Callaghan Investigations following Miss Alardyse about the hills and dales, and in turn being followed by the village policeman – probably on a bicycle. Not so good – hey? We shall have to find something better than that, shan't we?'

She said: 'Mr Callaghan, I've said all I'm going to say. I hope you'll be warned.'

Callaghan looked as near alarmed as was possible. Then he smiled beatifically at her. He said: 'Miss Alardyse, I *am* warned. I'm beginning to be scared stiff. And I think it was *very* good of you to come and see me.'

She moved towards the door. He opened it for her.

He said: 'Good afternoon, Miss Alardyse.'

She looked at him. Callaghan thought that he had never seen two such beautiful eyes so hostile.

She said: 'Good afternoon, Mr Callaghan.'

She crossed the outer office, opened the door, went out.

Effie Thompson looked at Callaghan out of the corner of her eye. She said nothing. Then she looked demurely at the typewriter in front of her.

Callaghan said: 'Yes, Effie?'

She said: 'I was just thinking, Mr Callaghan . . . I was wondering.'

'Wondering what?' Callaghan asked.

She smiled a little. 'Whether you still intended to go down to Waverley.'

Callaghan said: 'No, I shan't go down to Waverley. You'd better send another wire to Mrs Denys. Tell her that important business has detained me in town; that I'll get in touch with her as soon as I can.'

She said primly: 'Very well, Mr Callaghan.'

Callaghan went back to his desk. He called through the open door: 'Send Nikolls in to me, Effie.'

Nikolls came into the office. He said: 'Is she a looker, that one, or is she? I am walkin' around the passage outside when she goes along to the lift. Say, have you watched that babe walk? She don't walk – she floats. Is she a customer?'

Callaghan said: 'Not quite – at the moment. She might be.' He leaned back in his chair. He said: 'Windy, this Colonel Stenhurst who came through last night – tell me what happened.'

'He sounded like an old guy,' said Nikolls. 'He was a bit steamed up about somethin'. He said he'd gotta talk to you; that it was urgent. He said, "I gotta see Mr Callaghan. He's gotta come down here an' see me" – or something like that.'

Callaghan asked: 'Anything else?'

'Yeah,' said Nikolls. 'He said something about a letter. He said: "I got a letter . . ." and then he stopped.'

Callaghan said: 'So he had a letter – a letter that made him either excited or angry.'

Nikolls said: 'I thought maybe it was some business. I thought you might want the case. I didn't know whether you was comin' back, or whether you'd be here today, so I told him to call you at the Night Light Club. I gave him the number.'

Callaghan said: 'I see. It's funny that he hasn't been through today.'

Nikolls shrugged his shoulders. He said: 'Yeah. Maybe he's cooled off.'

Callaghan said: 'Get him on the telephone.'

'O.K.,' said Nikolls.

He went to the telephone in the outer office. Callaghan could hear him asking trunk enquiry for the number.

He relaxed in his chair; sat looking at the ceiling above him. He was thinking about Viola Alardyse.

Some minutes passed. Nikolls came in. He said: 'I got the number. It's Alfriston 76421. But Effie can't get through. There's a fault on the line.'

Callaghan nodded. 'I see.' He got up. He said to Nikolls: 'Get through to the garage and tell them to send the car round at once. Then get hold of the A.A. book and get me a route to Hangover. It ought to be fairly easy. I've got some things packed upstairs. Have them sent down. Then tell Effie to wire to Colonel Stenhurst. Tell him I'll be down this evening.'

Nikolls said: 'O.K.' He grinned. 'Are you gonna start somethin'?'

Callaghan said: 'Why not?' He went into the outer office. He said to Effie Thompson: 'Effie, get your book and make a note. The name is Stenhurst. It's too late to do any searching today, but tomorrow morning first thing, go down to the Probate Registry and find me a Will in that name – Mrs Stenhurst. The name's uncommon, so it should be easy, and it ought to be within the last twenty years. The beneficiary under the Will is Miss Viola Alardyse.'

She said: 'Yes, Mr Callaghan.'

Callaghan said: 'You know they don't like you taking copies at the Registry, but I want a copy, so you'd better ask for four or five other Wills after you've got the Stenhurst one, and whilst they're searching for them take a shorthand note of the Stenhurst Will. You got that?'

She said: 'I've got it, Mr Callaghan.'

He went on: 'You ought to have that by ten o'clock tomorrow. Come back to the office and type your note. Give it to Nikolls. He can hire a car and bring it down to me. Now give me the hotel guide.'

She got up, went to a shelf, handed him a book. He looked through it. After a minute's search he said:

'Tell Nikolls to contact me at the Two Friars Hotel at Alfriston at four o'clock tomorrow afternoon.'

Effie said: 'Very well, Mr Callaghan.' She went on demurely: 'I'll send the wires off now. Which one would you like to go first – to Colonel Stenhurst or Mrs Denys?'

Callaghan said: 'Mrs Denys. Didn't they tell you – ladies first!' He went back to his room.

*

At five o'clock Callaghan drove his open tourer car slowly up Berkeley Street. He was wondering about Colonel Stenhurst. He thought that it might have been a very good thing for somebody that Colonel Stenhurst hadn't talked to him last night, and that there was a fault on the telephone line today – not that faults on telephone lines matter; you can always use another phone. Callaghan wondered, if the matter was important, why the Colonel *hadn't* used another telephone. But you never knew. Country places are sometimes small. Sometimes people listened on telephone exchanges. Perhaps the Colonel was rather keen on speaking on his own line. Callaghan shrugged his shoulders.

It was ten past five when he stopped the car outside the little alleyway that led to the Night Light Club. He went in. There was only one person in the bar – a man sitting in the corner – half asleep.

O'Shaughnessy, the bar-tender, said: 'Good afternoon, Mr Callaghan. This is early for you.'

Callaghan nodded. He said: 'Perhaps I was wrong about that whisky last night.'

The bar-tender grinned. He said: 'You going to take another chance, Mr Callaghan?'

Callaghan nodded. He said: 'I'll take another chance.'

O'Shaughnessy poured out the drink; squirted in some soda. Callaghan put the glass to his lips, finished it.

He said: 'There's nothing much the matter with that whisky.' He took out his note-case; extracted two one-pound notes. He pushed them across the bar to O'Shaughnessy. He said: 'Keep the change. And tell me something. Last night, just before that telephone call came for me, a lady came and sat on the stool next to mine. I don't remember looking at her, but she wore a very heavy perfume. Who would that be?'

Patrick said: 'That's easy, Mr Callaghan. That's Miss La Valliere.'

Callaghan asked: 'Is *that* her name?'

O'Shaughnessy grinned. He said: 'It's the one she's using now. She's a scream.'

Callaghan asked: 'Where does she live, Patrick?'

The bar-tender said: 'She's got a flat – not far from here in Mayfield Street. I'll get you the number.' He fumbled under the bar;

produced a register of the club members. He turned over the pages. He said: 'Here we are – 14 Mayfield Street. The phone number's Regent 55443. Would you like me to get her on the phone?' He looked at Callaghan enquiringly.

Callaghan said: 'No, thank you.'

He went back to his car; drove to 14 Mayfield Street. The place was an ordinary apartment block on a side street. He went in; looked at the indicator in the hall. Miss La Valliere, it seemed, was on the first floor. Callaghan walked up the stairs. He found No. 14, put his forefinger on the bell-push, kept it there. He seemed to keep it there for a long time. He took it off when the door opened.

Miss La Valliere stood framed in the doorway. She was looking a bit tired. Her make-up had been put on very quickly. She was wearing a long black kimono covered with impossible silver dragons, very high-heeled red crêpe-de-Chine shoes, no stockings. Callaghan noticed she had small well-shaped feet.

She said: 'Well, what the hell goes on? Is the place on fire or something?'

Callaghan said: 'I don't think so. I just kept my finger on the bell. I'm in a hurry.'

Miss La Valliere looked at him with a little smile. She said: 'You don't say. So you're in a hurry and you kept your finger on the bell-push. You know what I think you are, don't you?'

Callaghan said: 'Don't tell me. Just get inside. I want to talk to you.'

He put up his hand as she began to speak. He said: 'Listen, if you know what's good for you, you're going to do what I say.' He smiled at her.

She said: 'Aw . . . what the hell! What goes on? Come on in.'

In the small sitting-room she turned and faced him. She said: 'Well, what is it? If you're in such a hurry you can get it off your chest and scram. I got a lot to do.'

'It won't take long,' Callaghan said. 'Just tell me something. Last night you came and sat next to me at the Night Light Club. Remember?'

'Why should I?' she asked acidly.

Callaghan said: 'I don't know, but you will.' He went on: 'A telephone call came through for me. You knew it was coming through. Somehow you knew that somebody was going to ring me at the Night Light Club and you got round there quickly. You sat next to me. In fact,' said Callaghan, 'you were just in time. When O'Shaughnessy, the bar-tender, told me I was wanted on the telephone you slipped something into my whisky and soda. You turned a perfectly innocent drink into a Mickey Finn.' He smiled reminiscently. 'A pretty good one too,' he said. 'I just got as far as the telephone room and went out cold. The point was,' he said, 'I never took the telephone call. Now *you* talk.'

She said: 'I don't know what the hell you're talking about.'

'All right,' said Callaghan. 'Listen to me. The name's Callaghan. I'm a private detective. I know the police pretty well and they know me. You're either going to talk or I'm going to take you round to Sackville Street.'

She said: 'You're talking rubbish.' But her eyes were scared.

Callaghan shrugged his shoulders. He said casually: 'I'm talking rubbish. But it's rubbish that I'm going to make stick. If you don't talk you're going round to Sackville Street.' He grinned at her. 'Maybe they've met you there before,' he went on, 'even if they don't know you as Miss La Valliere. Well?'

She shrugged her shoulders. She said plaintively: 'What the hell's a girl to do? I think I'm a mug. I'm always getting in bad.'

Callaghan asked: 'What did you get for it?'

She said sullenly: 'A fiver.'

Callaghan said: 'If you're a sensible girl and talk, you'll get ten. Who told you to do it?'

She thought for a moment; then she said: 'It doesn't matter a thing anyhow. It was some man I used to know. A chucker-out in a dump I worked in. A tough egg. I don't know a thing about it or what's behind it, but I was hard up . . . and . . . well . . . you know how it is.'

Callaghan opened his note-case. He produced two five-pound notes. He asked: 'Who's the boyfriend? Where does he live?'

'Off Macclesfield Street,' said Miss La Valliere. 'Grays Mansions – No. 24. The name's Grellin. You ought to watch your step. He can get bad-tempered sometimes and he's a big slob. Look . . . do you think you could keep me out of this?'

He gave her the money. He said: 'Why worry.'

It was half-past five when Callaghan rang the door-bell on the third floor at Grays Mansions.

Grays Mansions was an unsalubrious place. It was dusty. The walls were grimy; the passages unswept. There was an air of desolation about the place. After a moment somebody called out: 'Come on in. The door's open.'

Callaghan went in. The room in front of him was a bedsitting-room – one of those rooms which are converted by pushing the bed into a corner and putting a settee-cover over it. At the moment it was still a bedroom. Clothes lay on the floor. In the bed, an unprepossessing specimen with black hair and an unshaven face looked at Callaghan curiously.

He said: 'What the hell do *you* want? I thought you was Struby.'

Callaghan said: 'I'm not. My name's Callaghan. You're Grellin, aren't you?'

The man in the bed said: 'That's my name. And what the hell does that mean to you?'

'At the moment quite a lo,' Callaghan replied. 'I've got an idea that some time last night somebody telephoned through to you, told you I was going to the Night Light Club; and asked you if you could fix it that I didn't get a telephone call that was coming through for me there. Somebody evidently wanted to stall a little for time. You fixed it. You got through to your friend Miss La Valliere who you knew was a member of the Night Light. All right . . . well, who told you to do it and why – if you know why?'

Mr Grellin looked at Callaghan with supreme contempt.

He said: 'Why don't you get out of here?' He raised himself on one elbow. He looked almost ferocious.

Callaghan moved swiftly across the room. He put out his left hand and put the fingers into the neckband of Mr Grellin's rather soiled pyjamas. He brought his right arm up, hit Grellin in the face with the point of his elbow. The blow made a staccato noise like a mallet striking wood. Mr Grellin's head went back on the bed with a thud.

He said: 'Now, talk, Grellin, or I'm going to take you apart. I don't like you.'

The man in the bed put out a hand. He picked up a dirty handkerchief from the table by the bedside. He mopped his lips which were bleeding. He felt a tooth which was a little loose.

He said: 'This ain't so good. I didn't know there was going to be any strings to this.'

Callaghan said grimly: 'They always tell you that. Where did the call come from? Talk quickly; otherwise I'm going to start work on you.'

Grellin said: 'Yes . . .?' He said something else too. Not at all a nice word. He shot out of the bed as if he had been expelled from a cannon; aimed a blow at Callaghan that would have finished him if it had connected.

It did not connect. Callaghan side-stepped. He spun round as Grellin came in for his second *blitzkrieg*; ducked the terrific swing aimed at his head, stepped in and planted a nasty short-arm in the region of his opponent's navel. Mr Grellin gave a funny little gasp. He repeated it as Callaghan smashed in a left swing to his jaw and brought over another right to the stomach; turned it into a groan as Callaghan finished with a left-handed jab to Grellin's mouth that removed the loose tooth and loosened two more.

Grellin subsided on the bed. He said: 'I've 'ad it. This is not my bleedin' day!' He picked up the handkerchief and resumed first-aid operations.

Callaghan said: 'It looks to me as if it is. You'd better start talking, Grellin.'

Grellin sighed. Then he said something very rude under his breath. Then: 'Well, all I know is I got a call from a pal of mine. He's the head waiter at the Mardene Club – some place near Brighton. He said I was on to twenty pounds if you didn't get the call. So I fixed it. Maybe you know how I fixed it.'

Callaghan said: 'That doesn't matter.' He went on: 'What was the idea? What's the good of stopping one telephone call? How did your man know there weren't going to be some more?'

Grellin shrugged his shoulders. He mopped his mouth again. He said: 'I wouldn't know.'

Callaghan lit a cigarette. He asked: 'What's your friend's name?'

Grellin said: 'Charlie Maysin. He's not a bad guy. He did me a good turn once. I always like to pay a good turn back.'

'Very commendable,' said Callaghan. He went on: 'Take a tip from me, Grellin, mind your own business. Don't stick your nose into anything that doesn't concern you. If you do that, you're likely to stay all in one piece.'

He turned on his heel; walked out of the room.

Left to himself, Mr Grellin replaced his head on the pillow; pondered on the iniquities of life.

Callaghan drove slowly towards South Kensington. He sat at the wheel, relaxed, appreciating the dry, cold wind that stung his face. He was beginning to be very interested in Colonel Stenhurst, in Viola Alardyse, in the residents at Dark Spinney generally. And there were possibilities. Callaghan thought that someone was inclined to be nasty. He thought it possible that this same somebody might easily be even nastier. He wondered who it was that was going to get hurt.

Somewhere a church clock struck eight. The chimes sounded attractively in the still evening air. Callaghan stopped his car at the beginning of the private road that bounded the high wall round the Dark Spinney grounds; turned off the headlights; switched on the parking lights; began to walk back towards the entrance.

He was thinking about Colonel Stenhurst. It was obvious that some sort of situation was due to develop within the next hour or so. It was also obvious to him that Miss Viola Alardyse did not particularly like her trustee – Colonel Stenhurst – and by the same token Callaghan imagined that Colonel Stenhurst was not too taken with her. Well, that was fairly normal. When trustees and beneficiaries under Wills fell out, private detectives often stepped in.

Callaghan went up the carriage-drive, admired the rhododendron bushes that flanked it; thought how beautiful the drive would be when the flowers were in bloom. He went up the steps; rang the doorbell.

Two or three minutes went by; then one of the double doors opened. Sallins appeared. Callaghan noted with an appreciative eye the neatness of the butler's well-brushed evening clothes – the carefully tied black satin tie, the thin face, the sparse grey hair. Definitely an old-type family retainer, thought Callaghan.

He said: 'My name's Callaghan of Callaghan Investigations. I'd like to see Colonel Stenhurst.'

Sallins said: 'I'm afraid he's not at home, Sir.'

'When do you expect him to return?' Callaghan asked.

Sallins took a large gold watch out of his black waistcoat pocket. He said: It's just after eight now, Sir. Usually the family dines at nine. The Colonel ought to be back in time to change. Would you like to wait, Sir, or will you come back?'

Callaghan said: 'I think I'll come back.'

He was about to turn away when a figure appeared behind Sallins. It was Miss Wymering.

She asked: 'What is it, Sallins?'

The butler said: 'This gentleman – a Mr Callaghan of Callaghan Investigations – wishes to see the Colonel, Ma'am. I've just told him that he probably won't be back till half-past eight.'

Miss Wymering said: 'That is quite likely.' She said to Callaghan: 'Mr Callaghan, I wonder would you care to come in and wait. I don't think my brother-in-law will be very long. In the meantime I would like to speak to you. I am Miss Wymering.'

Callaghan said: 'Of course.' He stepped past Sallins into the hallway. He followed Miss Wymering down the long passage; turned to the left down a small passage; entered an oak-wainscotted room.

She said: 'Mr Callaghan, I'm glad I've an opportunity of talking to you before you see the Colonel. Will you sit down – and would you like to smoke? I'll get you some cigarettes?'

Callaghan said: 'Thank you very much, Miss Wymering. Don't bother. I'll smoke one of my own.' He took out his case, lit a cigarette. He said: 'Now tell me all about it.' He smiled at her. He went on: 'I think you're worried about something, aren't you? But I shouldn't if I were you.'

She looked at him closely. She thought she rather liked Mr Callaghan. His smile was kindly. He looked the sort of person you could trust – at least she hoped he was.

She said: 'Mr Callaghan, I'll say what I have to say quickly, because my brother-in-law might be back. He is rather inclined to be bad tempered. You know, he was in the Indian Army.' She smiled whimsically. 'Most of them seem to develop livers after fifty-five. But I don't want him to make a mountain out of a molehill. I don't want him to create a situation he might be sorry for afterwards.'

Callaghan said: 'That wouldn't be a good thing, would it? You can rely on my tact. Tact,' said Callaghan with a little grin, 'is the main part of the stock-in-trade of private detectives.'

'I'm very glad to hear it,' said Miss Wymering. 'The position is this: My sister – Colonel Stenhurst was her second husband – is the mother of the three girls here – Viola, Corinne and Patricia. She left a rather peculiar Will – perhaps not so awfully peculiar because she knew what she wanted to do. But it's placed the Colonel in a rather odd position. There are three trustees – he and I and a lawyer. At the moment, under this Will, Viola is the beneficiary and the life owner of this estate. The Colonel seems to have got an idea from somewhere or other that she and Corinne have got to know a rather unpleasant person or persons at Brighton. He doesn't like that. He talked to the girls about it at dinner last night and there was a little unpleasantness.'

Callaghan said: 'They didn't like it?'

'No,' said Miss Wymering. 'They didn't like it. That's quite understandable, isn't it? After all, Viola is nearly thirty and Corinne is twenty-eight. Times have changed and girls aren't like they were in my brother-in-law's young days. Quite naturally, they resent what they consider to be an unwarrantable interference on his part in their affairs.'

Callaghan said: 'I quite understand. They didn't like it – they probably said so – and there was a row?'

She nodded. 'There've been one or two rows lately,' she said. '*I* don't like them, Mr Callaghan. The position is made all the more difficult because Colonel Stenhurst has only his pension in addition to the two hundred and fifty pounds which he receives under my sister's Will. That isn't a great deal of money, especially in these days of high taxation. Viola allows him an additional thousand a year. That makes the situation a little more difficult.'

Callaghan said: 'Of course it does. In other words, if Miss Alardyse gets annoyed she can turn off the Colonel's thousand a year?'

She nodded. 'Precisely.'

Callaghan asked: 'Has she threatened to do that?'

She said: 'No.'

Callaghan knocked the ash from his cigarette. He said: 'I take it Patricia doesn't come into this.'

She said: 'We-ll . . . not really. You see, Patricia's only seventeen, but then she's a peculiar sort of young woman in a way. She's inclined to be a little dramatic, Mr Callaghan. She goes to the pictures a great deal and she adores situations.'

Callaghan grinned. He said: 'You mean she's rather liking this. Perhaps she enjoys a family row?'

'Ye-es . . .' said Miss Wymering. 'I think she does. You see, she likes to dramatize everything and see herself as the central character. Really, she's not concerned at all in this.'

Callaghan asked: 'And Viola and Corinne?'

She said: 'Viola is a delightful girl. It's no good my saying she's not my favourite because she is. Everybody likes Viola. Perhaps she's a little quiet; a little strange. Sometimes I think she is worried. Then again I think it's possibly just her temperament. She doesn't seem to want to live or do the things that girls of her age normally do.'

'I see,' said Callaghan. 'And Corinne?'

Miss Wymering said: 'Well, Corinne is quite a different type. She can be quite hard if she wants to. Lots of people think she is – it's rather an odd word to use,' said Miss Wymering diffidently, 'a little flighty, but I think that's normal. I don't think any of the girls have enjoyed the war much, and Corinne worked very hard at the war hospital near Herstmonceux. I expect she's just relaxing like so many other people.'

Callaghan nodded. 'I think I understand about Corinne. And as for Viola,' he went on, 'she's rather quiet – doesn't want to do the things that young women do in the ordinary course of events, except' – he added – 'this Brighton business in which Corinne also seems concerned. I suppose you don't know anything about that, Miss Wymering?'

She said: 'No. The Colonel didn't say anything about that, but he seems to know *something* about it.'

'I understand,' said Callaghan. 'You know, it struck me as a little bit extraordinary, Miss Wymering. It seems that the Colonel rang my office fairly late last night. He spoke to my assistant. He said he wanted to see me urgently; that he wanted me to come down here as soon as possible. He said something about having had a letter. My assistant gave him a telephone number at which he could get in touch with me later in the evening. A call came through for me which I imagine was from the Colonel,' Callaghan continued, 'but unfortunately I wasn't able to take it.'

She said: 'I expect, having failed to get you once, he thought he'd wait.'

'That would seem to be the normal thing for him to have done,' said Callaghan, 'but one would have imagined that as the matter was so urgent he'd have got through today. Yet he didn't telephone me.'

She said: 'No? Well, of course there's an explanation for that. There's been trouble here with the telephone. The man came out this afternoon and put it right. There was a fault or something – one of the connections was broken.'

Callaghan asked: 'Exactly what do you want me to do, Miss Wymering?'

She said: 'Of course you'll do whatever the Colonel asks you to do I expect. But I don't think that Viola will be prepared to stand for it. You see, he talked about having the girls watched which they naturally resented. I thought if I explained the situation to you, Mr Callaghan, you might possibly discount a *little* of what he says to you. He's rather inclined to exaggerate complaints against people. I don't think any of the girls are at all popular with him at the moment. I'm not asking you *not* to – to take any notice of what he says to you. I'm only asking you not to take him *too* seriously.'

Callaghan smiled at her. He thought he liked Miss Wymering. He said: 'Thank you very much, Miss Wymering. I think it would be a good idea if, after I've had my talk with the Colonel; after I've heard what he has to say, perhaps you and I could have another talk.'

She smiled at him. She was more certain than ever now that she trusted Mr Callaghan. She said: 'Yes, I think that would be a very good idea. But I don't think we ought to meet here. He'd be awfully angry if he thought I was talking to you behind his back.'

Callaghan said: 'We'll meet somewhere else. I'm staying at the Two Friars Hotel in Alfriston. After I've had a talk with the Colonel you might come and see me. We could talk things over.'

She said: 'That would be very nice.'

Callaghan looked at his watch. 'It is a quarter past eight,' he said. 'I think the best thing for me to do would be to telephone the Colonel after dinner – say at nine-thirty; tell him I've arrived at Alfriston; suggest that I drive over.'

She said: 'An excellent idea.' She held out her hand. 'Thank you very much, Mr Callaghan. I'm sure everything is going to be all right.'

Callaghan took her hand. He noticed that it was trembling. He wondered why. He thought perhaps Miss Wymering was a nervous type.

She said: 'Did you leave your car in the carriage-drive?'

He shook his head. He said: 'No, I left it fifty or sixty yards up the road, at the beginning of the little private road that leads round by the high wall.'

She said: 'Well, if you don't want to meet the Colonel on your way out; if you like to go through the side door in the hall passage, right across the garden path, across the lawn, you'll find a green door in the wall. If you go through that you'll arrive a few yards from your car.'

Callaghan said: 'Thank you.'

He walked out of the room, down the passage, into the hall. He picked up his hat from the stand, noticed the time on the grandfather clock – twenty minutes past eight. He walked down the side passage, opened the door at the end. Before him in the pale moonlight he could see the long well-kept path stretching across the lawn, skirting a flower garden at the end. He began to walk up the path. It was a fine night, cold but cheerful. The air tasted good.

Callaghan thought about Miss Wymering. He thought family life even in rural England was not as easy as people thought it was. He reached the door in the wall. His hand was on the latch. He stopped and listened. Behind him he could hear footsteps. He looked over his shoulder. Sallins was half-running, half-stumbling towards him along the path that ran at right angles from the one on which Callaghan stood.

Callaghan said: 'What's the matter?'

The butler stood looking at Callaghan. His mouth was working spasmodically, but no words emerged. He stood there, an almost grotesque figure mouthing unintelligible nothings.

Callaghan said not unkindly: 'Take it easy. What's the matter? Whatever it is, it could have been worse.'

The butler found his voice. He said breathlessly: 'After you'd gone with Miss Wymering, Sir, I noticed that the Colonel's hat was still on the hallstand. He always wears one hat – a soft brown hat. I wondered where he could be. I thought he might be in the grounds, so I went out to look to tell him that you were here. There is a summer house over there.' He pointed along the path from which he had come. 'We call it the pagoda. More out of habit than anything else I looked in. He was lying there. He's dead.'

Callaghan asked: 'What did he die of?'

The butler said: 'I think he's shot himself. There's a pistol there close by him.' He began to tremble again. 'It's not a nice sight,' he said.

'No, it never is,' said Callaghan. 'What's your name?'

The old man said: 'My name's Sallins, Sir. I've been here since I was a boy. My God, I never expected to see anything happen like this.'

Callaghan said: 'I don't expect you did. Look, Sallins, I'll tell you what you'll do. Just stay here and relax. When you feel better, go in and ring the police. Where are they?'

Sallins said: 'The nearest police officer, Sir, is at Alfriston.'

'All right,' said Callaghan easily. 'Wait here for a bit; then go back to the house. Ring the police at Alfriston and tell them what's happened. I expect they'll come out as soon as they can. You're sure the Colonel *is* dead?'

Sallins said: 'I think so, Sir.'

'I'll go and look,' said Callaghan. 'Do as I've told you, Sallins. Wait here for two or three minutes; then go in and phone the police.'

He began to walk along the path. Two minutes brought him to the edge of a coppice. The path ran through it. On the other side, in a little clearing, stood a pagoda-shaped summer house. A circular verandah surrounded it. A flight of wooden steps led up to the door.

Callaghan went in. Through a window on the other side of the circular room, which was furnished with garden chairs and a table, came a gleam of moonlight. Lying on the floor was the body of the Colonel. He was lying on his left side. His right hand was outstretched, the fingers extended almost in an attitude of supplication. Five or six feet from him on the floor was a pistol. Looking at it casually, Callaghan thought it could be a .38 R.I.C. police pistol. He knelt down by the body. One side of the Colonel's face was not at all pretty and was practically conspicuous by its absence. The other side was almost austere in the lines of death.

Callaghan sighed. As he rose from his knee he saw a gleam of white under the body. He snapped on his cigarette lighter, bent down again. It was a small lace handkerchief. He picked it up. There were two initials in the corner – V.A. He moved over to the window; stood leaning against the wooden wall, the wisp of lace in his hand, looking at the thing which had once been Colonel Gervase Stenhurst.

Then he moved to the body. He put the back of his hand against the good side of the corpse's face. He thought the Colonel had been dead for some little time.

He straightened up. He walked over to the door, went through it, closed it behind him, descended the five wooden steps. Then he stopped. He thought to himself that even if truth was at the bottom of the well it had an odd way of putting its head up in the long run. No matter what happened it eventually emerged. There . . .

Callaghan listened attentively. There was not a sound. Then after a minute he heard footsteps on a gravel path. That, he thought, would be Sallins walking back to the house. Callaghan turned. He went quickly up the wooden steps, back into the pagoda. He knelt down by the body, took the unused handkerchief in the left breast pocket of the coat. He spread the handkerchief over the palm of his right hand, picked up the pistol, wiped it. Holding the butt of the pistol in the handkerchief he took the Colonel's left hand; pressed the fingers on the barrel. He put the pistol down within two or three feet of the body; then carefully inserted the handkerchief between the open fingers of the Colonel's right hand. He went out of the pagoda, closing the door softly behind him. Outside he stopped to light a cigarette; then he began to walk slowly along the path towards the green door.

Callaghan thought life was damned funny. You did things and you weren't quite certain why you did them. At least you *thought* you weren't certain. Actually, at the back of his mind he knew perfectly well why. . . . He shrugged his shoulders.

He pulled up the latch of the green oak door and opened it. He stood there, the door held wide open, smiling. Viola Alardyse stood on the other side of the door on the dirt road. A few yards away he could see the rear light of his car shining in the half light.

He moved to one side. He said: 'Good evening, Miss Alardyse.'

It was quite a little while before she spoke. She looked at him steadily. When she did speak her voice was quiet but angry.

She said: 'This afternoon when I saw you, Mr Callaghan, I gave you some excellent advice. I'm very sorry that you haven't been wise enough to take it.'

He felt for his cigarette case, opened it, took a cigarette. He looked at her through the flame of the lighter.

'I never take advice, Miss Alardyse,' he said. 'I've found that other people's advice doesn't often interest me. I prefer to make my own mistakes.' He grinned at her, almost insolently.

She said in a low tense voice: 'I don't care what you prefer to do, Mr Callaghan, but I insist that you make your mistakes elsewhere and not in my house or grounds. If I find you here again I shall have you thrown out. You understand?'

'Perfectly,' said Callaghan. His grin was maddening. 'I wonder who's going to do the throwing out,' he asked. 'Is it to be Sallins – your ancient retainer – or Miss Wymering, or yourself assisted by your sisters? Then again,' he went on, 'I might not want to be thrown out. I might elect to go quietly.'

She stepped past him, through the door, on to the gravel path. She was standing quite near him. A suggestion of her perfume came to his nostrils. Callaghan thought it was extremely attractive.

She said: 'I hope you will be sensible enough to make the throwing-out process unnecessary. In any event, I am going to order that you are not to be admitted to the house or grounds. I don't like you, Mr Callaghan.'

Callaghan nodded casually. 'I understand,' he said. His smile was illuminating. 'You don't know what you're missing.'

She said: 'I have nothing to say to you and I want to hear nothing from you. Is that plain?'

'Perfectly,' said Callaghan. He drew on his cigarette. He said: 'Very well. You have it *your* way. But when you go to bed tonight I'd like you to spend a few minutes thinking this out:

'Last night your guardian telephoned my office from this house. I wasn't in. It was suggested to him that he telephoned me, at a number which was given to him, in half an hour. He did so, but I didn't get the call because somebody who knew he was coming through doped my drink. I went out before I could take the call. So somebody here listened in to his telephone conversation with my office and had time enough to fix things so that I didn't get the second call.

'That somebody knew that the Colonel would probably telephone me from this house today. They'd made up their minds that he wasn't going to. They cut the telephone wire here. They were playing for time; playing for time until they could fix something else. Something that would definitely – once and for all – stop the Colonel from telling me anything I wasn't intended to hear.

'This afternoon you arrived at my office and told me that I wasn't to see the Colonel. That if I did you wouldn't pay for it; that if I came down here and stuck my nose into something that didn't concern me you'd go to the police.'

Callaghan threw his cigarette stub on the ground and trod on it. Then he said pleasantly: 'Think those points out tonight, Miss Alardyse, and see how you feel. Then if you still feel like going to the police . . . well, get on with it.

'But you won't. You won't go to the police and you'll find that sooner or later you'll have to have a little talk – with *me*. And, if you're as sensible as I think you might be, you'll make it sooner – *not* later.'

He stepped through the door. On the road outside, he turned and looked at her. She had not moved.

'Good night,' said Callaghan cheerfully. He took off his black soft hat, walked over to his car; got in; started it. He backed it down the narrow road past the green door.

She was standing where he had left her. A moment afterwards he heard the door shut with a bang.

On the main road he swung the car round, drove towards Alfriston.

He began to whistle softly to himself.

Chapter Three
Enter Patricia

CALLAGHAN walked slowly through the open space at the end of Alfriston High Street. The afternoon sun shone on the old houses, and the tree in the middle of the little square threw a pleasant shadow.

He reached the Two Friars; went up to his sitting-room. He lit a cigarette, took a bottle of whisky from the corner of the wardrobe, drank four fingers. He thought that drinking in the day was rather a bad habit. He drank another four fingers.

He walked to the window, stood looking out on to the narrow street. The telephone in his bedroom rang. It was Miss Wymering.

She said: 'Mr Callaghan, you said that I could talk to you. I think I ought to. I'm *very* worried.'

'I expect you are,' said Callaghan. 'Where are you now?'

She answered: 'I'm at the call-box at the end of the High Street. May I talk to you?'

'Why not?' said Callaghan. 'Come through the side entrance and straight up to my sitting-room. It's on the first floor.'

He began to walk up and down his sitting-room. He wondered exactly what had happened at Dark Spinney after he'd left the night before. He remembered his interview with Viola in the garden. He grinned. Maybe Viola had changed her tune when she'd got back to the house and heard the news. That is, if she hadn't known it before.

And why shouldn't she have known it before? Any woman can put on an act if she wants to. One of the main businesses of women, thought Callaghan, is that of putting on acts. And if she had killed the old boy it was a certainty that she wasn't going to let him know by her attitude. Besides, if you've nerve enough to kill someone you've nerve enough for anything.

She could be the murderess. And why not? She had more reason – as far as was evident at the moment – than anyone else. She didn't like the Colonel and she was scared of his talking to Callaghan. Well . . .?

And then there was her handkerchief underneath the body. The handkerchief with her initials in the corner. There was that.

He shrugged his shoulders. Possibly he had already made himself "an accessory after the fact" – an accessory to murder. He grinned to himself. He remembered what Gringall had once described as the motto of Callaghan Investigations – '*We get there somehow and who the hell cares how.*'

But it might be tough sledding.

He had finished his cigarette, started another, when Miss Wymering arrived. Looking at her, Callaghan could realize that once on a time she had been very beautiful; that even now she was good looking; that her eyes were soft and kindly.

He said: 'Sit down, Miss Wymering. Smoke a cigarette and tell me all about it. Let me have the whole story.' He smiled at her. He went on: 'First of all, what's the point that's worrying you?'

She puffed at the cigarette. She said: 'The thing that's worrying me, Mr Callaghan, is just how much one ought to say to policemen.'

Callaghan cocked one eyebrow. He asked: 'Have they been asking you something you don't want to answer?'

She said: 'No, it's not like that *exactly*. When the police came last night they were awfully nice. They brought a police surgeon with them. He spent a lot of time in the pagoda examining my brother-in-law's body. They asked all sorts of questions but they all seemed to be leading in one direction.'

Callaghan said: 'They were leading in the direction of trying to find out if anybody particular disliked the Colonel, I suppose?'

She nodded. She said unhappily: 'Yes. In fact they were.'

'And I imagine,' Callaghan went on, 'they asked if you knew of any quarrels he'd had lately; if anyone had reason for wanting him out of the way?'

She said: 'Something like that.'

'Actually what did you tell them?' Callaghan asked.

She said: 'Well, the Inspector – a C.I.D. man, from Brighton I think they said – came over. He was awfully nice. When he asked those questions about the Colonel having any enemies or having had quarrels with people, I told him that my brother-in-law wasn't an awfully popular man; that he was irascible; that he lost his temper over quite small things.'

Callaghan asked: 'Didn't he try to narrow that down?'

She said: 'Ye-es, he did. He asked about people in the house; whether the servants liked him. He seemed reassured when I told him that our servants had been with us for many years.

'By this time,' she went on, 'the police surgeon had finished. He came to the house and he and the Inspector went off together. They took some photographs of my brother-in-law's body. It was taken away this morning. The Inspector said he would probably be coming back again – or perhaps another police officer.'

Callaghan asked: 'Do you expect them back today?'

She said: 'I don't know. They didn't tell me.'

'All right,' said Callaghan. He pulled up a chair; straddled across it. 'Miss Wymering, I take it you are very upset about this little difference of opinion between the Colonel and Viola and Corinne at dinner the other night?'

She said: 'Yes, but not really in connection with his death. After all, it was really a storm in a tea-cup, wasn't it?'

Callaghan asked: 'Was it? You know, lots of people have been killed because of storms in tea-cups. By the way, what actually started the trouble? Can you remember?'

She said: 'Yes, it started as most quarrels do over something quite different. Patricia had been very naughty. She'd taken one of Corinne's frocks. It was cut much too low for her and didn't fit her – a red frock. She wore it at dinner. Apparently, Corinne had seen her in it before dinner and told her to take it off. She hadn't done so. At dinner Corinne was very angry with her. They started a little slanging-match. That was the start of the trouble.'

Callaghan said: 'I see. Well, now let's get down to hard tacks, Miss Wymering. Possibly right at the back of our minds we're both thinking the same thing.' He grinned. 'When Miss Alardyse came in last night, did you see her?'

She nodded. 'Yes, she came straight to my room.'

Callaghan asked: 'What happened?'

Miss Wymering looked serious. She said: 'She was furious. She had met you in the garden, and she was awfully angry about you being here. She said some extremely rude things about the Colonel and she was a little rude about you, I'm afraid. It seems she doesn't like private detectives an awful lot. Why, I don't know' – she smiled diffidently – 'but she doesn't.'

Callaghan said: 'This was before she heard that the Colonel was dead?'

She nodded. 'That's quite right,' she said. 'Directly I had a chance – because she was very angry – I prepared her for it and then told her that he was dead. She was terribly shaken. She was *awfully* upset.'

'She would be,' said Callaghan. 'Naturally, having had a row with him about the business we've discussed, she hated to think that he was dead before she had time to put things right. Is that so?'

She said: 'Yes.'

'And then?' asked Callaghan.

'Well, we had dinner,' said Miss Wymering. 'It was rather a terrible sort of meal. Nobody said anything very much. I'm afraid that none of us had really been awfully fond of the Colonel when he was alive, but we'd been so used to seeing him sitting at the head of the table, we all felt very strange about it. It wasn't at all nice.'

Callaghan said: 'I bet it wasn't. And then I take it that you talked to the police after dinner?'

She said: 'Yes.'

'They didn't talk to anybody else except you?' asked Callaghan.

She shook her head. 'No. I rather think they're going to talk to other people today. I got that impression.'

Callaghan said: 'Perhaps they will and perhaps they won't.' He went on: 'I think you've been very wise, Miss Wymering. I think you've been very wise not to say anything about that little quarrel at dinner the night before. After all, as you say, it was only a storm in a tea-cup.'

She said seriously: 'Mr Callaghan, you don't think –'

Callaghan grinned amiably at her. He said: 'I don't think anything. I just think we ought to forget *that*.'

She said slowly: 'Very well, if you say so. But there wasn't very much to it, was there?' She seemed to be asking for reassurance.

Callaghan said: 'Miss Wymering, listen to me. There's a little more in this business than meets the eyes. Work it out for yourself. After dinner, on the evening of the disagreement, the Colonel telephoned my office. As far as he was concerned the matter was urgent. Also he said something else. He said something about a letter; that he'd had a letter. I suppose you wouldn't know what he meant by that?'

She shook her head.

'All right,' said Callaghan. 'Well, my office suggested that he might get me at a club. There's no doubt that he came through there. So it wasn't a matter only of bad temper. He'd had time to get over the bad temper. But he took the trouble to ring up again later that night in order to contact me. Unfortunately,' said Callaghan, 'for reasons which don't matter, I never took that phone call. Well, why didn't he ring through yesterday morning?'

She said: 'But I told you, the line was out of order. A connection was broken.'

Callaghan said: 'Either that or else someone had cut it.'

Her eyes widened. She said: 'Good God, Mr Callaghan. You surely don't think–'

'I don't think,' said Callaghan. 'I know. Somebody was trying to stop the Colonel getting in touch with me. Well, it looks as if they succeeded, doesn't it? And that seems to show us quite a lot.'

She asked nervously: 'What does it show us, Mr Callaghan?'

'It shows us that whoever wanted to stop the Colonel talking to me was either doing it to gain time or else they had a pretty good idea that the Colonel wasn't going to live for very long,' said Callaghan. 'Don't you realize that? Any normal person who wanted to delay a message reaching me would know that cutting telephone wires would only delay the matter for a little while; that eventually the Colonel would find some means of getting in touch with me. Did someone know what was going to happen to him; that he was going to commit suicide?'

She said: 'I'm beginning to see. So you think somebody might have had an idea that he was going to kill himself?'

'Exactly,' said Callaghan.

She said – and he noticed her lips were trembling a little: 'Mr Callaghan, you couldn't possibly think that any of the girls–'

Callaghan said: 'I don't think anything at all. All I know is that the Colonel had something he wanted to say to me; that he had a letter he wanted to talk to me about; that he hasn't been able to talk to me about it.' He went on: 'It's rather a pity that Miss Alardyse and I are not better friends, isn't it?'

She said quickly: 'Mr Callaghan, I think you're wrong there. I meant to tell you – when I was talking about her. I told you how she came in and was furious before she knew the Colonel was dead; how angry she was about you having been in the house. Well, I must say that late last night, after the police had gone, she came to me and she told me that she thought she'd been rather stupid about you; that she didn't really mean what she said.'

Callaghan said: 'Maybe I'll have a chance to talk to her after all.'

She said: 'I wish you could, Mr Callaghan.'

He asked abruptly: 'Why?'

She said: 'I'll tell you. Now that my brother-in-law is dead I feel more responsible about the girls than ever. It's quite obvious to me after what you've said that he was serious about this thing; that it wasn't just a matter of bad temper. I've been thinking . . . it's awfully difficult to know what goes on in young women's minds these days. I thought how odd it would be if there was some justi-fication for his suspicions; for his being so unpleasant about these people that Viola and Corinne had met at Brighton. After all, young women are never as clever as they think they are.'

Callaghan grinned at her. He said: 'So actually, Miss Wymering, *you're* asking me to try and find out what the Colonel wanted me to find out, but from a different motive. His was possibly anger and suspicion; yours is just kindness of heart. All right, I'll do my best.'

She got up. 'I think you're very kind,' she said. 'And I trust you, Mr Callaghan. I'm glad you're here. But I don't know how you're going to be paid.'

'We won't worry about that,' said Callaghan. He held out his hand. 'When I have something to talk to you about I'll let you know. In the meantime, if anything happens that you think I should know about you'll find me here. If I'm not here you can always talk to Mr Nikolls, my assistant. He should be here shortly.'

She said: 'Goodbye, Mr Callaghan. Thank you very much. You know, *I* haven't a great deal of money, but–'

Callaghan said cheerfully: 'You haven't a great deal of money and we can hardly ask Viola to pay for the pleasure of having Callaghan Investigations find out what she's doing. Let's wait and see what happens.'

She said: 'Thank you, Mr Callaghan.'

When she had gone Callaghan walked back to his sitting-room, closed the door, lit a fresh cigarette. He concluded that he liked Miss Wymering very much. But he wondered if she were telling the whole truth. He thought she was a little more concerned for the two girls than she was inclined to admit.

The door opened and Nikolls appeared.

Callaghan said: 'Well?'

Nikolls said: 'I had a swell trip down here. I hired a sweet car. Me – I like the country. The sunshine sorta makes me feel a different guy.'

Callaghan said: 'Yes? Apart from that, have you got that Will?'

'Yeah,' said Nikolls. 'Here it is.'

Callaghan took the sheets of paper; walked over to the window. He read:

This is the last Will and Testament of me Viola Corinne Patricia Stenhurst of Dark Spinney Hangover in the County of Sussex.

I hereby revoke all former testamentary dispositions.

I appoint my husband Gervase Stenhurst, my sister Honoria Jean Wymering and my Solicitor John Galashiels to be my Executors and Trustees and so long as each such Trustee shall continue to act in that capacity I bequeath to him or her £250 per annum and such additional sum as may be authorized as hereinafter mentioned.

During my lifetime I have observed that the possession of a large income may be dangerous to the marital prospects of any woman inasmuch as an undesirable type of man may be attracted by her money and may propose marriage to her merely in order to share her fortune and lead a life of idleness and selfishness and as it is my most earnest desire to save my daughters from such a fate which can only result in the deprivation of their proper happiness I direct my Trustees to distribute my estate in the manner following:

I direct that after payment of my debts and other liabilities my Trustees shall invest the residue of my Estate in Trustee securities and out of the income to be derived therefrom shall pay the bequests to themselves above referred to and £350 per annum to each of my three daughters Viola, Corinne and Patricia.

As to the rest of the said income (hereinafter referred to as 'the residuary income') I direct my Trustees to pay the same unto my eldest daughter Viola, provided that she is unmarried at the time of my death, until such time as she shall marry.

If my daughter Viola should be married at the time of my death or should become married thereafter or upon her death then in any such event the residuary income shall be paid to my second daughter Corinne (if then unmarried) on the same terms and conditions as those above stated in respect to my daughter Viola and in the event of my daughter Corinne failing or ceasing to become entitled thereto then the residuary income shall pass (again if then unmarried) to my third daughter Patricia again under the same terms and conditions.

In the event of all my daughters failing or ceasing to become entitled to the residuary income then my Estate both as to capital and income shall be distributed amongst such Charities as my Trustees shall select.

I direct that the bequests to my Trustees or any of them may be increased by an addition thereto from out of the residuary income should the daughter beneficially entitled thereto at the time so direct.

By this method of distribution of my Estate I am seeking to ensure that men who offer marriage to my daughters will realize that it will be their obligation and privilege duly to provide the means for their maintenance and support, but I am advised that these provisions may be invalid on the ground that they are in restraint of the marriage of my daughters and therefore contrary to Public Policy.

Therefore as I have no intention of allowing this Will to be the subject of legal controversy, I direct that should any beneficiary of this my Will seek in the Courts to contest its legality such person shall receive no benefit whatsoever hereunder.

In the event of any of my Trustees dying or ceasing to act a new Trustee shall be appointed by the continuing Trustees. In witness whereof the Testator has hereunto set her hand this 12th day of January 1943.

VIOLA CORINNE PATRICIA STENHURST

Signed by Viola Corinne Patricia Stenhurst as and for her last Will and Testament in our presence who in her presence at her request and in the presence of each other have hereunder subscribed our names as witnesses:

George Ernest Sallins (Butler)

Dark Spinney
Hangover
Sussex

Augusta Polly Stokes (Cook)

Dark Spinney
Hangover
Sussex

Callaghan folded up the papers, put them in his pocket. He said to Nikolls: 'Have you read it?'

Nikolls nodded. 'Yeah,' he said, 'I read it.'

Callaghan asked: 'Does it mean anything to you?'

'Sure,' said Nikolls. 'I reckon she didn't like the Colonel very much. It stands to reason, if she'd been happy with the Colonel she wouldn't have worried about some other guys takin' the girls for their money. Women can be odd about a thing like that. I reckon she got the idea in her head that he married her for what she'd got.'

Callaghan said: 'Yes, that's right enough.'

Nikolls went on: 'That's why she only leaves him two hundred and fifty a year. I bet that pleased the old guy. I don't wonder he gets excited and bad tempered. Anything else he gets he has to have from one of the daughters, whichever one is the heiress. I bet he didn't like that either.'

Nikolls fumbled in his pocket for a Lucky Strike. He found one, lit it. He said, with an attempt at whimsicality: 'Me – I *know* something. It's gonna kill you.'

Callaghan said: 'Yes?'

Nikolls went on: 'When I was drivin' along the main stem just now, who d'you think I see – standin' around in that little square where the tree is – smokin' a little pipe and lookin' up at the sky sorta innocent? I give you four guesses.'

Callaghan said: 'I don't want to guess.'

'Nobody else but Chief Detective-Inspector Gringall,' said Nikolls.

Callaghan said: 'I'm not surprised. Our client's had it. He's dead.'

Nikolls said: 'Does that account for Gringall? The local cops must have got a move on. He's down here pretty quick.'

Callaghan grinned. He said: 'That makes it really interesting. That means to say that the local police didn't like it and the Brighton C.I.D. don't like it either. That means to say that they're not quite certain it's suicide. They've got in touch with the Yard, and they haven't wasted any time.'

Nikolls said: 'No, I wouldn't be surprised if he didn't want to see you about something.'

Callaghan said: 'That wouldn't surprise me either.' He went on: 'Listen, Windy, according to this Will there are three trustees – the Colonel, who is no longer with us; Miss Wymering – I know about Miss Wymering; and the third trustee – a man by the name of John Galashiels, who was apparently Mrs Stenhurst's lawyer. See what you can find out about John Galashiels. I might like to talk to him.'

'O.K.,' said Nikolls. 'Do they know about it down here yet?'

'Not yet,' said Callaghan. 'It looks as if the C.I.D. man from Brighton told everyone up at Dark Spinney to keep their mouths shut about it. But it'll have to break in a minute; then everybody will start talking.'

'Yeah,' said Nikolls, 'and that's the time to listen.'

'Another thing,' said Callaghan, 'you might get into that car of yours and take yourself over to Brighton some time. There's a club somewhere on the outskirts called the Mardene Club. There's a waiter who works there called Charlie Maysin. Find out what you can about him and the club. Make it snappy.'

Nikolls said: 'O.K. I'll be seein' you.'

He went out.

When Chief Detective-Inspector Gringall came into the bar parlour of the Two Friars, Callaghan was sitting in the corner drinking whisky and soda. He watched as Gringall went to the bar, ordered a drink, began to fill his short briar pipe.

That makes it murder, thought Callaghan. Definitely murder. Gringall would not be down here unless it was; unless the Brighton police had thought so at first sight. Callaghan wondered just what the medical report had been. He took another look at Gringall.

George Henry Gringall – nicknamed the Jigger – was nearly fifty years of age. He looked like anything else but a police officer. He had that bland and innocuous expression which often distinguishes members of his calling. He was quiet, unassuming and pleasant. He was in fact a characteristic type of the senior police officer who is – when all is said and done, and when writers of detective novels have done their worst – still the finest type of police officer in the world.

If at times he preferred to look slightly stupid; if at times he seemed to be seeking for the right word; and if generally he gave the impression of concentrating on other matters, it was because that was a technique which he had developed over the years – the technique of making the 'other man' feel happy; that he was dealing with someone who was not quite as brilliant as he was.

Gringall, served with his whisky and soda, picked up the glass, came over to Callaghan. He said: 'Hallo, Slim. It's nice seeing you down here.'

Callaghan said: 'Yes, I like it too. How are you? It's a long time since I've seen you.'

Gringall said: 'Yes.' There was a pause, then: 'You know, Slim, I've got an idea. Two or three times on different cases, like the Denys case and the Vendayne case, you and I have run across each other. I've often thought about those two jobs, and then I've realized how much better it would have been if we'd got down to hard tacks from the start.'

Callaghan said: 'So that's what you've thought! You've got something on your mind, Gringall. If you think we could save any time by getting down to hard tacks go ahead.'

Gringall said: 'All right. Well . . . I'm not going to pretend that I think you're down here for your health. I know that you've been up at Dark Spinney. I take it that you were, or are, working for someone in the family; and I think you know why I'm down here?'

Callaghan nodded. He said: 'I take it that the Sussex police thought they'd like to have you down here over this Stenhurst thing – the suicide thing.'

Gringall raised his eyebrows. He said: 'Suicide? I hadn't thought of that.'

Callaghan grinned. He said: 'I haven't thought about it either.'

'No?' said Gringall. 'You know, Slim, you very seldom say anything you don't want to, and I've never known you talk about a client's affairs. But this case is rather different, isn't it? Your client's dead.'

Callaghan said: 'No? Now what do you think of that?'

Gringall asked blandly: 'Well, isn't he?'

Callaghan drank some whisky. He said: 'That depends on who my client is, doesn't it, Gringall? But aren't we rather flirting about with the subject?'

Gringall said: 'All right, don't let's flirt about with anything. Let's get down to hard tacks. The way I see it, the night before last there was a little bit of bad temper at dinner up at Dark Spinney. It seems that Colonel Stenhurst was rather annoyed with something that his stepdaughters had done – at least two of 'em. I mean Miss Alardyse and Miss Corinne Alardyse. It seems he gave them a pretty straight talking to.'

Callaghan said: 'Did he? I wonder where you got that from.'

'Naturally I've been talking to the servants,' said Gringall. He went on: 'It seems that the Colonel decided to employ a private detective. He was unhappy about the girls. He wanted to find out what was going on. He rang your office and I take it he rang your office immediately after he'd finished his dinner.'

Callaghan said: 'I wouldn't know about that, and I don't know how you know. Are you asking me or telling me?'

Gringall said: 'I'm *telling* you. You know, there's no automatic dialling down here in the call-boxes. You get through to the exchange. The girl who's on there at night isn't too busy and she's got a good memory.'

Callaghan said: 'It must be nice to be a telephone girl.' He grinned at Gringall. 'I wonder if she listened to the conversation.'

Gringall said: 'No, I don't suppose she'd do a thing like that. Anyhow,' he went on, 'the Colonel made another call to you at some other number – a Regent number.'

Callaghan said: 'I don't even know that either. Somebody rang me at that number but I don't know that it was the Colonel.'

Gringall asked: 'So you didn't take the call.'

Callaghan said: 'No, I didn't take the call.'

'All right,' said Gringall. 'But you decided to come down here yesterday evening, so I take it that some sort of message had been left for you at your office; that you considered it important enough for you to come down here. In other words,' he smiled cheerfully, 'you saw in Colonel Stenhurst a potential client.' He drew on his pipe. 'Now you don't work for nothing, Slim, and you knew that if the Colonel wanted to see you on urgent affairs he'd got to pay.' He smiled again. 'You charge a lot of money for your services – quite rightly I think. Who did you think was going to pay you? I ask that,' he said, 'because I think I know the technique of private detectives. If they're commissioned to do a job they like to find out that they're going to be paid.'

Callaghan said: 'I didn't have very much time to find out anything very much about the Colonel, did I?'

Gringall said: 'But you still came down. I wonder why.'

'What is this – a cross-examination?' asked Callaghan. 'Am I making a statement or is this just a little talk?'

Gringall said: 'It's just a little talk. Be reasonable, Slim. I've got to talk to you, haven't I? You know that.'

'Yes, of course,' said Callaghan cheerfully. 'I know you've got to talk to me, Gringall, because I was one of the first people to see the body. Sallins saw it first and then I saw it. I expect he told you about that too.'

Gringall nodded. He said: 'So that brings us back to the point. You thought that it was sufficiently to your advantage to come down and see the Colonel. Would I be asking too much if I asked why?'

Callaghan said: 'No, I'll tell you why. Just let me sort my ideas out.' He thought quickly. If Sallins had told Gringall as much as he knew he might easily have told him that Viola Alardyse had been away from Dark Spinney most of the afternoon on the day of the Colonel's death. It was a certainty, thought Callaghan, that somebody would have seen her driving away from Dark Spinney. If he knew anything about Gringall, Gringall would find out one way or another that she'd been to see Callaghan that afternoon.

He said, with that bland expression he invariably wore when lying: 'Listen, Gringall, when we started this conversation you said something that I rather agreed with. So if I tell you exactly what's happened I shall be doing my duty as a good citizen. In other words, nobody will be able to threaten me with "withholding information from the police", or the "obstruction of a police officer in the execution of his duty".' He smiled amiably.

Gringall said: 'I think you're very wise Slim, and it's going to save an awful lot of trouble.'

Callaghan said: 'Yes, well here goes. This is what happened: Colonel Stenhurst did ring me after dinner – that would be the night before last. It was well after nine o'clock and I wasn't in my office. Nikolls was there. Apparently, the Colonel was rather angry and excited about something. I don't think that's unusual in these elderly ex-Indian Army officers. He wanted to see me and of course he wanted to see me as soon as possible. Nikolls didn't think I'd be particularly interested, but actually we hadn't very much business on hand at the moment so he suggested to the old boy that he might ring me up at a number – a club I was going to – later.'

Gringall nodded.

Callaghan said: 'He did ring up. I was told there was a telephone message for me. Well, I didn't take it. I didn't see why I should. You see, I didn't know it was a potential client, and people who ring me up round about the region of ten o'clock at night in night clubs aren't usually potential clients.'

'No, they wouldn't be,' said Gringall. He smiled.

'Exactly,' said Callaghan. 'Between you and me I thought it might be a lady and I didn't think I wanted to talk to her. So I didn't.'

Gringall said: 'That's all right, but you still came down yesterday evening in spite of the fact that you hadn't talked to your potential client. You still thought it would be worth your while to talk to him.'

Callaghan said: 'Aren't you rather jumping ahead with things? Let me finish my piece. The next morning when I went into the office, Nikolls of course told me about the call from the Colonel. I told him I wasn't interested. Then something happened which made me a little more interested.'

Gringall said: 'No? What?'

Callaghan thought: That's good enough. He doesn't know yet. He said: 'Actually I was so disinterested in the Stenhurst business that I'd planned to go to Waverley in the afternoon, but I had a caller. Miss Alardyse came to see me at the office.'

Gringall raised his eyebrows. He said: 'Now this *is* getting interesting.'

Callaghan said: 'That's what I thought – very interesting. That's why I came down.'

Gringall said: 'So it wasn't because of anything that Colonel Stenhurst had said in the message he'd left for you, but as a result of your conversation with Miss Alardyse, that you came down.'

Callaghan said: 'That's right. After talking to her I came to the conclusion I didn't want the Colonel as a client.' He stopped speaking abruptly.

Gringall said: 'What does that mean? You didn't want him as a client but you still came down.'

Callaghan said: 'That's right. I decided that my client was Miss Alardyse.' He grinned at Gringall. 'You see, she's the owner of Dark Spinney. She's a rich woman.'

Gringall said: 'I see.'

Callaghan continued: 'As you know there'd been some sort of unpleasantness at dinner the night before. The Colonel had talked rather stupidly. I think he was rather inclined to exaggerate things.' He shrugged his shoulders. 'I expect you've talked to Miss Wymering about that,' he said. 'The point is,' he went on, lying with an expression of complete candour, 'that this little unpleasantness at the dinner table had rather brought things to a head – so far as Miss Alardyse is concerned I mean. It seems to me that the Colonel had made some rather silly suggestions about all sorts of things. Well, you know what the position is. He was a trustee, together with Miss Wymering and another person, for the estate. Miss Alardyse was beginning to wonder whether he was fitted to hold such a responsible position. At the same time she didn't want to do anything that would hurt or displease him, or her aunt for that matter, until she was certain of her facts. She told me the Colonel was talking a lot of rubbish. She employed me to come down and see him; to hear what he'd got to say, check up generally on the situation, and when I'd done so to advise her as to what steps she ought to take.'

'I see,' said Gringall. 'Are you suggesting that she thought the Colonel wasn't quite right?'

Callaghan said slowly: 'Well, yes . . . I *am* suggesting that. You know what these elderly ex-Indian Army Officers are. They get livers; they get very bad tempered; they say all sorts of stupid things they don't mean.'

Gringall drew on his pipe. He smoked silently for a few moments. He said: 'But you didn't see the Colonel?'

'No,' said Callaghan, 'I didn't see the Colonel. When I arrived at Dark Spinney he wasn't there. They expected him back for dinner. The idea was that I should ring up and go and see him after dinner, but I didn't get the chance. I parked my car away from the front gates. I went out the back way. *En route* I met Sallins. He'd found the Colonel. He didn't like it a bit.'

Gringall said: 'So you decided to go and have a look at the Colonel?'

'No,' said Callaghan. 'Not exactly. I was going to tell Sallins to get through to the police; then I thought of something. I asked him if the Colonel was dead and he said he didn't know.' Callaghan shrugged his shoulders. 'I didn't want to start anything unnecessarily,' he said, 'so I thought I'd better take a look. I told Sallins to wait until I came back. He was in rather a bad way,' he added, 'very frightened and excited naturally. I went and took a look at the Colonel. I saw he was dead. Well, there was only one thing to do. Sallins got through to the police and that was that.'

Gringall nodded. He said: 'Quite. Tell me something, Slim. What made you think it was suicide?'

Callaghan looked at him in amazement. 'It was *obviously* suicide,' he said. 'There he was on the floor, the gun not far from the body. It had obviously fallen out of his hand. I naturally took it to be suicide. What else should it be?'

Gringall said: 'Well, I'll be perfectly straight with you. There's just one thing I don't like. If the Colonel shot himself there ought to have been fingerprints on the gun.'

Callaghan asked: 'Weren't there any fingerprints?'

'No,' said Gringall.

Callaghan said: 'Well, there's an explanation for that. The old boy had a handkerchief in his right hand. He'd held the gun in the handkerchief.'

Gringall looked at him. He said: 'Why should he want to do a thing like that?'

Callaghan said: 'It's obvious. He didn't *want* there to be any fingerprints on the gun.'

Gringall raised his eyebrows. He asked: 'Why?'

Callaghan shrugged his shoulders. He said: 'Well, isn't it reasonable to suppose that there might be a lot of people's fingerprints on that gun? It had probably been lying about the house. Probably lots of people had handled it and the old boy knew that the police would probably check for fingerprints. He didn't want anyone else to be involved so, I imagine, he took out his handkerchief and wiped the gun. Let's visualize him doing that. He'd hold the gun by the butt first of all and wipe off the barrel and the cylinder, and when he'd done that he'd be left holding the gun by the butt. He would have the handkerchief in his left hand and the gun in the other. Being a tidy sort of person he didn't want either to drop the handkerchief on the floor or put it back into his pocket – it must have been oily – so he just wrapped the handkerchief round the butt, holding the barrel in the fingers of his left hand, and then shot himself. That way, he knew that the only prints on the gun would be his own. The prints of his fingers on the barrel.'

Gringall nodded. 'Strangely enough,' he said, 'there were a couple of his fingerprints on the barrel. But it's still very odd.'

Callaghan said: 'Gringall, you're looking for a motive, aren't you? You've got to try and pin this on somebody. You're looking for somebody who wanted to kill the Colonel. *I* don't think anybody wanted to kill him, but I think it's very likely he wanted to kill himself. Work it out for yourself,' he continued. 'He was getting on. He was pretty unpopular with the family. He knew that. In fact,' said Callaghan, 'I wouldn't mind betting he was pretty unpopular in the village and everywhere else. All right. He makes a scene at the dinner table. Carried away by bad temper he rings me up. The next day he realizes he's started something. He thinks there's a chance that I might even come down to see him. He realizes that there is going to be a very unpleasant situation. He gets fed up with the whole business. He decides to put an end to it. It seems reasonable enough to me.'

Gringall said: 'Yes, that's reasonable enough.' He got up.

Callaghan said: 'Have another drink, Gringall?'

The police officer shook his head. He said: 'No thanks. Not just now. You know, your theory isn't a bad one. In point of fact, I don't mind it a bit. At least I *wouldn't* have minded it but for one fact.'

Callaghan said: 'Yes? Something interesting?'

'Something quite interesting,' said Gringall. 'It seems that the Colonel telephoned your office from an extension line in his own room. That was the first call. But the next time he telephoned was from outside Dark Spinney. He went for a walk. He must have telephoned you from a call-box on the Alfriston road.'

Callaghan said: 'Well?'

Gringall said: 'The point is that if Miss Alardyse came to see you the next afternoon she must have known that the Colonel had telephoned you asking you to come down. That's why she came to see you. In other words, somebody must have been listening to his first telephone call. I wonder why they wanted to do that.'

Callaghan said: 'I wouldn't know.'

Gringall said: 'It's just an odd point that occurs to me. Well, good night, Slim.'

Callaghan said: 'Good night.'

Gringall went out.

Gringall was no fool, Callaghan thought. He believed the Colonel had been murdered. And he would do his damndest to prove it. Callaghan began to think about the Colonel's telephone calls. So the second call had been from a call-box on the Alfriston road. Why? That one was easy, thought Callaghan. Whoever had listened in to the first call had made up his mind to hold up the second call for as long as possible. The telephone line at Dark Spinney had not gone out of order next day. It had been cut that night, *immediately after the first call* to Callaghan's office.

He ordered another whisky and soda.

The evening shadows began to lengthen. Callaghan took the side road that led out of the High Street; began to walk up the hill towards Hangover. Like Wilkins Micawber, he was waiting for something to turn up. He realized that the crux of the whole business was the letter which Colonel Stenhurst had received – a letter which had made him angry – a letter which had made it imperative that he get in touch with Callaghan. Somebody had been in a position to tell the Colonel something that was both urgent and important.

He began to walk up the narrow road that led round by the high wall that bounded Dark Spinney. The road wound uphill; led through a wood – a sombre, shadowy place. The evening shadows made grotesque shapes on the moss-covered ground. Callaghan, busy with his thoughts, took a small path that led through the heart of the wood, came out into a clearing, leaned on a gate that led into a field. He lit a cigarette.

Somebody said: 'Good evening, Mr Callaghan.' Callaghan turned. Behind him, her hands demurely behind her, stood Patricia Alardyse. She was neatly dressed in a tweed coat and skirt; a small felt hat framed her pretty face. She was smiling.

Callaghan said gravely: 'Good afternoon. And who might you be?'

She said: 'I'm Patricia Alardyse. I know all about you. You're a private detective. I think that's most exciting.'

Callaghan said: 'I'm glad somebody thinks it exciting, Miss Alardyse.'

She said: 'Please call me Patricia. You know, I think I could be of great help to you. I feel that within me I have all the makings of a first-class woman spy.'

Callaghan nodded. He said: 'That's very interesting. But I wonder what makes you think I need the services of a first-class woman spy at the moment?'

She put her head on one side. She said: 'Well, *I* think you do.'

Callaghan said: 'All right. For the sake of argument, I do. Now exactly what could a first-class woman spy do for me?'

She said: 'I don't know, but I can guess quite a lot.' She went on: 'It's an awfully funny thing about Gervase – my stepfather – isn't it?'

'Is it?' asked Callaghan. 'Why?'

She moved beside him. She leaned against the gate quite close to him. He noticed that her eyes were very blue – very wide. A delectable young woman, thought Callaghan, and no fool.

She said: 'I'll tell you why. First of all there was this row at dinner. It's quite obvious that Gervase had got something on Viola and Corinne – at least he thought he had. He threatened to have them watched, but he didn't say who was going to watch them. Nobody knew then that he intended to get in touch with you.'

Callaghan said: 'No? Well, how would somebody find out?'

Patricia said: 'That wouldn't be difficult. You see, the Colonel always used to make telephone calls from his own room upstairs, but there's an extension in the hall. Anybody who was in the hall could pick up the telephone and overhear what he was saying.'

Callaghan said: 'I see.' He asked: 'Was it a very serious quarrel – the one at dinner-time I mean?'

'No,' said Patricia. 'We've had them before. You know, Gervase was *always* slightly angry. He always seemed to be upset about something. But he hasn't always had it in for Viola. The person he *didn't* like was Corinne. He disliked her like hell. He wasn't *very* fond of me but I always thought he was *for* Viola until fairly recently.'

Callaghan said: 'So he disliked Corinne. Do you think he was justified?'

She nodded vigorously. 'Between you and me,' she said, 'Corinne is the utter end, extremely poor value and, in fact, a perfect bitch. Actually I don't know *anything* good about her – even if she *is* my sister. And she's awfully scare-making. She frightens me sometimes. Of course I never let her know. Another thing,' she went on, 'she's rather the Italian type – dark and beautiful in a heavy sort of way. I have been wondering if it was *she* who killed Gervase.'

Callaghan asked: 'Why should she kill your stepfather?'

She shrugged her shoulders. 'Ask me another,' she said: 'but then I don't know why *anybody* should want to kill him. It's awfully wrong to say anything about the dead, but he really was a very stupid old man – at least that's what I've always thought.'

Callaghan nodded. He said: 'This quarrel . . . it was about some club Viola and Corinne went to, wasn't it?'

She said: 'That wasn't the start. The start was about *me*. Actually,' she went on confidentially and with a certain satisfaction, 'I started most of the rows in this house. It was rather fun. You see, there wasn't very much else to do.'

Callaghan said: 'Quite. So it started about you?'

'Yes,' she said. 'You see, I'd taken one of Corinne's evening frocks – a red frock, cut very low. She saw me wearing it before dinner. She was furious. She's done everything she can to stop me wearing her clothes, but I always get at them somehow.'

Callaghan said with a smile: 'Quite obviously you have the makings of a first-class woman spy. Why didn't she lock her clothes up?'

Patricia smiled. 'She did. At least she used to lock her bedroom door. She didn't know I had a key. In fact,' she went on, 'I think I've got keys to practically *everything* that Corinne can lock up.'

Callaghan asked: 'Why?'

She put her head on one side. She said: 'I don't know, except that I've always sort of distrusted Corinne. You know, I'm awfully fond of Viola. I think she's a sweet. Everybody likes her. Corinne doesn't seem to like *anybody*. I've often wondered why that was. I've often thought she's been up to something and I've always wanted to keep an eye on her. Is that odd?'

Callaghan said: 'No, not particularly. You're curious and fond of dramatics.'

She nodded. 'Yes. Poor stepfather used to say I went to the pictures too much.'

Callaghan said casually: 'Listen, Patricia. How would you like to do something for me?'

She smiled at him. She intended the smile to be languorous and mysterious. She said: 'I'd love it. What do you want?'

Callaghan said: 'I'm curious about something and I think you're the only person who could help me. I'll tell you exactly what it is. On the night before the Colonel died – that is on the night of the quarrel – he received a letter from somebody. He wanted to talk to me about that letter. Well, just at the moment, with police officers all round the place, it isn't very easy for me to look for a letter. I thought perhaps you might like to try.'

She said: 'But of course. That means to say I'd have to start off with stepfather's rooms. I wonder if it would be in his desk.'

Callaghan thought: You've got to take a chance sometimes. He thought he might as well take it now.

He said: 'Listen, Patricia, I trust you, and I know you won't let me down.'

She said: 'No, I'd never do that. By the way, what's your first name? I'm rather *for* you. I feel I've known you for a long time.'

Callaghan said: 'The name's Slim.'

She said: 'How lovely. O.K., Slim.'

He went on: 'It seems to me that it might have been Corinne who listened to that telephone conversation in the hall. You see, Viola came to see me the next day in my office. She must have found out from somebody to whom the Colonel was speaking – that is unless *she* listened in the hall.'

Patricia said: 'She didn't. She was in her room. It *must* have been Corinne.'

Callaghan said: 'All right. If it was Corinne she'd know that the Colonel had had a letter, wouldn't she? She'd be interested in what was in the letter obviously; she must have thought that it concerned herself as well as Viola – because, remember, the Colonel had said he was going to have *both* of them watched. So she'd want to get that letter, wouldn't she?'

Patricia nodded again. She said: 'Of course she would.'

'In those circumstances,' said Callaghan, 'I should think that when she heard that the Colonel was dead, she might make a search to see if she could find it. Perhaps she *has* found it. Do you see what I'm getting at?'

Patricia said: 'I see. You mean that the first place I should look is in Corinne's room?'

Callaghan nodded.

Patricia said: 'That's easy, Slim. You just don't know how easy that is. She hasn't anything that I couldn't get at.'

Callaghan said: 'You'll have to be careful. It wouldn't do any good if she found you snooping about the place.'

Patricia said: 'You're telling me! She won't find out.'

'All right,' said Callaghan. 'You see what you can do. If you have any luck, ring me at the Two Friars, at Alfriston. But don't say you're Patricia Alardyse.'

'I won't,' said Patricia. 'I'll say I'm Madame "X".'

Callaghan grinned. 'That's just as bad,' he said. 'Just say you're Miss Brown.' He lit a fresh cigarette. 'There's another thing,' he went on. 'I want to have a little talk with your sister Viola – but not at the house.'

She said: 'Well . . . I can tell her, can't I? We usually dine about nine. I don't see why she can't slip out and meet you here after dinner, say at a quarter to ten. I'll tell her she's *got* to come.'

'That's nice of you,' said Callaghan. 'I think it might be a good thing for her if she did.'

Patricia said seriously: 'So it's like that . . . is it?'

He nodded.

'All right, Slim,' said Patricia. 'Well . . . I'd better be getting along now otherwise they'll wonder where I am.' She held out a small hand. 'This is *terrific*,' she went on, 'working for you, I mean. It's marvellous. I love it just for the hell of it. And it's got the movies beaten to a frazzle.'

Callaghan said: 'I'm glad you're glad.'

'If Corinne's got that letter I'll find it,' said Patricia. 'By fair means or foul. Probably foul.' She became serious. 'It's a bit stinking of me to feel so happy now that the Colonel's dead. But I do think it's good for him – being dead, I mean. He was always *so* miserable when he was alive.'

She gave him an alluring smile.

'*Au revoir*, Slim,' she said. 'I'll be seeing you.'

She tripped off. Callaghan watched her until she disappeared amongst the trees.

CHAPTER FOUR
A NICE EVENING

CORINNE sat in front of her dressing-table, looking at her reflection in the mirror. She wore a scarlet dressing-gown; velvet mules that matched. The robe had fallen open, showing the whiteness of her neck and throat, the beauty of a silk-clad leg and ankle. The single electric lamp beside her, pink shaded, lent a subtle and mysterious light to the picture. Outside the circle of light, the room was in darkness.

Corinne concluded that she was beautiful in a Borgia manner. Her dark hair falling about her shoulders framed an oval face which, in the subdued light, seemed Italian; her luscious mouth, the almost heavy languor of her eyes, looked back at her from the mirror. A Borgia murderess might have looked like this, thought Corinne. She concluded cynically that the murderess might have felt like she did too.

She was not pleased. Like most people who are prepared to deal with facts – no matter how unpleasant the facts may be – uncertainty set her nerves on edge. And she was uncertain. Some things she knew and could deal with. But the things she did not know. . . .

The letter. *Who had sent that letter?* And why? Who – with the exception of two people whom she knew – had the knowledge that would allow them to send the letter? And like a damned fool she had acted before she knew what was in it. The time had come, she thought, when it was necessary that she should be clever.

And there was Viola. Viola, who was worried to death and who might fly off the deep end at any moment and talk. Because she sought relief from worry. Definitely, thought Corinne, Viola would, at the moment, be considering making a clean breast of the whole damned bag of tricks to Aunt Honoria. After which the *fat* might be in the fire so far as she, Corinne, was concerned.

And one had to be careful. There were police snooping about the place. Being unostentatious and courteous and all that sort of thing, but snooping nevertheless. And even if policemen were as stupid as some people liked to believe, they couldn't help seeing something if it was stuck right in front of their noses.

Corinne began to think about Callaghan. Callaghan was a private detective, and private detectives, she had heard, were often unscrupulous. They thought usually in terms of money, not morals. She wondered whether she could use Callaghan and if so whether he could be bought with money – or anything else? Possibly, if things looked *not* so good, she would have to consider doing something about this Callaghan. She would have to think up some sort of act for his benefit. Perhaps he'd have to be vamped a little, but it would be worth it if she could find out what she wanted to. *If she could find out for certain who had written that letter.*

She began to think about the Colonel. She thought *that* was damned funny. For Gervase to die at this moment. Perhaps that was as well. Or was it? Now . . . one wasn't quite sure. And it seemed the police were not satisfied that he had killed himself. Not *quite* satisfied. Of course the Chief Detective-Inspector from Scotland Yard had said that the continued inquiries were really only a matter of form . . . a matter of routine. But they suspected . . .

Who would they *think* had killed Gervase? All things being equal, suspicion ought to fall on Viola. It ought to. Hadn't she gone rushing off to town to see the detective, to threaten all sorts of things if Gervase's instructions were carried out. Obviously, she was angry with Gervase, hating him. Would they *think* that she might have done it? Was it possible that they might think that Viola *could* have done it?

Of course it was possible. Anything was possible. Whenever someone was murdered, friends of the murderer often found it difficult to believe that he *could* have done such a thing. Yet he *had* done it.

In any event, if Viola was getting scared; was feeling that she ought to confide in someone like Aunt Honoria, then she had to be stopped. Corinne smiled cruelly. She thought she could manage that all right. Viola was really rather sweet and nice, and people who were sweet and nice were a damned sight easier to scare than people who weren't.

There was a tap at the door. Corinne turned slowly on her stool as Viola came into the room. She smiled at her sister.

She said: 'Darling, of course you're *quite* beautiful. I wish to God I looked like you do. And you always look so wonderful in black. That black frock's divine. But you're tired, aren't you . . . and worried?'

Viola closed the door behind her. She came forward, stood a few paces from Corinne, outside the circle of light. She said: 'I *am* worried. Aren't you?' She went on, without waiting for an answer: 'I can't understand the attitude that the police officers are taking about Gervase. It's awfully odd. They haven't said in so many words that he was murdered, but it's quite obvious that they believe it. Well . . . supposing that's true. Who could have wanted to kill him? Who could have done a thing like that?'

Corinne yawned delicately. 'Practically anybody,' she said, 'that is if they had the nerve. I've often felt like killing him myself. And you never know, there might be other people who didn't like him, too. Someone from out of Gervase's remote past. But in any event I don't see why you should worry about it. He's gone and that's that.'

Viola shuddered a little. She said: 'You're very hard, aren't you, Corinne? Poor Gervase . . . whatever he did or said he's dead. We ought to remember only the good things about him.'

'Nuts,' said Corinne. 'And if I'm hard, why not? It did you a hell of a lot of good – being soft I mean – didn't it?' She smiled cruelly at Viola. 'Take a tip from me, my dear, and give up worrying about Gervase.'

There was a silence. Then Viola said: 'Corinne, when you were listening to Gervase speaking on the telephone to the detective office what did he say? Did he say something about a letter?'

Corinne thought: So that damned detective's been talking to her. I shall have to do something about *him*. She said: 'Gervase was fearfully excited. I don't really remember what he said. The only thing that interested me was that he apparently intended to carry out his threat of having us watched. *That* was the thing I concentrated on. Not so much for my sake as *yours*.'

'And when he'd finished speaking,' said Viola, 'why didn't you come and tell me at once? What did you do? Where did you go?' She watched her sister intently.

Corinne said casually: 'I put on my raincoat and went out and walked about the grounds. I was trying to make up my mind what *I* was going to do about Gervase – quite apart from anything you did. I was considering telling him that if he employed a detective to watch me I was going to clear out. Well . . . I thought it over and decided that I wouldn't; that the best thing I could do was to come to you and tell you about it. I did just that. Why do you ask anyway? What did you think I did?'

Viola said: 'I don't know what I thought.'

'You're not considering doing anything really stupid, are you?' said Corinne cheerfully. 'What's in your mind, my dear? Are you sure you're not making a mountain out of a molehill? Believe me, everything will straighten itself out. In a few days these police people will get tired of asking questions and getting answers that don't help. They'll go away. They'll decide that Gervase killed himself – which he obviously did. Then all you've got to do is to get rid of this stupid private detective who seems to be hanging about on the chance of making something out of our troubles – and get back to normal – *without* Gervase – thank God!'

Viola said: 'I don't know whether you'll think it's stupid or not, but I'm going to tell Aunt Honoria the truth.'

'Really?' said Corinne casually. 'Then I think you're going to feel a great deal more unhappy. I think it's a fatuous idea – especially at *this* moment. Just imagine what the consequences are going to be! Allow your mind to wander over what might happen if you *do* talk to Aunt! *What* a marvellous scandal.' She laughed cynically.

'I don't know that I mind about that,' said Viola. 'This thing has gone on long enough. I don't think I can stand a great deal more of it.'

Corinne said impertinently: 'Is it that or is it because you were asked to produce a little more money? Possibly if you hadn't got to pay you wouldn't feel so badly about things.'

Viola said miserably: 'Corinne, how *can* you say such things?'

'I *can* and I do say them,' said Corinne. 'All right, so you've made up your mind to talk to Aunt Honoria. But I shouldn't do that if I were you. I think you'll find it would be a very bad thing to do.'

Viola looked at her. She said: 'Why?'

Corinne got up. She went to the mantelpiece, opened a box, took a cigarette, lit it. She stood, her back to the fire, looking at her sister.

'Listen to me, Viola,' she said. 'I think it's time that you and I understood each other – not that we haven't understood each other before fairly well. The point is this: If any harm's been done to anybody it's been done to me – not you.'

'Has it?' said Viola wearily. 'I wonder. You wanted it that way. You've always said –'

'Right,' said Corinne. 'I wanted it that way and I want it to go on that way. If you go to Aunt Honoria and tell her all about it just as a salve to your rather school-girlish conscience, don't think I'm going to back you up.'

Viola said: 'My God, you don't mean to say that. . . .'

Corinne interrupted. 'I mean to say I'm going to tell Aunt Honoria that I knew nothing about it,' she said calmly. 'I'm going to throw it all on to you. Then there's going to be a fine how-d'you-do. Do you realize,' Corinne went on with a certain satisfaction, 'that if I knew nothing about this you'd be in the position of having committed *fraud* for years. Supposing I say I don't know anything about it; that I never knew a thing; who's to prove that I did? You don't think the boyfriend's going to let me down, do you – any more than he'd let you down, whilst it's worth his while *not* to?'

Viola said: 'Corinne, there are moments when I think you're the most horrible person in the world.'

'Possibly,' said Corinne, 'but I don't know that I mind very much about your opinion. You know, you'll be well advised, Viola, to do as I suggest. Incidentally, I don't think we want to start any fresh trouble. I think there's likely to be quite sufficient for all of us in a minute what with one thing and another.'

Viola said: 'Do you really mean what you said? Do you really mean that if I went to Aunt Honoria and told her everything, you'd say you knew nothing about it?'

'That's right,' said Corinne. 'That's exactly what I do mean. I've been a damn good friend to you, Viola, and I'm going to insist that the situation remains as it is. Be advised by me . . . let sleeping dogs lie. And now, if you'll excuse me, I'll change.'

Viola said nothing. She turned; walked slowly out of the room.

Callaghan stopped pacing the floor of his sitting-room at the Two Friars; gave himself another four fingers of whisky, lit a fresh cigarette, looked at his watch. It was nine o'clock. He was thinking about Gringall. Gringall had the definite idea in his head that somebody had killed Colonel Stenhurst. Callaghan thought he was probably right. An interesting situation, because no one had any *apparent* motive for murdering the Colonel – at least not any adequate motive. Actually the person who would want him out of the way most at the moment – the person who disliked him most – would be Viola.

And somebody else had thought of that one. Or had they? Callaghan remembered the scene in the pagoda when he had found the Colonel's body. The set-up was almost too good to be true. The pistol lying well out of reach of the Colonel's hand and the handkerchief with the initials 'V.A.' – obviously Viola's – nearly hidden under the body. A complete set-up; Callaghan thought that the décor had been too carefully arranged, which was the reason why he had, as carefully, upset it.

Yet that same somebody still knew what the situation had been. Possibly some other red herring would be produced intended to lead Gringall back to Viola.

In any event, what was Gringall going to do? Callaghan thought he could find the answer to that one. Gringall would lay off and do nothing; he would indulge in a little masterly inactivity. Gringall believed – as Callaghan believed – that if you give people enough rope they will eventually hang themselves. Believing this, he would lay off and see what happened. He would think that somebody would have to do something; that the big lead would eventually emerge.

As Callaghan finished his whisky, the telephone rang. It was Nikolls. He said: 'Is it all right for me to talk?'

'Yes,' said Callaghan. 'And I hope you've got something to talk about.'

Nikolls said: 'I got plenty. Me . . . I am the complete sleuth. I am the Eye that Never Sleeps. Anyway, here's how it goes: This Mardene Club . . . it's a swell place all right. I got the idea that it was on the other side of Brighton. Well it's not. It's on this side. Just past Rottingdean. If you turn right off the coast road just after you've run through the village, keep right on, take the dirt road to the left, you run right into it. A house on its own – about two miles from the sea.'

Callaghan said: 'I see. What about Maysin?'

Nikolls said: 'This is good. D'you remember a dump called the Yellow Anchor?'

Callaghan said: 'Do I?'

'O.K.,' said Nikolls. 'There used to be a guy there employed as a head waiter – his name was Tony Empli. He was knocked off one time on a dope charge. Remember?'

Callaghan said: 'I remember.'

'O.K.,' said Nikolls. 'Well, that makes it easy, because Charlie Maysin is nobody else but Tony Empli.'

Callaghan asked: 'Who told you?'

'Nobody told me,' said Nikolls. 'Here's how it was. I was hangin' around this dump an' got talkin' to one of the girls who works there. She's the typist; sort of secretary to the boss. Well, I know this baby . . . see? I usta know her when she was hat-check girl at the old Mayflower before she learned to punch a typewriter. While I am talkin' to her, Tony Empli comes into view. He don't see me but I see him. I asked her who he was because I reckoned that he'd changed his name anyhow. She says Charlie Maysin. I reckon that's good enough.'

Callaghan said: 'I think so. You'd better keep in touch with your girlfriend.'

'That's what I thought,' said Nikolls. 'I made a date with her tonight. She's gonna meet me over at Brighton. Before I'm through with her I'll know all the answers includin' how she got the birthmark on the back of her neck. Maybe it's gonna be worth while to flog the expense account, hey?'

'But not too hard,' said Callaghan. 'We don't know who's paying us yet.'

'No?' said Nikolls. 'Ain't that a pip? It looks like we'll have to get another client.'

Callaghan asked: 'Who does the Mardene Club belong to, Windy?'

Nikolls said: 'Some guy called Donelly – Lucien Donelly – a wise guy. He seems to run the place fairly straight and keep his nose clean. He gets his extension permits when he wants them. The liquor is good and he seems to pay his bills. This babe I was talkin' to said that everybody likes him. He's a terrific guy – sort of cute, if you get me. Women fall for him just for the hell of it.'

'I see,' said Callaghan. 'Anything else?'

'You bet,' said Nikolls. 'There's this bit. Two of the Alardyse girls come here. Viola an' Corinne. Corinne's a member an' Viola's been out here with her as a guest. But Corinne goes for the place in a big way. The girlfriend sorta suggests that there might be somethin' on between this Donelly an' Corinne. She reckons that Corinne is stuck on him. An' he seems to be for her too.'

'All right,' said Callaghan. 'That's enough for now. By the way, where do the Club staff live and where does Donelly live? Do you know?'

'Yeah,' said Nikolls. 'All the staff, the waiters an' cooks an' such-like, are livin' in Brighton. They pick up the Rottingdean 'bus on the main road at night. The last 'bus. On extension nights Donelly lays on a car to take 'em in. He lives in the Club. He's got an apartment on the first floor. That's where his office is too . . . where the girlfriend works.'

Callaghan said: 'All right, Windy. You get to work on your typist friend and see what else she knows. But don't throw a scare into her.'

'What, *me*?' asked Nikolls. He sounded aggrieved. 'Me . . . with *my* technique. I'll be seein' you . . . maybe tomorrow. I reckon I'm gonna be late tonight.'

Callaghan hung up.

He poured another drink; lit a fresh cigarette. He thought Nikolls was right. It was time that they got a fresh client.

Callaghan looked at his strap watch as he turned out of the main Alfriston road; took the secondary road that led towards Hangover. It was a quarter to ten. He drove slowly along the road.

It was a fine night. He slowed down as he approached the dirt road that bounded Dark Spinney. His headlights picked up a figure coming towards him. It was Viola Alardyse.

He drove the car to the edge of the grass verge, stopped it, got out. He went towards her. In the moonlight he noted the pearly whiteness of her face. Viola, he thought, was very beautiful. He wondered if she was as clever.

He touched his hat. He said: 'Good evening, Miss Alardyse. I'm glad to see you. It's time we had another talk.'

She stood still, regarding him silently. She was wearing a beaver fur coat over her black dinner-frock. Callaghan noted that her shoes were thin georgette shoes; that they were stained and damp from the moss. Viola, he thought, had been walking in the woods.

He said: 'I haven't a long time to talk now, but I have time enough to say this. There is somebody round here who isn't a particularly good friend of yours – someone who doesn't like you very much.'

She said: 'Yes?'

Callaghan said: 'Yes. Would you like to do anything about it?'

She asked: 'What do you mean by that?'

Callaghan said: 'I mean this. It is time you knew anyway. When I met Sallins and he told me that your stepfather was dead, I went to the pagoda, and took a look at the body. You can take it from me that Colonel Stenhurst didn't commit suicide. He was killed. The pistol was lying several feet from him, and if he'd shot himself there ought to have been some sort of powder marks round the wound. There weren't any. Of course there don't *have* to be powder marks, but they are usually there in cases of suicide.'

She said slowly: 'I see.'

Callaghan went on: 'Supposing I was working for you, I might get the idea in my head that somebody wanted to plant this kill-ing on you.'

She looked at him. Her eyes were wide with astonishment. She said: 'Who should want to do a thing like that?'

Callaghan shrugged his shoulders. 'I don't know. I can only guess. The point is,' he went on, 'that I suppose there was some sort of motive for your wanting the Colonel out of the way. You were angry with him. You had quarrelled with him.'

She said: 'But this is ridiculous. Even supposing all that were true; even supposing that I hated him – which I didn't – why should I want to kill him?'

Callaghan said: 'I'm not concerned with whether you wanted to kill him or not. I'm concerned with the fact that *somebody* killed him. I'm also concerned with the fact that somebody had created a set-up that was deliberately intended to pin that killing on you.'

She said: 'My God . . . is this true?'

Callaghan asked: 'What were you doing on the evening of the Colonel's death? Presumably you left my office and came back here. Is that right?'

She said: 'Yes, I drove back. I put the car away and had some tea.'

'Then what?' asked Callaghan.

She said: 'I went for a walk in the woods up here.' She pointed behind her.

Callaghan said: 'I take it you went out of the green door – the door in the wall just down here?'

She said: 'Yes.'

Callaghan asked: 'Did anyone see you?'

She shook her head.

He said: 'Where was everyone else in the house that afternoon?'

'I don't know,' said Viola. 'I think everyone was out. I wasn't concerned. I was angry. I'd seen you and my interview with you hadn't made me any less angry. I went for a walk because I intended to talk very severely to my stepfather before dinner. When I came back I met you. When I got to the house I heard about it.'

Callaghan said: 'Yes?' He put his hand into his pocket. He produced the small lace handkerchief. He held it out to her. He asked: 'Is that yours?'

She nodded. 'Yes . . . why?'

Callaghan said: 'I found that under the Colonel's body.'

She stood looking at him, the wisp of lace and cambric in her hand. Now she was frightened. Her face was very white. He noticed the shadows under her eyes.

She said: 'And you took it away?'

Callaghan nodded. 'I took the handkerchief. I moved the gun,' he said.

She asked: 'Why did you do that?'

'I'm not quite certain,' said Callaghan, 'but I think I know. Possibly there were two reasons. The first reason was that the whole thing looked like a set-up to me. It looked to me as if that handkerchief had been planted there. It looked as if somebody had thought that just at that time you might be sufficiently angry with Colonel Stenhurst to have wanted him out of the way. It looked as if somebody might have arranged things. In any event, I thought I'd take a chance.'

She said: 'That might be very dangerous for you.'

Callaghan said nothing.

She asked: 'Do you want this?' She held out the handkerchief towards him.

He said: 'Yes, I'll keep that if you don't mind. And,' he continued, 'I don't think we ought to stand here talking. There is just a chance that a car coming round the main road might see us. Perhaps that wouldn't be too wise.'

She said: 'No.' She turned; began to walk up the dirt road towards the trees. He walked by her side.

She went on: 'Mr Callaghan, you haven't told me the second reason.'

Callaghan grinned in the darkness. He said: 'I'm not quite sure about it myself. Maybe I'll talk to you about that some other time. In the meantime I'm going to suggest that you are fairly careful. Make certain, if you talk to anybody in the house, that they really are your friends.'

She said: 'You believe that somebody is trying to make out that I did this?'

Callaghan said: 'That's my impression. Don't you think it's possible?'

She said softly: 'I don't know.' Her voice was tired. She went on: 'I'm weary of thinking, Mr Callaghan.' She stopped suddenly in the shadow of some trees. She said: 'I've been thinking that I might one day want to talk to you. You might help me.'

Callaghan said with a smile: 'Our client's dead. We've always got room for another one.'

She said: 'I see. You don't mind very much who you work for?'

'No,' said Callaghan. 'Somebody pays the bills . . . some time . . . somehow. . . .'

She said: 'I suppose I ought to be very grateful to you, Mr Callaghan.'

He said: 'I don't know. We'll wait and see, but if there's anything you think you ought to talk to me about, Miss Alardyse, I think it should be soon. I know Gringall. I take it that he's questioned everybody in the house. He's got such information as he can get. I don't think he's very satisfied. The fact that he's gone off means nothing. He'll be making further inquiries; finding out all sorts of things. You know, I've always believed that as between a client and a private detective there is nothing like the truth, the whole truth and nothing but the truth. So if you're going to talk to me, Miss Alardyse, I'd think seriously first of all.'

She smiled bitterly. She said: 'Do you think I ever think *not* seriously, these days? Everything is terribly serious.'

'It could be worse,' said Callaghan. 'Incidentally, there's something you should know. When I was talking to Gringall it seemed to me a good idea that he should not know everything about the interview we had in my office. If he'd known that you came up to London for the purpose of – he grinned – 'trying to threaten me to keep away from Dark Spinney, not to work for your stepfather, and generally the truth of our talk, he'd have a still stronger motive for your wanting your stepfather out of the way. I didn't like that idea much, so I did something about it.'

She looked at him in astonishment. 'What did you do?' she asked.

Callaghan said: 'I invented a little story. I told Gringall that in fact you weren't very pleased with your stepfather's attitude – not only towards you but towards things in general. I suggested that he had been behaving a little strangely for some time and that this strangeness had culminated in the row at the dinner table. I said that you had come to see me because you wanted me to come down to Dark Spinney to keep an eye on your stepfather; to find out what was going on and then to report to you.'

He produced his cigarette case; took out a cigarette; put it in his mouth. He did not light it.

He went on: 'This was a good story for two reasons. It removed the additional motive from Gringall's mind and, in a way, it substantiated the theory that your stepfather might have committed suicide. Remember that. And remember that if you *are* going to have a talk with me it had better be as soon as possible. I've got an idea in my head that something is going to happen fairly soon. I'd like it to be as nice as possible – for you, I mean.'

She said: 'That's kind of you. You're rather a strange person, aren't you?'

'I wouldn't know,' Callaghan replied.

She said: 'Mr Callaghan, when I met you, you were going off somewhere. When will you be coming back?'

'I don't know,' said Callaghan. 'Between eleven and half-past, I should think – maybe a little later . . . a quarter to twelve at the latest.'

She said: 'Very well. At a quarter to twelve I'll be waiting for you inside the green door. I'll take the latch off. If you can meet me there we can go into the house. Everybody will be in bed.'

He said: 'All right. I'll be there.'

He touched his hat, walked away; left her standing amidst the trees.

Callaghan turned the car off the coast road on the Brighton side of Rottingdean. He drove down the long road leading inland; took the first turning – a dirt road – to the left. He drove on for five minutes; then he saw the house. It stood on the right-hand side of the road in what had once been a small park. A circular carriage-drive led up to what he could see was an imposing portico. He parked the car in the shadow of some bushes.

He walked up the carriage-drive. Somewhere in the house a gramophone or panatrope was playing. He could hear the sound of voices. To the left were some tennis courts; a swimming pool. He saw no one.

He walked round the side of the house, which had once been an imposing country mansion, past the tennis courts. At the back was a courtyard. A door was open and the light inside reflected on the stone courtyard.

Callaghan sat down on the running-board of a car. He lit a cigarette. He waited. Half an hour afterwards figures emerged from the door – men and women. They walked round past the tennis courts, down the carriage-drive. Callaghan could hear their voices dying away in the distance. Another ten minutes went by. A figure came out of the lighted doorway; stood for a moment. The man was tall and thin. He wore a small black moustache and a soft black hat.

His overcoat was padded at the shoulders, cut in at the waist. He stood there whistling. Callaghan saw him take the cigarette case out of his pocket, light a cigarette. Then he moved off.

Callaghan got up. He walked quickly after the man; caught up with him as he turned round the corner of the house. He said: 'Good evening, Tony.'

The man stopped. He turned and looked at Callaghan. He said: 'You're making a mistake. My name's Maysin.'

Callaghan said: 'I'm not making a mistake. You're Tony Empli. I want to talk to you.'

The man said: 'I don't know what you want to talk to me about.'

Callaghan grinned. 'Of course you don't,' he said. 'That's what I'm here for. I'll tell you what I want to talk to you about; then you'll tell me what I want to know.'

Empli said: 'Yes?' His tone was insolent. Callaghan said: 'My name's Callaghan. I'm a private detective. You know that. You've seen me before. You remember what happened at the Yellow Anchor Club, Tony, don't you?'

Empli shrugged his shoulders.

'What do I care what happened at the Yellow Anchor Club?' he said. His English was almost perfect. 'It had nothing to do with me.'

Callaghan said: 'That's a nice story. Maybe the police believed it then because they were after bigger fry. But if you're thinking about that drug charge I'm not worrying about that. I'm thinking about something else.'

Empli said: 'Yes?'

Callaghan went on: 'There was a girl who disappeared just about that time – a very good-looking girl – Carlotta Eames I think her name was. She used to go to the Yellow Anchor. She left a letter for her parents saying she was going off to the country. They didn't see her again. They had some sort of idea she'd gone off and married a man.'

Empli said impatiently: 'Yes? What's this got to do with me?'

'I'll tell you,' said Callaghan. 'She wrote me a letter. She wrote me a letter three months after she was supposed to disappear. It came from Buenos Aires. When I'd read the letter, I'd got the idea

in my head that her people might prefer to believe she was married
– or dead. I thought I wouldn't show it to them.'

Empli said: 'I see . . . an interesting letter, I've no doubt.' His
voice was uncertain.

'Damned interesting,' said Callaghan. 'She had one or two very
interesting things to say about you.'

Empli said: 'What is this?'

Callaghan said easily: 'I'll tell you what it is. I expect you've heard
about Colonel Stenhurst committing suicide at Dark Spinney. The
night before that happened he got into touch with my office and
arranged to telephone me later. Actually, he tried to but I never
got the call. Somebody hocked a drink of mine – a woman. She
had been paid to do it by a man who got his instructions from you.'

Callaghan smiled. 'I'm curious,' he continued. 'I'm curious to
know whether it was your idea or whether somebody else put you
on to it. I think it was somebody else. I think perhaps you'd like
to tell me.'

Empli said nothing. He stood there looking at Callaghan. His
eyes were narrowed and angry.

Callaghan went on: 'It's no good your getting annoyed. All you
have to do is talk. If you don't talk I'll tell you exactly what I'm
going to do. I'm going to show that letter – the one from Carlotta
Eames – to Chief Detective-Inspector Gringall. I'm going to suggest
to him that there might even be a connection between one or two
odd things that have been going on in the district and you. I'm
going to suggest that it might be a good thing if he had a talk with
you. You know, if Gringall has a talk with you I think you're going
to be for it, Tony. I think you'll go inside. I don't think you'd like
that, would you?'

Empli shrugged his shoulders. He said: 'All right. What the hell
do I care anyhow? I'm sick of this set-up. I'm sick of this goddam
place too. I telephoned Grellin. I didn't tell him to get a woman
to hock your drink. I told him that if he could stop you getting a
telephone call it might be good for him. I don't know a goddam
thing about anything else. But I know who pays me.'

Callaghan said: 'All right. So it was your boss here who asked
you to do that?'

Empli nodded. 'That's right,' he said. 'Why don't you go and talk to him?'

'Maybe I will,' said Callaghan. 'In the meantime do you know what *you're* going to do?'

Empli said: 'No. You tell me.'

'I'm going to tell you,' Callaghan said. 'You go home and pack your bag and get out of here. You understand that? I don't want to see you here again. If I do see you here again, I'm going to make a lot of trouble for you. See?'

Empli said softly: 'I see. You're a sweet bastard, Callaghan.'

Callaghan went on: 'It's no good feeling like that. You'd like to stick a knife in me or carve me up. But you know you can't do it. The thing is you'll do as I say. If I see you here again you're for it. Now get out.'

Empli stood for a moment looking at Callaghan. Then he said a very rude word. Then he turned on his heel; walked away.

Callaghan stood by the side of the tennis court, inhaling cigarette smoke. He felt almost happy.

Callaghan walked slowly round the house, along the carriage-drive, keeping in the shadows. He found the place where he had left his car, got inside, lit a cigarette, sat smoking, wondering about Corinne.

Corinne provided a great deal of food for speculation, he thought. In any event, even if she wasn't quite as beautiful as Viola she was an interesting type. She *had* to be. Callaghan tried to piece together the odd pieces of the jigsaw puzzle which were in his possession; to try to make some sort of sense out of a certain number of vague and rather inexplicable actions.

Life was sometimes like a problem in algebra, 'x' being the unknown quantity. And the unknown quantity was invariably the reason *why*. To determine 'x' one had to know motive; and the motives operating in the business at Dark Spinney were very vague and mysterious – or were they? Possibly they were simple – provided you knew what 'x' stood for.

But he knew *some* things. He could guess a few more. It was obvious to him that on the night of the scene at the dinner-table

Corinne had gone into the hall. She had known that her stepfather intended to telephone Callaghan's office. She had taken off the hall telephone receiver; had listened to his conversation with Nikolls. She had heard Nikolls tell him that Callaghan could be telephoned later at the Night Light Club.

Then she had acted quickly. She *must* have acted quickly.

She had, apparently, gone out and telephoned her friend Lucien Donelly. She had told Donelly that her stepfather would probably be ringing the Night Light Club in half an hour or so. She had told Donelly that somehow that call mustn't go through; that it must be stopped. Donelly had, it seemed, agreed to do what he could. He had probably spoken to Empli, who had remembered that the woman La Valliere was a member of the Night Light Club; and that she could be got at through Grellin. Empli had telephoned to Grellin and Grellin had laid it on. La Valliere had put some Dutch drops in Callaghan's drink and that was that.

But why? What was the motive in Corinne's mind? If she had been the inceptor of the plan – and it must have been she – she had a reason for holding up the call. She must have known that the Colonel would get into touch with Callaghan by *some* means eventually. Therefore she was simply stalling for time. Why?

Callaghan thought that there might be two answers to that one. The first one was that she thought that by cutting the telephone wire next day she could still prevent the Colonel from talking to Callaghan on the telephone. That presupposed that she knew sufficient about the Colonel's intended movements on the next day to know that he did not propose to leave the house. If he had left the house he could have telephoned from anywhere.

And if she had some reason for knowing or believing that he would not leave the house next day, had she any reason for thinking that, by the evening, he would be dead and not interested in telephoning anyone?

The second answer was, thought Callaghan, much more plausible. Supposing Corinne had wanted to gain time merely for the purpose of finding out what was in the letter? She must have heard the Colonel mention it. He had said to Nikolls – after saying that he *must* see Callaghan – '*I've had a letter*,' and the fact had made him angry, or irritated, or scared. Corinne must have realized that there must have been some connection between the letter that the Colonel had received and the fact that he had decided to call Callaghan in because he was worried about his stepdaughters. So the letter had something to do with Corinne, or Viola, or, more probably, both of them.

Had Corinne thought that, at all costs, she must find out what was in the letter before the Colonel had a chance to talk to Callaghan?

This seemed a reasonable theory to Callaghan. Anyhow, he thought, sitting in the darkness, you had to start from somewhere, and why not from there?

The moon had gone behind a cloud. It was quite dark. Callaghan could hear, in the stillness of the country night the sound of cars being driven down the Club carriage-drive. None of them passed him. They turned right at the Mardene gates and took the secondary road that ran parallel with the coast, towards Brighton. He thought that the Club was probably closed for the night. The last customer had gone.

He lit a fresh cigarette. The time had come, he thought, for a direct action. You could always make a guess, and even if you were wrong it didn't matter; if you were you made another guess. He started the engine, turned the car, drove along the road into the drive. He stopped the car before the portico of the house, walked up the wide steps, rang the bell. He stood there, relaxed, the cigarette hanging from the corner of his mouth, his black soft hat at a jaunty angle, an amiable expression on his long face.

The door opened. Inside, Callaghan could see that the wide hall was still brilliantly lit. But the music had stopped and the house was silent.

A man in an alpaca coat stood in the doorway. He was broad, full-faced. A dead pan. His fish-like eyes regarded the caller without curiosity. Callaghan thought that he looked like a professional chucker-out in any one of the small night dives that abound in the Shaftesbury Avenue area.

He said: 'I'd like to see Mr Donelly.'

The man in the alpaca coat said: 'P'raps you would . . . but it's late. He's gone up to his own rooms. The Club's closed anyway. What's the matter with tomorrow?'

'Nothing so far as I know,' said Callaghan cheerfully. 'And there isn't anything the matter with tonight either . . . *yet*. Go and tell Donelly that Mr Callaghan wants to see him, and make it snappy.'

The man in the alpaca coat leaned against the doorpost. He was grinning. He seemed pleased with life. He said: 'Ain't you the little pip? You hate yourself, don't you? Go an' do this an' go an' do that! You tell me something . . . why?'

Callaghan said: 'That's a good question. It should be answered. There are several answers. Here's one of them.'

He blew a cloud of tobacco smoke into the man's face. Then, very swiftly, he stepped back, brought up his foot, planted it somewhere in the region of alpaca-coat's navel and pushed hard.

The man fell backwards into the hall. Callaghan stepped in after him, closed the door quietly behind him. He said: 'Start something if you want to. But I'm still going to see Donelly even if I have to kick your teeth in first.'

Alpaca-coat got up warily. He looked at Callaghan carefully; measured him with a professional glance from head to foot. He said: 'O.K. I'll go an' tell him. But if he don't want to see you I'm goin' to fix you good when I come back.'

He turned, crossed the hall, disappeared into the dimly-lit passage on the other side. Callaghan stubbed out his cigarette and waited.

Two or three minutes passed. The man appeared, behind him a tall, slim figure. They came towards Callaghan. Alpaca-coat said: 'This is the one. I don't know him. An' he ain't a member. An' he thinks he's tough.'

The other man laughed. He said: 'Mr Callaghan, I don't know why, but your name's familiar. You must excuse my rough friend here. He's inclined to be very suspicious and doesn't like people who aren't members gate-crashing. My name's Donelly. I think you wanted to see me.'

Callaghan thought Donelly was almost too good to be true. He had a superb figure, lithe, slender. He moved with the quick grace of an athlete. His face – except for a peculiar strained expression about the eyes – was devastatingly handsome. His mouth, chin and jaw might have been carved by a sculptor. His hair was black and wavy, and a small moustache, trimmed down to a mere line, completed an almost perfect figure of a matinee idol. Only the eyes were strange. They were light blue – expressionless.

Callaghan said: 'I want to see you particularly.' He grinned. 'Actually I think you want to see me too. I'm a friend of Corinne Alardyse.'

There was a pause. Then Donelly said: 'Well . . that's funny, because she's never mentioned your name to me.'

'That's possible,' said Callaghan. 'Possibly I'm one of those friends that she likes to keep in the background. Perhaps she doesn't even realize that she knows me. But I'm still a friend – for better or worse.' His grin was insolent.

Donelly said coolly: 'This is very interesting. Exactly what was it . . .?'

'Do we have to talk in front of this moron?' Callaghan asked, indicating the man in the alpaca coat. 'I don't think I want to do that. If we're going to have an audience I could suggest a better place.'

'Really?' said Donelly casually. 'May I ask where?'

'The C.I.D. office at Brighton Police Station *might* be a good place,' suggested Callaghan. He was still smiling.

The man in the alpaca coat said acidly: 'There you are – what did I tell you – a bleedin' nark!'

'Shut up, George,' said Donelly. His voice was cheerful. 'I think I like Mr Callaghan. He wants to talk and he shall. Come this way, please, Mr Callaghan.'

He turned, crossed the hall. Callaghan followed him along the carpeted passage into the small, well-furnished room at the end. Inside the room a fire burned brightly. The Mardene Club was an expensive place, thought Callaghan, with a lot of money behind it. He wondered whose money it was.

Donelly went to the sideboard. He said: 'A whisky and soda? I'm sorry that George was troublesome. He has a complex about late visitors. One or two people who aren't members sometimes try to get in for a drink. He doesn't like that. It means trouble with the police.'

He brought the glass to Callaghan; indicated a chair. Callaghan sat down. He thought that Mr Donelly was a remarkably cool, clever and possibly very dangerous individual, in spite of his good looks.

Donelly mixed his own drink; sat down. He said: 'Well . . . here's to us both. And now, what's the trouble? If it *is* trouble?'

Callaghan said: 'I'll make it as short as possible. I'm a private detective. I came down to Alfriston originally because Colonel Stenhurst wanted me to do an investigation for him. Well, as you know, he's dead. However, I'm still working for the family, and there's one little point which you might like to clear up.'

Donelly said: 'So you're working for the family. Now just what does that mean?'

'It doesn't matter what it means,' said Callaghan amiably. 'Because whatever it means doesn't make any difference to facts. Here are the facts. They affect you. Last Tuesday night Colonel Stenhurst rang my office after dinner. He telephoned through to speak to me personally; to ask me to come down as soon as possible. He was told that I wasn't in but that if the business was urgent he could get me at another number later.

'Someone listened to that telephone call. The someone was, I think, Miss Corinne Alardyse. She realized that the Colonel would telephone through later and for reasons best known to herself she didn't intend that he should speak to me. Not at *that* time, anyhow. I imagine she was stalling for time. All right. She either came here or telephoned through here and asked you if you could fix it somehow so that I didn't get the call. She told you where I should be. You spoke to Tony Empli – now calling himself Charlie Maysin – and Empli knew a woman – La Valliere – who was a member of the Club where I was to be telephoned. La Valliere hocked my whisky so that I couldn't take the call. Is that clear so far?'

'Perfectly,' said Donelly. 'Please go on. I think you're being *frightfully* interesting.'

Callaghan said: 'I'm glad you like it. Next day the telephone line at Dark Spinney went wrong. It's my guess it was cut. Anyhow, I couldn't speak to the Colonel from London, so I decided to come down. Well . . . I still didn't speak to him. He was dead by that time.'

Donelly said: 'Don't say that he found that to commit suicide was a more pleasurable alternative than to meet Mr Callaghan?' He showed his even white teeth in a caustic smile.

Callaghan said: 'So you think he committed suicide?'

'Well . . . didn't he?' asked Donelly.

Callaghan said: '*That* doesn't matter just at this moment. What does matter is this: Whose idea was it to stop the Colonel speaking to me last Tuesday night? I'd like to know that. Was it yours or was it Corinne Alardyse's idea? I'm curious.'

'Curiosity killed the cat,' said Donelly pleasantly. 'In any event, I don't know what you're talking about. I've never heard such nonsense in my life. Wherever did you get this ridiculous story from?'

'From La Valliere, the man Empli telephoned, named Grellin, and finally Empli,' said Callaghan smoothly. 'Empli told me tonight – not long ago – that he acted on your instructions. Well . . .?'

'Empli's a very stupid person,' said Donelly. 'I must talk to him seriously. Have another drink?'

'No thanks,' said Callaghan. 'And you won't have the chance of talking to Empli again. I don't think he'll be here any more.' He smiled cheerfully at Donelly.

Donelly went to the sideboard. He mixed himself another drink. Callaghan could see the dark shadow on his face. He went on: 'I've got something on Empli . . .. something I could make stick. He's a pretty rotten type, the sort of lousy hanger-on that people like you use in a business like this. I told Empli that if I saw him again I'd put him inside. I meant it too.'

Donelly leaned against the sideboard. He said with a half-smile: 'It seems that Mr Callaghan can be tough if he wants to be. Am I supposed to be scared?'

'What do I care?' asked Callaghan. He drew on his cigarette. 'I can be tough if I have to be,' he went on. 'I haven't even started yet. But if you *want* it to be tough . . .'

Donelly drank his whisky. He said: 'It's very nice of you to take such an interest in my private affairs, Mr Callaghan. But I shouldn't go on doing it if I were you.'

'No?' said Callaghan. 'Well, what are you going to do about it if I do?'

'I don't know,' said Donelly. 'But whatever it is it's going to be good. Possibly one thing, possibly another. In any event, I don't intend to be intimidated by any cheap squirt of a so-called private detective who is trying to chisel off a little money by sticking his nose into something that doesn't concern him.' He went to the fireplace, pressed the bell.

Callaghan said nothing. He lit a fresh cigarette, smoked placidly.

The man in the alpaca coat appeared. Donelly indicated Callaghan. He said: 'George . . . you can have your wish. Throw him out!'

George grinned. He said: 'Right . . . I knew he was a bleedin' nark. Come on, feller.'

He advanced on Callaghan.

A lot of things happened very quickly. As George put out an immense hand to take Callaghan by the coat collar, Callaghan put his fingers, quite gently it seemed, on George's wrist. George stiffened; then he began to bellow. As Callaghan, without getting up from his chair, increased the pressure of the *judo* thumb-lock, the bellow changed to a near shriek. Sweat ran down George's face. He began to give at the knees.

Callaghan got up. He released George's wrist; stepped back and, before the unfortunate George realized what was happening, shot a neat short-arm jab to his stomach; then, as George's head shot forward, followed with an upper cut that connected on the mouth. George, minus two teeth, and with smashed lips subsided on the floor – out.

Callaghan said: 'It's too bad about George, Donelly. You'll have to try and get somebody really tough to do your throwing out.'

Donelly said quietly: 'You think you're damned clever, don't you, Mister Callaghan? You think . . .'

Callaghan said: 'I think a hell of a lot of things. But I'm beginning to *know* one or two things. Good night, Donelly.'

He stepped over the recumbent body of George, whose neat alpaca coat was now somewhat bloodstained; opened the door, went out.

He walked along the passage, across the hall, through the front door. He got into the car, drove slowly along the carriage-drive. He turned left for Alfriston.

The moon had come out from behind the clouds. It was cold and the moonlight was cheerful.

The Lagonda purred along the road; the breeze stung Callaghan's face. The moonlight, silvering the pasture land, gave the country-side the appearance of a Christmas card.

Callaghan thought that something would happen now. Donelly, good looks or not, had brains. He had not even bothered to use them. Faced with Callaghan's original query, he could have manufactured a quite simple explanation to account for Corinne's wanting to gain a little time before the Colonel saw Callaghan. There could have been half a dozen innocent reasons produced.

But Donelly had not *bothered* to lie. He had not even bothered to concern himself with the question. Beyond a rude denial he was unconcerned. Which meant that he thought he was sitting pretty; that he held the cards; that *he* was all right; that in any event *he* had nothing to be afraid of.

But in any event, concluded Callaghan, he would have to do something. Certainly he must do *something*. Even if the some-thing merely consisted in telephoning Corinne and telling her to watch her step.

Callaghan thought that, all things considered, it had been a nice evening.

It was a quarter past eleven when Callaghan unlocked the side door of the Two Friars Inn in Alfriston; went up to his room. He opened the door of the sitting-room; stood smiling at Miss Patricia Alardyse, who sat in the big chair by the side of the fireplace.

Patricia had dressed for the occasion. She wore a tweed coat and skirt, well-cut brogue shoes, a small tweed hat pulled well over one eye. A voluminous tweed cloak lay on the other armchair.

Callaghan said: 'Well . . . this is a pleasant surprise. How long have you been here? And how did you get in?'

'I came before they closed the side door,' said Patricia. 'I slipped in and came straight up to your sitting-room. I knew there was only one suite in the Inn and I guessed you'd have it. I've just sat here and waited. I had to. There's going to be hell and blazes popping in a little while.'

'No?' said Callaghan. 'Why?'

She dropped her voice. She said: 'Slim . . . I've found the letter.'

'Nice work, Patricia,' said Callaghan. 'Where did you find it? Was it Corinne?'

She nodded. 'She had it,' she said. 'It's pretty damned awful, Slim. I don't know what we're going to do if it's true. But . . .'

Callaghan said: 'Where was the letter? How did you find it?'

'Corinne went out tonight,' said Patricia. 'I watched out of my window and saw her take her car from the garage. She's got a Ford 10 Tourer that Viola gave her for a birthday present. She had about a gallon in the tank and so when I saw her putting another tin of petrol in I knew she was going to be away for some time. Please give me a cigarette, Slim.'

He gave her a cigarette; lit it.

She went on: 'I got into her bedroom – I've got a key – and went straight to the little old bureau in the corner of the room. There are two pedestal drawers; but one of them has a false back. I knew that. I'd looked there before when I'd been snooping. When I tried the drawers they were locked, but I managed to get a paper knife under the lock and opened it. I found the letter in the drawer with the false back. It had been pushed behind the back of the drawer. It was in the envelope addressed to Gervase. It was posted in Brighton on Monday night. I opened it and read it and I nearly fell over. I tell you,' continued Patricia, 'it's a fair *basket*, that's what it is.'

She opened her brown leather handbag; produced an envelope; handed it to Callaghan. She said: 'Read that. . . .'

Callaghan looked at the envelope. It was postmarked 'Brighton' with the previous Monday's date stamp. It was typewritten, addressed to Colonel Gervase Stenhurst, at Dark Spinney, Hangover, near Alfriston.

Callaghan opened the envelope, took out the sheet of white typing quarto paper that was folded inside. He read the note. It said:

Dear Colonel Stenhurst,

The time has come when, I think, as a trustee of Dark Spinney, Estate Trust, you should know that, in direct opposition to the terms of the Will of her mother, Mrs Stenhurst, the present beneficiary – Miss Viola Alardyse – was married, on the 23rd August, 1939, at the Registry Office in Marloes Road, Kensington, to Mr Rupert Ellingham Sharpham.

It will of course be obvious to you that under the directions of Mrs Stenhurst's Will the Estate and Income from the Trust should have, on the date above-mentioned, passed automatically to Miss Corinne Alardyse who, it would seem, has, for some six years, been defrauded of her rightful inheritance.

Perhaps, in due course, when you have had time to digest and act on this information, I may telephone you.

A Friend of the Family.

'Well?' asked Patricia. 'Is that a fair basket or is it?'

Callaghan said: 'I'm inclined to agree with you. Relax for a minute.'

He went into his bedroom, reappeared in a minute or so with a typewriter and a square magnifying glass. He put the anonymous letter on the table, placed the magnifying glass on top of it. He took a sheet of paper, wrote down the characteristics of the machine on which the letter had been typed. The 'a' was slightly worn on one side. The 't' had dropped a little below the alignment. The 'r', 'e' and 'i' differed from normal inasmuch as they sloped slightly, under magnification, to the left or right.

Callaghan wrote for several minutes. Then he placed a sheet of paper in the typewriter; sat down; copied the letter. He replaced the letter in the envelope; handed it back to Patricia.

He said: 'Get back to Dark Spinney as quickly as you can. Put that letter back where you got it from, and do it before Corinne gets back. Make it snappy, Patricia.'

Patricia got up. She put on her cloak. She said: 'O.K. Slim. And for God's sake look after Viola . . . won't you? She must be in some *awful* sort of jam. All these years and none of us has ever even *guessed.*'

Callaghan said: 'All right . . . but get a move on.'

She said, at the door, breathlessly: 'You know, if this is true, Viola will be broke. But *broke*. She won't have a bean. Perhaps you won't even be paid. . . .'

'Get cracking,' said Callaghan. 'Callaghan Investigations never worries about money . . . well, not much. . . .' He grinned. 'And telephone me tomorrow morning. Not from Dark Spinney.'

'Right,' said Patricia. 'So long, Slim.'

She disappeared.

Callaghan looked at his strap-watch. Then he went to the corner cupboard, produced a bottle of whisky. He put the neck of the bottle in his mouth; took a long swig. He lit a cigarette.

He thought it had been a *very* nice evening.

CHAPTER FIVE
SHOW-DOWN

HANGOVER church clock struck a quarter to twelve as Callaghan pushed open the unlatched green door in the Dark Spinney boundary wall. He stepped through on to the path; closed the door quietly behind him. A few yards away, walking towards him, he saw the figure of Viola. She was wearing a fur coat and a scarf about her hair.

Callaghan thought: You're in a jam, my beautiful, and it's beginning to get you down, I think. I wonder why the hell you did it. Maybe Mr Sharpham had something – or knew something. In any event, if you're not *very* lucky you'll be for it.

He said: 'It's a lovely evening, isn't it – cold but romantic?' He smiled at her. 'The sort of night on which things happen.'

She said: 'Too much has happened for my liking, Mr Callaghan. Let's go into the house. I want to talk to you.'

He followed her along the gravel pathway, through the side door into the hall, along the corridor. They went into the room in which he had seen Miss Wymering. A fire burned brightly in the grate.

She said: 'There's whisky and some cigarettes on the sideboard if you'd like them.' She threw off her fur coat. Beneath she wore a long dove-grey velvet housecoat with a cerise sash. Her shoes were cerise georgette with high heels. Callaghan lit a cigarette. He looked at her through the flame of the lighter.

He thought: You're a hell of a woman. You've got everything. But looking like that, and having all you've got, is going to be of little use to you. The funny thing is I'm damned sorry for you.

He said: 'Well, Miss Alardyse, what have we got to talk about?'

She said: 'I'm sick of lies and pretence. I don't know what to do. I've worried so much during the last few days that sometimes I've thought that I should go mad.'

Callaghan said: 'Why don't you sit down and relax? Whatever happens, it could always be worse.'

She shook her head. She said quietly: 'I don't think so. I don't think that anything could be worse than this. I'm in a fearful predicament. It's my own fault and I don't think that there's any way out.'

Callaghan said: 'You must think there's some way out; otherwise you wouldn't be talking to me. People don't talk to private detectives when they think they can get out of a jam themselves. It's when they want the way out – the one *they* can't find – that people like me come in.'

She sat down. She crossed her legs; rested her fair head wearily against the back of the chair. Callaghan noted with appreciation the beauty of her feet and ankles. Small, well shaped feet, superbly cut ankles. All the external marks of breeding, not one of which was of any practical value at the moment.

She regarded him seriously. Her lovely eyes looked straight into his face. He thought: She's wondering whether she can take a chance and tell me. Maybe she thinks that if *I* get to know something she'll find herself in another jam. He moved over to the fireplace; stood, opposite her, his elbow on the mantlepiece, the cigarette hanging from his mouth, looking at her.

She said: 'Mr Callaghan, I *must* do something and it must be done quickly. The death of my stepfather has made it necessary. But just what I'm going to do I haven't the remotest idea. I cant think any more. I'm too tired of thinking. I'm putting myself in your hands because all I can do now is to save as much scandal as possible. And I'm not even sure that I'm doing right. I don't even know that I can trust you.'

Callaghan grinned. He said: 'All right. You don't know that you can trust me, but you're in such a devil of a jam that you've got to take a chance. You're looking for the way out and you're going to talk to me just because you're not certain if you *can* trust me.'

She said: 'What do you mean by that?'

He shrugged his shoulders. 'If you could trust me you'd know all about me. If you knew all about me and I sized up to being the sort of man you felt you *could* trust . . . well . . . you'd probably realize that I wouldn't be any damned good to you at all. It's because you think that I'm not *quite* trustworthy; that I'd take a chance if necessary; that I'd *do* something that one of your *trustworthy* friends wouldn't have the nerve to do, that you're sitting there talking to me at the moment.'

'Possibly so,' she said. 'But Aunt Honoria trusts you. She likes you. For myself, it doesn't matter very much, does it, whether I like or dislike you?'

Callaghan smiled. He knocked the ash from his cigarette into the fire. He said: 'No. It doesn't really matter. Although it *might*. The thing that *really* matters is whether *I* like *you*.'

She moved – a little uneasily, Callaghan thought. She said: 'Why?'

He shrugged his shoulders again. 'If I don't like you,' he said casually, 'it's a certainty that I'm not going to take any chances over you. And somebody's got to take a chance. However, the question doesn't arise. It doesn't arise because I *do* like you. There are moments when you are damned stupid, but all women are stupid occasionally. So let's have the story. And smoke a cigarette while you're telling it. That makes things easier.'

He brought her a cigarette; lit it.

There was a pause; then she said: 'I'll tell you everything. Just before the war started in 1939, I went to London for a month's holiday. I suppose now it sounds rather ridiculous to say that I was not a very experienced young woman. Most of the time when my mother was alive I led what is usually called a sheltered existence.'

Callaghan said: 'Yes?'

She went on: 'In London I met a man – Rupert Sharpham. He seemed to me a most charming and delightful person. Actually I know now that I didn't love him, but he had the most extraordinary fascination for me. It's rather difficult to explain, but when I was with him I was almost entirely dominated by his personality.'

Callaghan said: 'I know. It can happen.'

She hesitated for a moment. Then she said: 'I married him a week later. God knows why. When I try to think back to those days it often seems that I was a little mad. I married him in the afternoon and returned home an hour afterwards. We'd arranged to meet in London a fortnight later.'

Callaghan said: 'Tell me something . . . when you married Sharpham did he know about you and your family? Did he know that you were an heiress; that you might one day have a great deal of money?'

She said: 'No, I didn't tell him.'

Callaghan asked: 'Why not?'

'The reason may sound odd,' she answered, 'but my mother was very unhappy in her second marriage. I think she always had the idea that my stepfather married her for her money. It made her cynical and bitter. She'd always said that it was very bad luck for any girl to have money; that it always attracted an undesirable type of man.'

Callaghan said: 'I understand. So you thought you wouldn't say anything about it to Sharpham, and in spite of the fact that he thought you had no money he still wanted you to marry him?'

She nodded.

He asked: 'What then?'

She said: 'I never saw him again. A week afterwards, war was declared. He went immediately into the Royal Air Force. He was a pilot. He was killed in 1944 – two weeks after my mother died.'

'I see,' said Callaghan. 'So when your mother died you were married?'

She nodded. 'That's the point,' she said miserably.

Callaghan looked at the glowing end of his cigarette. He said: 'You needn't tell me about the Will. I know all about it. I've read it. In fact,' he continued, 'you inherited the estate under false pretences, because at the time of your mother's death, when the Will became operative, you were married, even if your husband died a fortnight later; even if you'd never lived with him, you were still married.'

She nodded. 'Yes. That's fearfully bad, isn't it?'

'It's not so good,' said Callaghan.

'You must think badly of me,' she went on. 'But try and understand. I've said I was inexperienced and a fool. In 1943 my mother made that Will in which she expressly laid down that in the event of my being married on her death, the estate was to pass to Corinne; that I was to have only three hundred and fifty pounds a year. Immediately after my mother's death – directly I knew of the existence of that Will – I sat down and wrote to my husband, who was then a prisoner of war in Italy. I told him about it. I said that because I was married to him I should only have three hundred and fifty a year.'

Callaghan asked: 'Did you ever get a reply to that letter?'

'No,' she replied. 'I never heard from him right throughout the course of the war. The next intimation I got was a month after my mother's death, saying that he was killed after having escaped from the prison camp.'

Callaghan said: 'Sharpham seems to have been an odd sort of man. But perhaps not so odd.'

'What do you mean by that?' she asked.

He said: 'Well, the probability is that when he met you in London before the war, he knew all about you and just who you were. He hoped that one day you were going to inherit this estate. I bet he wasn't very pleased to know that just because you were married to him you *weren't* going to inherit. I don't suppose he liked that a bit.' Callaghan grinned at her wryly.

'I don't know. You see, I knew so little about him,' she said.

Callaghan said: 'No, you couldn't have known very much about him, could you? And then what happened? The position is that a fortnight after your mother died in 1944, and presumably before the probate of her Will was granted in your favour, your husband was killed. So you decided to say nothing. You thought as he was dead you might just as well let sleeping dogs lie and inherit Dark Spinney. Is that right?'

She said: 'No.' He saw that her eyes were filled with tears. 'I've no doubt you'll think I'm the most awfully selfish person; that I withheld this information merely to inherit Dark Spinney and the money. You're quite entitled to think that if you want to.'

Callaghan said: 'It isn't a matter of what I want to think. It's a matter of what's true. Of course' – he looked at her sideways – 'you may have had some very good reason for not informing the trustees that you were married at the time of your mother's death.'

She said: 'I did inform them – or one of them.'

Callaghan raised his eyebrows. He said: 'No!'

She nodded. She said: 'I told my aunt, who, with Colonel Stenhurst and my mother's lawyer, Mr Galashiels, is a trustee. I told her that at the time my mother died I was married and that I was not entitled to succeed to the estate; that it should go to Corinne. I told her everything.'

Callaghan said: 'She must have been interested. What did she say when she heard it?'

'She entreated me to say nothing . . . she begged me to say nothing,' she said quietly. 'She said it was essential that the estate and the money should come to me. She said that although I'd legally been married, morally and actually I hadn't been; that if my husband had been killed three weeks earlier – a week before my mother's death instead of two weeks afterwards – I should have been entitled to succeed.'

Callaghan said: 'Was that her only reason?'

She shook her head. She said: 'No. The other reason was much more important – it was Corinne.'

He asked: 'What had Corinne to do with it?'

She shrugged her shoulders. 'Corinne's a strange girl,' she said. 'She isn't really like the rest of us and she's always been a little funny about men. She's had affairs – one after the other – with not very nice people sometimes. You don't know what a terrible time Aunt Honoria has trying to keep an eye on her. When I told her about my having been married she realized what a terrible thing it would be for Corinne if she came into Dark Spinney and the money.'

Callaghan said: 'I think I see. What you mean is that Miss Wymering knew sufficient about Corinne to know that if she came into this money she'd take damned good care *not* to get married, and that she'd play ducks and drakes with the money and probably go to hell in the process?'

She nodded. 'That is exactly what she thought,' she said. 'She told me that she considered it would be very much better for Corinne to go on living here as she was; to have an additional allowance from me. She thought it would be better for all of us.' She said miserably: 'I did my best to make things right for her. I gave her everything she wanted – money, a car, anything that she could have. I thought I was doing the right thing. I wish to God I hadn't.'

Callaghan grinned. 'Somebody once said that the road to hell is paved with good intentions,' he said. 'Your motives weren't bad, Miss Alardyse. Neither were Miss Wymering's. The unfortunate part is that both of you have acted illegally, no matter what your motives were. In fact,' he went on, 'I wonder what Corinne would have to say if she knew. She might suggest that you'd defrauded her.'

'No,' she said. Her voice was very low. 'She wouldn't suggest that. You haven't heard the rest of the story.'

Callaghan threw his cigarette stub in the fire. He said: 'So there's some more. I think if you don't mind I'll have a drink.' He walked to the sideboard; mixed a whisky and soda. He lit a fresh cigarette; came back to the fire. He said: 'Let's have the rest of it.'

'In March 1945 – last year,' she said, 'Corinne came to me one day in a great state of excitement – if Corinne could ever really get excited. During the War she'd been working at one of the Convalescent Homes for Officers near Herstmonceux. She was a V.A.D. there. While she was there she met a man – a man who had been in the prison camp in Italy with Rupert Sharpham – a man who escaped with him and who managed to get through after my husband was killed. He told Corinne that he knew that I had married Rupert Sharpham. He knew all about our marriage. He told Corinne that unless he was paid, and well paid, he was going to tell the trustees.'

Callaghan blew a smoke ring. He said: 'That put the fat in the fire. How did Corinne like that?'

She said: 'Her attitude amazed me. I should have thought she'd have been terribly angry about it, but she wasn't. In point of fact,' she went on, 'she was really nice to me for the first time in her life.

She said that whatever happened this man must be kept quiet. She said she didn't mind about the estate and the money; that I had been more than generous to her. But she said it would be a terrible thing if the scandal came out; if my stepfather knew. She said it would be awful – that whatever the cost that mustn't happen.'

Callaghan nodded. 'So you began to pay?' he said.

She looked into the fire. Callaghan could see once again that her eyes were filled with tears.

She said; 'I started to pay. I've been paying ever since. Lately his demands have been getting bigger and bigger. Corinne has acted as a sort of go-between. I've given her the money and she's given it to him.' She sighed. 'I knew,' she said, 'that eventually something would have to happen.'

Callaghan asked casually: 'Well, what has happened?'

'I can't go on with this,' she said. 'The night before my stepfather died – before that scene at the dinner-table – I spoke to Corinne. She said that he wanted more money again. I told her that I was sick and tired of the whole business. I made up my mind to tell my stepfather about it. I went so far as to go to the study and knock on the door, but he was angry and bad tempered, so I went away. The next day he was dead. Then,' she went on, 'I had a talk with Corinne. I told her that I couldn't go on any longer. I told her I intended to tell Aunt Honoria. Of course you understand I had to keep from her the fact that Aunt Honoria knew already. Then her attitude was most peculiar.'

Callaghan asked: 'What did she say?'

She sighed. 'She said that the situation suited her quite well; that she didn't want it altered. She said that if I told the trustees she'd say she knew nothing about it; that I'd defrauded her for all these years. I can't understand her.'

Callaghan shrugged his shoulders. He said: 'Well, maybe she thinks she's better off as she is. But it puts you in a rather bad spot.' Callaghan pitched the remains of his cigarette into the fire. He finished his whisky and soda. He sat down on the club fender. He said: 'I'm glad you've told me the truth, because I knew a little of it.'

She looked at him in amazement. '*You* know! But how?'

Callaghan put his hand in his pocket. He brought out the copy of the typewritten letter. He said: 'The night before the Colonel died, when he telephoned my office, he spoke about a letter he'd received. It obviously had some connection with his quarrel with you and Corinne at dinner. It was a letter which apparently he had picked up from the hall table – it had come by a late post – on his way up to his room. I happen to know what was in that letter. I have a copy of it. Here it is.' He handed her a sheet of paper.

She said in a low voice: 'My God. . . . So he knew.'

Callaghan said: 'Yes, he knew, but he didn't have time to tell anybody, did he? And he can't tell anyone now.'

She said: 'No.' She looked at him. She asked: 'Mr Callaghan, how were you able to get that copy?'

Callaghan thought quickly. Then he began to lie with that expression of frankness which he could adopt at will. He said: 'The Colonel was cleverer than people thought. When he made his *second* telephone call and failed to get me, he put the letter in an envelope and posted it to me at my office. It arrived the next afternoon.'

She said: 'So you have the original?'

Callaghan said: 'Yes, it's in my office safe.' He went on: 'So you understand why you're in rather a bad spot – quite apart from the estate I mean?'

She stiffened. 'You mean . . .?'

Callaghan got up. He stood looking down at her. He said: 'Don't you realize what all this adds up to? It gives you a first-class motive for wanting the Colonel out of the way. *If you had known what was in that letter*. The devil of it is somebody took the trouble to put him out of the way.'

She said: 'But I didn't know. How could I know?'

'I believe you; some people wouldn't,' said Callaghan. 'A lot of people might believe that immediately the Colonel received such a letter he would talk to *you* about it.' He grinned at her. He said: 'I'm beginning to be rather glad that I moved your handkerchief.'

She got up. She looked at him. She said slowly: 'But you couldn't think that . . . that . . .'

Callaghan shook his head. He said: 'No, I couldn't, but what would a jury think?'

She swayed a little. Callaghan went to the sideboard: mixed a small whisky and soda. He brought it back to her. He said: 'Drink that.'

She took the glass; drank a little of the whisky.

He said: 'All right. I'm working for you. You're going to do what I say. You've got to. This thing's got to be played carefully or else there'll be the devil to pay. You're to say nothing to anyone.'

She asked quickly: 'But what's going to happen? What . . .?'

Callaghan grinned. He said: 'Plenty is going to happen, and I hope it's going to be something that *I* want. All *you* have to do is to keep quiet. And don't pay any more money to your blackmailing friend. No matter how tough he becomes or how much he threatens. If Corinne says that he's got to have money your answer is . . . nothing doing.'

'I'll do what you say,' she said. 'But supposing he carries out his threat. Supposing he talks. . . .'

Callaghan said quietly: 'He's not going to talk.'

She was silent for a little while. Then she said: 'Whatever you may do, one day this thing has got to come out. It *must*.'

He nodded. 'One of these days it will,' he said. 'Truth has a way of coming up from the bottom of the well, but we'll try and bring it up when *we* want.'

She said: 'When it does come out, Mr Callaghan, I shan't have any money. And I believe you're a very expensive detective.'

Callaghan said: 'You'd be surprised! I charge a lot for my services, Miss Alardyse.'

She said miserably: 'How do you know you'll be paid?'

Callaghan said: 'I don't.' He smiled at her. 'I'm taking a busman's holiday,' he went on. 'The other thing is I like you.'

She smiled a little. She said: 'That's kind of you. But supposing you don't get any money?'

Callaghan put out his hand. He put his fingers under her chin; turned her face up. He kissed her on the mouth.

He said: 'Let's call that a payment on account. Good night. Don't worry. Callaghan Investigations never lets its clients down . . . well, not much . . .!'

He went out. She heard the hall door close quietly behind him.

She stood motionless, her hands on the mantelpiece, looking into the fire. Then, suddenly, she sat down; buried her face in her hands; began to sob bitterly.

It was ten o'clock next morning when Callaghan awoke. He lay in bed, his hands folded behind his head, looking at the ceiling.

He reached for a cigarette and lighter; began to smoke; to blow smoke rings and watch them sail across the room.

It seemed to him that the original quarrel at the dinner-table at Dark Spinney had developed into a series of events which might lead anywhere, and end – unless a lot of care was taken – in the Central Criminal Court. With Callaghan Investigations tailing along as accessories 'before and after'. He grinned a little ruefully. You liked the look of a woman; the way she walked; spoke and behaved generally, and you took a chance. Every chance you took meant, usually, that you had to take half a dozen more. Life was like that.

His mind switched to Corinne. An interesting personality, thought Callaghan. A girl who was beautiful; had most things that young women wanted, but who was unpopular with her own family; a girl who, as Patricia had said, seemed to like no one. He wondered why Corinne should be so bitter. What was the reason for her peculiar attitude towards life?

Possibly, he thought, Corinne was a little too experienced. She was a young woman who was fond of *affaires*; sometimes, as Viola had said, with people who were not particularly nice. An unhappy, dissatisfied person, Corinne. One who was, perhaps, trying to get everything in too much of a hurry. And one who, if things went wrong, and she did not get her way, might be very nasty.

He smiled a little cynically as he thought of the situation that existed between Viola and Corinne. It seemed to him that by and large Viola had not had a very good deal. Talked into doing something which she did not want to do – not to divulge the fact that she had married, she had placed herself in a position where she was open to blackmail. The humorous part of that aspect, if it could be called humorous, thought Callaghan, was that Corinne – the girl who had been kept from her inheritance by Viola, no matter with what good motives, had been the person whom the blackmailer had contacted – the person used as the go-between.

Callaghan began to wonder again about Corinne. Was she as black as she was painted? Patricia had said that Corinne disliked everyone. Therefore she disliked Viola. If this was so she was in an excellent position to vent any spite she felt against her sister. She had only to divulge to the trustees the story of her sister's marriage and the fat would be in the fire. Viola would be dispossessed and in a very odd position. Perhaps, thought Callaghan, Corinne wasn't so bad after all.

He got out of bed. He was wearing the top half of a pair of ash-grey silk pyjamas dotted with black *fleur-de-Lys*. He began to walk up and down the bedroom, admiring the morning sun which came through the open window and illuminated the drab carpet. There was a knock at the door. It was Nikolls.

He closed the door behind him; said: 'Would you have a drink around here? I feel sorta faint.'

Callaghan said cynically: 'I know – your usual morning faintness! There's a bottle in the cupboard over there.'

Nikolls went to the cupboard, produced the bottle. He poured himself out a neat drink, swallowed it. He sighed. He said: 'That's better. I reckon if you'd been workin' like I was workin' last night you'd feel faint.'

Callaghan asked: 'Did she talk?'

Nikolls nodded. He sat down in an armchair, produced a Lucky Strike, lit it. He said: 'Yeah . . . this babe keeps her eyes open. I reckon being a hat-check girl in a London night club is a good trainin' for anybody. She says it's a funny sorta set-up over there at the Mardene.'

Callaghan said: 'Yes? What does she think of Donelly?'

Nikolls said: 'She's a bit vague about that guy. She says she likes him, but there's somethin' odd about him. She don't know what it is, but it's there. An' he's got dough. He runs the place there in a pretty good way, and the dames fall for him like skittles. That boy has certainly got what it takes.'

Callaghan said: 'Any special woman?'

'Yeah,' said Nikolls '– Corinne Alardyse. She's nuts about this fella. My girlfriend says you've only gotta watch her lookin' at Donelly to see that she'd jump off the end of the pier for that one.'

Callaghan said: 'Does she know about the other women?'

'I asked her that one,' said Nikolls. 'She thinks not. She says this guy Donelly is a very leery sort of cuss. He never lets his left hand know what his right one's doin'. Besides, she don't meet the other dames who go over there. I reckon he's got one or two pieces in Brighton – sort of on the side. The boy seems to have a big time.'

Callaghan said: 'Where do you think your girlfriend will be now? Does she work there in the mornings?'

'Yeah,' said Nikolls. 'She gets there at a quarter to ten, goes through the correspondence and checks the accounts for the day before. Donelly gets there around twelve.'

Callaghan looked at his wrist-watch. He said: 'Get on the telephone to her. Tell her some story. Get her to type something out for you.'

Nikolls said: 'O.K. What is it – the typewriter?'

Callaghan said: 'Yes. I had a look at a letter that was sent to Stenhurst. It might have come off Donelly's typewriter.'

Nikolls said: 'O.K.' He went to the telephone.

Callaghan went into the bathroom. Nikolls dialled a number. He waited; then he said: 'Hallo, is that you, babe? How're you feelin' this morning? We had a big night last night, didn't we? Yeah, I know . . . I know. . . . Me – I always get like that when I've had a few doubles . . . sort of passionate. There was an Italian Countess I usta know years ago. She said . . . O.K. . . . I didn't know I told you that one last night. Look, will you do something for me? Here's what I want . . . there's a guy in Brighton owes me some dough. I wanta write him a sort of formal letter giving him four or five days to pay. I wanta tell him that if he don't pay I'm gonna get my lawyer to do something about it. Type that out for me, willya? Put this address on it . . . the Two Friars Hotel, Alfriston . . . and here's the letter. Will you take it down, kid?

'Willie Strevens, Esq., 1214 Kings Road, Brighton. . . . Dear Mr Strevens. . . . This is to inform you that unless you pay me the thirty-seven pounds which you borrowed from me last June by

Thursday next, I propose to place this matter in the hands of my lawyers and to proceed against you with the utmost rigour of the law. . . . Yours truly. . . .'

Nikolls went on: 'Get that typed out for me, babe, an' do an envelope. You got me . . . sorta classy. I reckon that'll scare the pants offa that heel. An', look, drop over here this afternoon when you're off an' leave it for me, so's I can sign it an' mail it to him tonight. . . . Thanks, honeylamb. . . .'

Nikolls breathed what was intended to be a rapturous sigh but which sounded like a whale coming up for air. He continued: 'Every time I think about you, babe . . . I go sorta dizzy. An' I'll be seein' you tomorrow maybe. I'll call through in the mornin'. So long, lambie. . . .'

He went to the door of the bathroom. He called out: 'It's O.K. She's writing a letter for me. . . . She's bringin' it over here this afternoon.'

Callaghan stopped brushing his teeth. He came out of the bathroom. He said: 'Windy, get into that car of yours and get up to London. Go and see Frane, John Elliot, Stevens and Lullworth – if he's out of the Army. Here's the thing. I reckon those four boys can get going in a big way if they use all their operatives.'

Nikolls said: 'Yeah. . . . What's the story?'

Callaghan said: 'On 23rd August, 1939, at the Marloes Road, Kensington, Registry Office, Viola Alardyse was married to a man called Rupert Sharpham.'

Nikolls whistled. He said: 'For cryin' out loud! What do you know about that one? And she inherited the estate, didn't she? Hey . . . hey . . . hey . . .!'

Callaghan said: 'Yes. A couple of weeks after the war started Sharpham went into the R.A.F. He was a pilot. He was killed escaping from an Italian prison camp in '44. I want a check-up on him. I want to know everything they can find out. It doesn't matter what it costs. The great thing is speed.'

Nikolls said: 'O.K.'

'There's something *you* can do,' Callaghan went on. 'When you get up there go and see Aynesworth. He's well in with the Air Ministry. Get him to fix it so that you go round there and get Sharpham's complete flying record. Try and get copies of all his official documents. Get cracking, Windy.'

Nikolls said: 'O.K. But, look, what about the babe?'

Callaghan said: 'Never mind about the babe. She'll keep. Get a move on.'

Nikolls said: 'O.K. O.K.' At the door he stopped. He said over his shoulder: 'Some guy once told me that absence makes the heart grow fonder. I hope the mug was right. I'd hate anybody to muscle in on my territory while I'm doin' leg work in London.'

Callaghan put on a dressing-gown, lit a cigarette. He walked up and down the room, stopped to give himself four fingers out of the whisky bottle. He thought it was a very bad thing to drink on an empty stomach. He had another drink. He began to think about Sharpham. He wondered what sort of man Sharpham had been. Maybe he'd been in love with Viola Alardyse. Why not? Callaghan could understand that. Maybe he hadn't even been interested in the fact that she was an heiress. But supposing he *had* been. Supposing he had thought that he was on a good thing? Even then he could not have known about the Will; could not have known that the very fact that she had married him would reduce Viola's income to a mere three hundred and fifty pounds a year. He could not have known about the Will, because it was not produced until after Mrs Stenhurst was dead.

Callaghan grinned. Sharpham must have been surprised when he received Viola's letter in the Italian prison camp informing him of the true facts.

The telephone rang. It was Patricia. Her voice was bright and cheerful. She said: 'Good morning, Slim. Any instructions for today?'

Callaghan said: 'So that's Madame "X", is it? How are you this morning?'

She said: 'I'm fine. And life is thrilling. I think I ought to tell you that I think you're rather a *good* type, Slim. There's something about you like George Raft – either him or Clark Gable – I'm not sure which.'

'Thanks, Patricia,' said Callaghan. 'If it's all the same to you, I'll go on being like myself. Now to business . . . . What's happening at Dark Spinney?'

'Nothing very much,' said Patricia. 'I'm not talking from there, of course. That wouldn't be wise. I'm in the call-box on the Alfriston road. There's just one little thing. I think Corinne is a little bit interested in *you*.'

Callaghan said: 'You don't say? Why?'

She said: 'Well . . . for once she was quite nice to me this morning. She was asking about you. She knew you'd been down, of course. She knew you'd found Gervase. She knows you're still down here. I think she wonders why.'

'Maybe she's only curious,' said Callaghan.

'I don't think so,' said Patricia. 'You know, I've got an idea in my head, Slim, that she wants to talk to you. She knew you were staying at the Two Friars. Possibly she's seen you. She asked me what you did, where you went, so I thought I might as well make a suggestion just in case she *did* want to talk to you. I said that I believed that in the morning you walked down the Herstmonceux road, had a drink at the Crown Inn – usually about twelve o'clock.

'I thought,' said Patricia, 'that if she *really* wanted to talk to you she might be about there at that time.'

Callaghan said: 'That was clever of you, Patricia.'

'There's only one thing,' she went on, 'if you *do* get talking to Corinne. You be *careful*.'

Callaghan said: 'I'll be very careful. But what do I have to be careful about?'

'She's awfully clever, Slim. She's as clever as a wagonload of monkeys, and, you know, she's very beautiful in a quiet, dark sort of way. And she's got great charm and when she lays herself open to vamp anybody I should think she was very, *very* good. I imagine,' she continued airily, 'that her technique would be rather like that of Ingrid Bergman in the Saratoga Trunk film. I don't know if you saw the film, but Ingrid was marvellous in it – very attractive and a most terrific vamp.'

Callaghan said: 'Thanks for the warning. I promise to be careful. By the way, how's Miss Wymering?'

'Quite well as far as I know,' said Patricia. 'In point of fact the whole household is settling down very nicely.'

Callaghan said: 'That's good. Where's Corinne going to be this afternoon? Do you know?'

Patricia said: 'If I know anything about her she'll be over at Brighton or Eastbourne. She usually takes her car and goes off in the afternoon. She seldom comes back before dinner-time. I've often wondered where she went. She's supposed to be fond of driving.'

Callaghan said: 'All right. Well if she *does* go out in the car this afternoon leave that green door in the wall on the latch so that I can come in the back way.'

'Marvellous,' said Patricia. 'Do you want to see me, Slim?'

Callaghan said: 'No, I don't. That's a pleasure I might have later in the day. But if Corinne goes out this afternoon leave that door open.'

'All right,' said Patricia. 'I'll do that. Is that all?'

'That's all,' said Callaghan.

She said good-bye; hung up. Callaghan thought she sounded a little disappointed.

It was soon after twelve o'clock when Callaghan turned off the main road; walked along the rutted roadway that led to the Crown Inn. He wondered if Patricia's guess had been right. If Corinne was keen to meet Callaghan and wanted to talk to him it was either because she wanted to *know* something or wanted something done.

Callaghan's guess was that she wanted to *know*.

He turned into the long, low-roofed bar parlour; went to the small service hatch in the far corner; ordered a double whisky and soda. He was given the drink, turned and moved towards the window.

A voice said: 'Good morning, Mr Callaghan!' The voice was very low, very soft and had a peculiarly attractive *timbre*.

It was Corinne. She sat, almost hidden by one of the wings of the old settle bench by the window. Now, leaning forward, her lovely, oval face, turned almost impishly towards him, radiated charm and *bonhomie*.

He took off his hat. He noted with satisfaction that there was no one else in the bar parlour.

He said: 'Good morning, Miss Alardyse. I'm very glad to meet you. In fact, I've been looking forward to meeting you.'

'Yes?' she said. 'Please tell me why.'

He looked at her. He thought she was a perfect foil for Viola. Her dark hair, grey-green eyes were beautiful and more than attractive in a manner which belonged entirely to Corinne.

She wore a green dress of velvet cord, beneath a coat of snow leopard. A matching scarf of green *chiffon* set off her hair. Her figure, feet and ankles were as near perfect as mattered, Callaghan thought.

He said: 'I've heard that you were a very beautiful person. I didn't believe anyone could be quite as beautiful as you *are*.'

She laughed. She said: 'Aren't you delightful? When I first heard about you I thought I was going to be fearfully scared of you. Now I've met you I'm not a bit scared. I think you're *quite* charming. Please come and sit down and have your drink with me.'

Callaghan said: 'Thank you.' He sat down beside her on the oak settle. He gave her a cigarette; lit it.

She said: 'I'm awfully glad you came in this morning. I've been wanting to talk to you ever since I heard that you were down here – that is if you *want* me to talk to you.'

Callaghan said: 'Of course. I like listening to you. Why shouldn't I want you to talk to me?'

She said: 'Well . . . actually I wondered if you were working for the family. If you weren't too awfully busy I thought perhaps you wouldn't mind doing a little work for me.'

Callaghan said: 'I'd like to. What exactly is the work?'

He thought: She's clever, this one. She isn't going to waste words. She's coming straight to the point in a minute and she's going to make it sound like the truth. She's *good*.

She turned towards him. The movement was sudden as if she had, as suddenly, made up her mind about something. Then she put a small hand on his. She said: 'I've made up my mind about you. I *like* you and I *trust* you. People say that I'm impulsive; that I come to conclusions too quickly. Possibly that's true. But in this case I know I'm right about you.'

Callaghan said: 'I think you're being very kind.' He lit a cigarette, drank some whisky. He went on: 'There's only one thing I'd like to say before you go any further. There's an old proverb that says you ought never to tell a lie to your doctor, your lawyer or your bank manager. The same remark ought to apply to private detectives.' He smiled at her.

She smiled back. 'I couldn't tell a lie to *you*,' she said. 'There's something about you . . . something . . . oh well; of course I must tell you the truth. It wouldn't be any good if I didn't.'

Callaghan said nothing. He thought that Corinne had, in about four minutes, managed to convey to him that in her opinion he was the one man in the world she had been waiting to meet. She'd done it quickly and cleverly. Definitely, thought Callaghan, she was *very* good.

She said: 'What I am going to say to you is, of course, in complete confidence. I want you to do something for me. It might be difficult and it might not. I don't know. But I'm certain that you'll find a way of doing it. I'm certain that you're *fearfully* clever. And you mustn't mind if I suggest that you must be paid very well for your work.'

Callaghan said: 'Thank you. I shan't mind that a bit. Providing I want to do the work.'

'I'd better tell you about it,' she said. 'You know that on the evening when my stepfather tried to telephone you at your office, the evening before he died, there'd been a little unpleasantness at dinner. Colonel Stenhurst was very old fashioned and, I'm afraid, inclined to be foolish. He thought that my sister Viola and I were just a pair of gadabouts and that we'd got to know some people of whom he did not approve. Did you know about that?'

'I'd heard something to that effect,' said Callaghan vaguely.

She went on: 'Actually, at dinner, my stepfather behaved rather foolishly. He threatened to have Viola and me watched. After dinner, when he had gone to his room, I was in the hall. I heard the extension telephone tinkle and I gathered from that that he was telephoning to someone about *us*. I thought he might even be going to talk to a detective.' She threw a sudden radiant smile at Callaghan. 'He was. He was trying to talk to you.'

Callaghan asked: 'How did you know?'

She smiled at him. She said demurely: 'I did a very naughty thing. I took off the receiver of the hall telephone and listened. I heard him speaking to your office and being told that he might get at you at some place later. But the thing that intrigued me was that he spoke about having received a letter.'

'And that made you curious?' asked Callaghan.

She nodded. She got up, picked up his empty glass, took her own and went to the service hatch. She moved quickly and gracefully.

After a minute she returned. 'I've got myself a double Martini and you a double whisky and soda,' she said. 'I heard you order that the first time. And please, you are to call me Corinne, and I'd like to call you by your first name. I feel I've known you for *years*.'

Callaghan said: 'Thank you, Corinne; the name's Slim.'

'How lovely,' she said. 'I think Slim is absolutely charming. Very well, Slim, I'll go on, shall I? Well . . . when I heard him talking about having received a letter I was fearfully curious. I'll tell you why. You see, the post usually comes before dinner and everyone has their letters in their rooms whilst they are changing. But on this occasion it was late and Sallins, the butler, had left the post in the hall. My stepfather must have picked up that letter, gone to his room, read it, and telephoned you immediately. Directly I heard him mention a letter I had the idea that this mysterious missive must have something to do with what had happened at dinner, and his threat to have us watched. Do you understand, Slim dear?'

'Perfectly,' said Callaghan. He thought: She's damned good. She's going to tell enough of the truth to carry the packet of lies that's coming later.

'So,' continued Corinne, 'I wanted to do two things. I didn't want him to see any detective about us and/or that letter until I'd had a chance of seeing what was *in* the letter. I felt that I ought to know and that it might be something that Viola should know.' Her voice became serious. 'I'm awfully glad I did think that,' she said, 'for Viola's sake.'

'Go on,' said Callaghan. 'I'm *very* interested.'

'The first thing I had to do,' said Corinne, 'was to stop stepfather talking to you later. I did a very wicked thing. I cut the telephone connection so that he couldn't use the telephone again until it was repaired. Then I felt a little better.'

Callaghan said: 'I'm sure you did. You mean that you felt you had time to think.'

'Yes, Slim dear,' said Corinne. 'That's perfectly right. I felt that I had time to think.'

Callaghan asked casually: 'You didn't take any other steps – beyond cutting the telephone line I mean, to stop your stepfather getting into touch with me?'

She looked at him with wide eyes. He thought that they were very beautiful. Grey-green and limpid and *very* innocent.

'But of course not, Slim,' she said. 'What *could* I have done beyond that? There wasn't anything else I could do ... was there?'

He agreed that there wasn't.

She went on: 'The next thing I had to do was to get a look at that letter. I felt I *must*. So I waited until Gervase had gone to bed and then, when the house was quiet, I sneaked into his study and began to search. I found the letter. It was in the letter rack in his desk. I read it and got the most *awful* shock. I was so shocked I hardly knew what to do.'

Callaghan said: 'Was it very tough?'

'Awful, Slim,' she said. 'I don't know if you know anything about our mother's Will, but if you do, you'll know that if any of her daughters marry they lose their inheritance – except three hundred and fifty pounds a year. Viola, of course, was the beneficiary under mother's Will, and no one had ever known that she was married!'

'Good heavens!' said Callaghan. 'And was she?'

'Well ... that's what the letter said,' Corinne went on. 'It was an anonymous letter signed "A friend of the family" and it said that Viola had married some man in 1939 and had therefore contravened the terms of mother's Will and done me out of my inheritance.'

Callaghan whistled softly: 'Not very good,' he said.

'Quite,' said Corinne. 'It made Viola out to be a fearful person, didn't it? And I could imagine how furious and excited Gervase must have been when he received it, and I knew just why he wanted to talk to a detective about it.'

'Did you?' asked Callaghan. 'Tell me why, Corinne.'

She came a little closer. Callaghan could feel the softness of her thigh against his. She dropped her voice. She said: 'Quite obviously, my stepfather's first thought was *who* had written that letter. He probably thought of the scandal that would get about if the thing got known, that is if it was true. So he first of all wanted to find out if it was true and then he wanted to find out who had written the letter so that he could do something about it.'

Callaghan asked: 'But supposing he had found out who had written the letter, what could he do about it?'

Corinne shrugged her shoulders. 'I'm not sure,' she said. 'But knowing Gervase, and knowing how he *hated* any sort of scandal, I imagine he would have tried to bribe the writer of the letter to keep quiet.'

'That wouldn't have been so good, would it?' Callaghan asked. 'After all, even if he didn't like scandal he couldn't very well make himself a party to defrauding you out of your inheritance. Because if Viola was married, then the estate should have come to you.'

'But I shouldn't have *cared*,' said Corinne. 'Slim, dear, I shouldn't have *cared*. I'm so fond of Viola. I wouldn't have cared *what* she'd done. I'd have been quite happy to have gone on and said nothing.'

'Maybe,' said Callaghan. 'But the Colonel wasn't to know that at the time, was he? Of course,' he went on, '*you'd* never had any idea that Viola had been married? Before you saw that anonymous letter, I mean.'

She shook her head. She looked at him with wide eyes. 'Never, Slim,' she said. 'I'd never even *thought* about such a thing.'

Callaghan said: 'Tell me some more. This is all very exciting.'

'Isn't it?' said Corinne. 'I think it's rather romantic, really. Well . . . I read the letter and I put it back in its envelope and replaced the envelope in the letter rack and slunk off to bed. I felt terrible. I was so worried about Viola I didn't know what to do.'

'Did you tell her about it?' asked Callaghan.

'No,' said Corinne. 'I thought I ought not to. If it wasn't true it didn't matter and if it was true I didn't see why the poor darling should be worried about it. Because, obviously, as she's been living here all the time there must have been some trouble of *some* sort between her and her husband. I thought I'd better say nothing at all.'

Callaghan nodded. 'And then,' he said, 'next day the Colonel killed himself.'

'Yes,' said Corinne, sadly. 'That poor old man, who hated any sort of excitement or scandal or anything like that, just came to the conclusion that it was all too much for him and so he decided to end it all. Poor dear Gervase. . . .'

A tear stole from Corinne's eye. She dabbed at it with a small, perfumed handkerchief.

'And then . . .?' asked Callaghan.

'Well . . . then,' said Corinne, 'when I heard that he was dead I thought I must act quickly. I thought whatever happens I must do my best to save Viola. I knew that Gervase hadn't been able to talk to you, because I'd cut the telephone line, and obviously nobody else in the family – no one at all for that matter – except the writer of the letter, Gervase who was dead, and I, knew about it. So I sneaked into Gervase's room and luckily the letter was still there in the rack on his desk. I took it and I've still got it. So nobody knows – no one at all.'

'Except you and the writer of that letter,' said Callaghan.

Corinne nodded. 'That's right, Slim,' she said. 'And this is where I want to ask you to help me. *Please* help me, Slim dear.'

Corinne came even closer. A suggestion of her very subtle and attractive perfume came to Callaghan's nostrils. Corinne, he thought, could be a very tough proposition.

'What do you want me to do?' he asked.

She said: 'I'll tell you, Slim. I've got the letter. I've got it with me in the pocket of this coat. It's typewritten, and the envelope is postmarked from Brighton. Slim dear, I want you to find out who sent that letter. I want you to find out who the writer was so that we can stop him from hurting Viola; so that she can be *safe*.'

Callaghan asked: 'Have you any idea . . . any idea at all, Corinne, who might have sent such a letter?'

She shook her head. Then, after a moment, she said: 'Of course this is just guessing – or intuition – or whatever it's called, but there's a man who owns a club near Brighton – it's called the Mardene Club, and his name is Lucien Donelly. D'you know, Slim, once or twice when I've been there with Viola, I've thought that he was a dangerous sort of man. I don't know why I should think that, but immediately I saw that letter I thought of him. A picture of him came to my mind. D'you think there might be anything in that, Slim? Or am I just being foolish?'

Callaghan said: 'You never know. Anyhow, it's somewhere to start looking. Give me the letter, Corinne.'

She produced the letter from her coat pocket; handed it to him. He read it; put it into his pocket. He said: 'I dare say I could check up with any typewriter he's got at this club. But it's going to be a ticklish job.'

She said: 'I know you'll be able to do it, Slim. I know you will. And if my guess is right, then we'll be able to do something about him. We'll be able to look after Viola.'

'Shall we?' asked Callaghan. 'How?'

'We'll think of something,' said Corinne. 'We must think of something. But we've got to find out first.'

She got up. She said: 'I've got to go, Slim. They'll miss me. If you want to get into touch with me telephone me at Dark Spinney and say that you're Vones of Brighton. I get things from them. It's a shop.'

Callaghan said: 'I'll do my best. And I'll let you know what happens.'

She said: 'Thank you, Slim. You're such a sweet. *Thank you*. Find this out for me and I'll do anything for you . . . but anything.' She looked at him with eyes that promised a great deal.

He said again: 'I'll do my best.'

She produced another envelope. She said: 'There's some money there, Slim. Something to be going on with. If you want more, ask for it. *Au revoir, dear* Slim.'

She went out. Callaghan heard her car start outside.

He went to the service hatch; ordered a double whisky and soda. He carried the glass back to the settle. He sat down, opened Corinne's second envelope. Inside, were fifteen five-pound notes.

Callaghan lit a cigarette. He began to grin. Then he said to himself: 'Well . . . I'm damned!'

CHAPTER SIX
RED HERRING

CALLAGHAN turned out of the High Street; began to walk towards Hangover. The afternoon sun was brilliant; somewhere a bird was singing. Callaghan thought that it was an ideal country afternoon – a pastoral scene – that is if you liked pastoral scenes. He grinned cynically. He concluded that you might as well have trouble in the country as anywhere else.

And there was going to be trouble. He was perfectly certain of that. It was sticking out a foot that trouble *must* start shortly. In a big way.

He began to consider the point of view of the individual – whoever he was – who had written the anonymous letter to the Colonel. Why had the letter been written? Obviously, because the writer wanted to *start* something. He wanted to make things hot for somebody, that somebody being Viola Alardyse. Now what was his attitude going to be?

First of all, thought Callaghan, he (or she) would wait and see what happened as the result of the Colonel's death. He (or she) would wait patiently, or impatiently, for the letter to be discovered amongst the Colonel's effects. When it was not discovered and nothing happened what would be the result?

Quite obviously, reasoned Callaghan, the writer of the anonymous letter would start something else. It being impossible for the Colonel to do anything about it, somebody else must be prodded into action. Who would that someone else be? Callaghan thought life would be a great deal simpler if it were possible to answer questions as easily as it was to ask them.

He began to think about Donelly. To add together the things he had heard; the things he knew about Donelly. First of all Donelly had seemed pretty certain of himself. He was not a man to scare easily. Then there was the tie-up between Corinne and Donelly. Nikolls' girlfriend had suggested that Corinne was stuck on Donelly; that she was a little crazy about him. Yet she suspected him. She thought it possible that Donelly might have written the letter. She wanted to know. Very well . . supposing she did know. Supposing it appeared that Donelly *had* written the letter . . . well . . . what was *she* going to do about it?

Callaghan found himself concerned with motives. If Donelly had written the letter what had been his motive? Obviously to dispossess Viola of the estate and the money that went with it and, as a result of this, Corinne would be very much richer than she was. Did Donelly – if he *had* written the letter – think it was going to be easier to get money from Corinne than it was from Viola? Hardly. Corinne was tough and Viola had, up to the moment anyhow, paid when she had been asked to pay.

He shrugged his shoulders. Theories were all very well in their way. They helped sometimes. But it was action that got results.

The green door in the Hangover boundary wall was unlatched. Callaghan pushed open the door, went into the garden, closed the door behind him. He began to walk along the gravel pathway towards the house.

Viola came out of the side door. Callaghan took off his hat. He said: 'It's a lovely afternoon and I'm glad I've met you. I want to talk to you.'

She said: 'I want to talk to you too. I've been thinking. I've been wondering if we ought not to do something about all this.'

Callaghan raised his eyebrows. He asked: 'Something such as . . .?'

She began to walk slowly along the pathway. She said: 'This idea of my being a possible suspect of having killed my stepfather – the motive would be because of the Will, wouldn't it? The motive would be because Gervase had found out about my being married, and that I'd quarrelled with him and killed him. Wouldn't that be the idea?'

He nodded. 'I suppose it would,' he said. 'But as you didn't see the Colonel after you came back from my office I don't see how you could have killed him, and so the motive doesn't really matter.'

'It's nice of you to say that,' she said. 'But the point is that no one knows that I didn't see Gervase. *I* know I didn't. As I told you, I was unhappy and went for a long walk in the woods, but I didn't see anyone. There isn't anyone who could prove that I was there. I *might* have killed him and I might have had a good motive.'

Callaghan smiled at her. He said: 'You're beginning to lose your nerve, aren't you? Supposing we don't worry about your motives for wanting, or not wanting, to kill your stepfather. The fact remains that you didn't and somebody else did. If I were you I should forget it for the time being.'

'You're very comforting,' she said. Then: 'What did you want to tell me – or ask me?'

Callaghan said: 'Has Mr Gringall been about? Has he been asking any more questions? Have you heard anything more from the police?'

She shook her head. 'Only that the inquest has been adjourned once more. I don't know why that is.'

Callaghan thought: That's Gringall. He's still stringing along. He's still not satisfied. He wondered what Gringall's next line of inquiry would be.

He said: 'Well . . . there's nothing to worry about. Nothing at all.'

'I wish I could believe you,' she said. 'I think there's a great deal to worry about. First of all there's Corinne. I think her attitude is extraordinary. I don't know what to do about it.'

'When in doubt, don't,' said Callaghan cheerfully. 'You're suffering from a spot of reaction, that's all – just sheer nerves. Remember that you promised to do as I tell you and I'm telling you to do nothing.'

He lit a cigarette. 'Where can I find Sallins?' he asked. 'I want to talk to him.'

'He'll be in his room,' she said. 'If you go down the stairway on the right of the hall there's a room at the bottom. He'll probably be there. I think he rests in the afternoon.'

'Thanks,' said Callaghan. 'I'll see you soon – I hope.' He grinned at her; went towards the house.

Sallins was lying on his bed when Callaghan opened the door. He looked very old and tired. There was a pencil and a sheet of foolscap paper on the dressing-table.

Callaghan said: 'Don't get up, Sallins. I don't want to disturb you. Just relax. You look as if you needed a rest.'

'Yes, Sir,' said Sallins. 'I must admit I'm a little tired. And worried too. I hate all this business, Sir. It's all terribly disturbing.'

Callaghan nodded. 'I expect the police have been at you, haven't they?'

'They've been very nice to me, Sir,' said Sallins. 'Very nice and polite. Actually I'm afraid I've been able to be of very little use to them. I've been able to tell them hardly anything.'

Callaghan grinned. 'You'd be surprised, Sallins,' he said, 'what you can tell a policeman without even knowing it. How did you like Mr Gringall?'

'A very charming gentleman,' said Sallins. 'Very kind and considerate. I believe he thinks the Colonel killed himself. A terrible thing to do, Sir, but I'd rather believe that than that anybody else killed him.'

Callaghan nodded. He thought: Like hell Gringall thinks the Colonel killed himself. He wondered just how far Gringall had led the old butler up the garden path; just how far Sallins, swayed by Gringall's kindness and the charm that he could put on like an overcoat, had gone. Just how much he had talked and surmised and suggested.

He said: 'Sallins . . . I want to ask you just one question. When you went back to the house to telephone the police – after you'd seen me in the garden; just after you'd told me about the Colonel – what did you do? Did you telephone right away or did you tell anyone?'

Sallins said: 'I told Miss Wymering, Sir. I was in the hall. I was just going to telephone and I saw her at the top of the stairs. I went to the bottom of the stairs and told her. She said she would go at once and look at the Colonel. Then I telephoned the police.'

'I wonder why I didn't see her?' asked Callaghan. 'If she went straight to the pagoda she ought to have passed me.'

'She went the other way, Sir,' said Sallins. 'When I told her, she was at the top of the staircase. She turned and walked along the first floor corridor. She would go out from the back of the house by the other path.'

'I see,' said Callaghan. 'And then you telephoned the police?'

'Yes, Sir,' said Sallins. 'Then I telephoned the police.'

'All right,' said Callaghan. 'I'm much obliged to you, Sallins.' He went out of the room, closed the door softly behind him, slowly mounted the circular stairway that led to the hall. He thought: None of this is so good. There's going to be a *lot* of trouble in a minute.

He was crossing the hallway to the side door. A voice said: 'Hallo, Slim.' It was Patricia. She was standing at the top of the main staircase. She wore a simple linen frock; a demure expression.

Callaghan said: 'Come down here, Patricia. I want to talk to you.'

She tripped down the stairs. She stood two or three steps from the bottom looking down at him. She said softly: 'Slim . . . I think you're a *sweet*. The way I go for you is nobody's business.'

'Good,' said Callaghan. He grinned at her. 'Listen Patricia,' he said. 'Have any of the policemen who have been asking questions here asked you whether you saw Viola on the evening of your step-father's death?'

She shook her head. 'I was fearfully disappointed in them,' she said. 'They asked me practically nothing. I might have been the village idiot so far as they were concerned.'

Callaghan asked: 'Can you see the pathway outside the green door – the one that leads up to the woods where you and I first met – from anywhere in this house?'

She nodded. 'You can see it from my bedroom,' she said. 'Quite easily.'

Callaghan said: 'Good. Well, remember that you saw Viola going up that path for a walk on the evening that your stepfather was killed. That would be about seven-fifteen or seven-thirty. Have you got that?'

She said gravely: 'Yes, I've got it, Slim. I see what you mean.' She came down the stairs, stood close to him.

'You don't think anyone's going to suggest . . .' There were tears in her eyes.

Callaghan said: 'I don't think anyone's going to suggest anything.' He smiled down at her. 'But someone may try a bluff. You never know and I always like to have an ace up my sleeve. You'll remember that, won't you?'

'I couldn't forget it,' she said. 'I was standing by my window at about seven-fifteen or seven-twenty and I saw Viola go out by the green gate and up the path to the wood. That's my story and I'm sticking to it.'

'Good,' said Callaghan. 'And thank you for the tip about Corinne. She and I had an interesting little talk.'

'No! But how thrilling,' said Patricia. 'Was it nice? Did she try to vamp you? Was she terribly clever with you?'

Callaghan said: 'I wouldn't know. All I know is I'm working for her.'

'What *do* you know!' said Patricia. 'I think you're pretty good, Slim. I do really. So you're working for Corinne too!'

Callaghan said: 'Listen, Patricia. I don't like going behind Viola's back, but I've got to. If I were to play straight with her just at this time and tell her what's in my mind I'm not certain that she wouldn't upset the apple-cart. She's nervy, you understand that, and a little scared.'

Patricia nodded. 'I know,' she said. 'What do you want?'

Callaghan said: 'Do you know Viola's bank? Do you ever go there and cash cheques for her?'

'Often,' said Patricia.

He went on: 'Do you think you could put this over? Drop into the bank tomorrow morning casually; say that Viola has mislaid some banknotes that she drew not very long ago. Ask them if they have the numbers of the notes. They will have. Get them. And try and do it without Viola knowing anything about it.'

'All right,' said Patricia. 'I know the cashier well. He's awfully nice. And he won't think it odd. It's just the sort of thing Viola *might* ask me to do for her.'

'If you get them,' said Callaghan, 'make a note of the numbers on a piece of paper, put it in an envelope and leave it for me at the Two Friars. Try and do that tomorrow morning, but for the love of Mike play it carefully.'

'O.K., partner,' said Patricia. 'I'll fix it if it can be fixed.'

Callaghan said: 'I don't know what I'd do without you. I'll be seeing you.'

He went out through the side door.

Patricia stood for a little while at the foot of the hall stairs. She was thinking about Callaghan. She emitted a heavy and somewhat theatrical sigh.

She decided that she was in love. But *definitely* in love. Not like any of the hundred and one times she had been in love before, but in a very big way. This was different.

She thought that she would go to her room, finish off the chocolates and think about it.

*

It was six o'clock. Callaghan sat in the deserted bar parlour, looked at the sporting print on the wall opposite. He thought: Those were the days – the good old bad days when there were only Bow Street runners, no Gringalls, no police laboratories and no private detectives. Life, he thought, must have been quite interestingly uninteresting.

He remembered the pencil and the sheet of foolscap paper on Sallins' dressing-table. That was Mr Gringall, that was. Callaghan remembered, from a previous occasion, the Gringall technique of giving a witness a long time to think and a pencil and a sheet of foolscap paper to think on. Callaghan had seen the Stationery Office mark on the foolscap. A police issue, that piece of paper, and Sallins was thinking hard trying to remember something that Gringall wanted him to remember.

He finished his drink; got up; began to walk along the oak passage that led to the stairway. He stopped at the letter rack. There was a typewritten envelope addressed to Nikolls and a fat telegram for Callaghan.

He took them both; went to his room; sat down and opened the letter from Nikolls' girlfriend at the Mardene Club. It contained the typewritten letter that Nikolls had asked her to write.

Callaghan took one look at it. He whistled softly to himself. There was no doubt about it. The anonymous letter written to Colonel Stenhurst had been written on the same machine.

So it *was* Donelly. Donelly was the key. Donelly was the boy who wanted to start something; who *had* started something; who might easily start something else unless he was stopped.

Callaghan lit a cigarette, opened the telegram. It was from Nikolls. It read:

'*John Elliot has uncovered dope stop R. Sharpham early 1939 when Sharpham involved action with old lady he took for a packet. Smart, good looker, man-about-town type lots of charm what it takes very keen on women stop Came from Cape Town South Africa where was one time working as dancing instructor Rosehill Dance Hall stop Arrived England 1938 got some dough means unknown took up flying and took civilian pilots ticket late 1938 nobody knows why stop Information re marriage with our client correct stop Aynesworth pulling strings Air Ministry re full record flying service and or other lines stop Sticking around for this hope arrive tomorrow with works – Nikolls.'*

Callaghan began to pace up and down the room. His cigarette, which had gone out, hung limply from the corner of his mouth. So Sharpham had been of the gigolo type – a man about town – clever, charming, with the remains of the money which he had got from the old lady and the rather romantic background of a pilot. Callaghan could understand how Viola had fallen for all that. He shrugged his shoulders.

He picked up the telephone; asked for his office number in London.

Effie Thompson's voice came demurely over the line.

Callaghan said: 'Well, Effie, how are things with you?'

'Very well, thank you, Mr Callaghan,' she said. There was a little pause; then: 'I hope they're well with you.'

Callaghan said: 'Not too bad. Now get your notebook, Effie, and take a note.'

'Very well,' said Effie. There was a pause, then: 'Ready, Mr Callaghan.'

'Get a telephone call through to Cape Town, South Africa,' said Callaghan. 'Make it a business priority call – you ought to be through at latest in three to four hours. Get John Friquet – his cable address is "Investigator, Manzanilla, Cape Town". Speak to Friquet himself or, if he's not there, his wife, Eleanor. Tell him to get cracking and get me the fullest possible information on the background, and anything of importance that he can uncover, on Rupert Sharpham who was at some time in or, before 1938 employed as an instructor at a joint called Rosehill Dance Hall in Cape Town. Tell Friquet that expense is no object and remind him that he owes me a good turn for something he'll remember. Tell him really to get cracking and telephone you as soon as he's got something that matters. Have you got that, Effie?'

She said: 'Yes, Mr Callaghan. I'll get on to it right away.'

Callaghan said: 'O.K., Effie.' He hung up. He threw his dead cigarette into the fireplace; lit another: began to walk up and down the room.

A quarter of an hour went by. Callaghan was so engrossed in his thoughts that he did not hear the tap at the door, or even see it open. He suddenly became aware of the presence of Chief Detective-Inspector Gringall.

Gringall stood in the doorway, a pleasant little smile playing about his mouth, his soft brown trilby hat in one hand, looking at Callaghan.

He said: 'Hallo, Slim.'

Callaghan said: 'Well, this is a pleasure. Come in, Gringall. What can I do for you?'

Gringall closed the door quietly behind him. He came into the room, put his hat on the table. He sat down in the chair Callaghan indicated.

He said: 'I don't know, Slim . . . I don't know whether you can do anything for me or not, but I think you ought to try.'

Callaghan said: 'Well, you know me well enough to know that I'd do anything for you. What is it?'

Gringall said: 'I'm having difficulty in getting the right sort of evidence, but perhaps you can help me.' He went on: 'You see, the butler at Dark Spinney – Sallins – he's an old man and very upset about all this business. I haven't liked to jog his memory too much. I've given him lots of time to think.'

Callaghan said: 'Yes, I thought you'd do that.'

'The point is,' said Gringall, 'that I showed Sallins the police photograph of the body of the Colonel – one of those we took after we'd seen it. The old boy was a little bit surprised.'

Callaghan said: 'No? I wonder why.'

'He's beginning to remember why,' said Gringall. 'There was a difference. In fact, there were several differences.'

Callaghan said: 'This is interesting. You mean . . .?'

Gringall said: 'I mean that the body wasn't in the same position as when he found it, and there were other things. You see, he was awfully surprised to see that handkerchief in the Colonel's hand. He says he's certain that handkerchief wasn't there. He also says that he's certain he saw another handkerchief under or very near the body. He also says the pistol was some way from the Colonel and not as near as it seemed in the photograph.'

Callaghan said: 'Is he sure about these things?'

Gringall nodded. 'He's sure enough,' he said. 'It's not very good, is it, Slim? I'm a little worried about your client.'

Callaghan asked: 'Why?'

Gringall said: 'Well, after Sallins found the Colonel he came down the path to go back to the house. He met you. You went to look at the Colonel and Sallins went into the house. He was in the hallway when he saw Miss Wymering at the top of the stairs. He told her what had happened. She went along the corridor, down the back stairs, out of the back of the house and along the path to the pagoda. She looked at the Colonel. The next people to see the body were the local police and they had a man on there until we arrived. Nobody else went in. So there's only one deduction to be drawn, isn't there?'

Callaghan said: 'Is there? What's the deduction?' He thought to himself: This isn't so good.

Gringall said: 'The obvious deduction is that for some reason best known to herself, Miss Wymering moved the pistol, put the handkerchief into the Colonel's hand after probably wiping the prints off the butt, removed the other handkerchief which Sallins thinks he saw there. It must have been Miss Wymering,' Gringall went on, 'because it couldn't have been you. Why should you want to do a thing like that, Slim?'

Callaghan said: 'Quite. But why should *she*?'

'That's the point,' said Gringall. 'I'm not suggesting for a moment that Miss Wymering had anything to do with the Colonel's death. In point of fact we know she couldn't have. But she might have done what she *apparently* did because she wanted to shield somebody.'

Callaghan asked: 'What are you getting at, Gringall? Who should she want to shield and why?'

Gringall produced his short briar pipe. He began to fill it carefully from a rubber pouch. He took quite a time over the process. When the pipe was filled he lit it, drew on it with obvious pleasure.

He said: 'Of course, Slim, I'm holding out on you; there are one or two angles in this case that you don't know. You see, you didn't talk to the Colonel, did you?'

Callaghan said: 'No. I didn't have a chance. I told you about that.'

Gringall nodded. 'Well,' he said, 'it seems that the Colonel really *was* worried when he telephoned you. Apparently, he wanted to talk to you in the first place about some fairly small incident, but it seems that between the time he had dinner and the time he went upstairs he received a letter.'

Callaghan raised his eyebrows. 'A letter . . .?'

'An anonymous letter,' said Gringall, 'from somebody or other giving him some information which upset him very much. I imagine he wanted to talk to you about that too.'

Callaghan said: 'Well, that's that. I wonder what was in the letter.'

Gringall said: 'I can tell you that. I know.'

Callaghan looked surprised. 'You know? How the devil do you know, Gringall?'

'Well,' said Gringall, 'the person who sent the original anonymous letter wasn't very pleased at the Colonel's death. They thought maybe nothing would be done about it, so they sent a copy of it. They sent a copy of it to me.'

Callaghan nodded. He said: 'That was a break. What was the anonymous letter about?' His voice was casual.

Gringall said: 'The letter was a funny sort of letter. It suggested that Miss Viola Alardyse had been married some time in 1939 and as a result thereof had inherited the Dark Spinney Estate and Trust Fund illegally. That was all.'

Callaghan shrugged his shoulders. He said: 'Probably somebody being funny. There are always a lot of people trying to start something by writing anonymous letters. This is just another nitwit trying to pull something.'

'No,' said Gringall. He relit his pipe. 'This wasn't a nitwit. This was somebody who knew what he (or she) was talking about. I've checked the information and it's correct. That isn't so good, is it?'

'All right,' said Callaghan. 'It's not so good. But I don't see that it matters – not at the moment anyhow.'

Gringall drew on his pipe. He said: 'You know better than that, Slim. I've adjourned the inquest because there wasn't anything much in the way of evidence to go before a Coroner's jury. I've never believed the Colonel committed suicide. He was murdered. And murderers always have a motive. I've been trying to find one. This might be it.'

Callaghan said nothing. He went over to the window, stood looking out on to the quiet street. He thought: I wonder how the hell you play this one. This looks like the end of the story.

Gringall went on: 'This writer of anonymous letters seems to have known a thing or two. He wrote a letter to the Colonel. Then the Colonel dies and the writer thinks that he's going to be short-circuited. So he writes some more letters. For all I know he may have written to Miss Wymering. If he did, that might explain why she tried to dicker about with the evidence after the Colonel was dead. It might explain why she moved the handkerchief that Sallins saw; *and* the pistol, and why she put the Colonel's handkerchief in his hand after she'd wiped the prints off.'

'You mean she was trying to shield Viola Alardyse who, having illegally inherited the estate, had a good motive for killing the Colonel?'

Gringall said evenly: 'I don't mean anything. I mean that it's my job to place all the relevant evidence before the Coroner's jury. They've got to find how the Colonel died. It's their business, not mine, to bring in a verdict. But I've got to do my best to help them.'

Callaghan said: 'That's as maybe. But I think it's damned silly to suggest that Viola Alardyse had a motive for knocking off Stenhurst. The idea's ridiculous.'

Gringall shrugged his shoulders. 'I've known some murderers and murderesses who've been awfully nice people. So have you, Slim. You never know. And anyhow, facts are facts.'

'Right,' said Callaghan. 'Facts are facts. Well . . . what are you going to do about it?'

Gringall said slowly: 'There's only one thing I can do. I'm going back to Dark Spinney now and I'm going to have a heart-to-heart talk with Miss Wymering. I'm going to tell her what Sallins says and show her the police photographs. I'm going to ask her why she moved the gun and the handkerchief. I'm going to tell her that we know all about Miss Viola Alardyse's marriage. I'm going to tell her that so far as I'm concerned that doesn't matter to me except as it affects the case. I don't care who married who or why. I'm not a lawyer. I'm a police officer investigating a murder. If she's wise she's going to talk. If she moved the gun and the handkerchief and likes to admit it, all right. Probably I'm not going to do anything about that. I'm merely going to find out *why* she moved them. Especially the handkerchief. Handkerchiefs can be important. Very often they have people's initials, or scent, or lipstick on them.'

Gringall paused and smoked for a few seconds. Then he went on: 'My attitude is that *she* moved those things. *You* didn't, so she *must* have. In any event, I'm going to find out quite a few things that I don't know at the moment. That is, of course' – Gringall paused and looked whimsically at Callaghan – 'that is unless you've got something to tell me – something that you haven't mentioned before because you didn't think it mattered. Something possibly that you considered to be your client's private affairs. See . . . Slim?'

Callaghan said: 'I see. Well . . . what have I got to tell you? I don't know a thing.'

Gringall nodded. 'Then that's that,' he said. 'I know that you're clever enough not to buck up against the police, Slim. You've sailed near the wind once or twice and got away with it. But this case is a serious one. It's murder. If you get in the way, no matter what your motives may be, you're going to get hurt. You know that.'

Callaghan said: 'I know. I fancy I've heard that some time before.' He grinned. 'Anything else?' he asked.

Gringall said: 'No. I don't have to remind you, Slim, about that old-fashioned Police Act of ours – "withholding information", etc. If you know anything that is likely to help the police in this case it's your duty to produce it.'

Callaghan sighed. He said: 'Life can be tough.' He grinned at Gringall. 'I don't know a thing,' he said. 'And if I did I'd tell you. So that's that.'

Gringall got up. He walked over to the fire, knocked his pipe out carefully on the top bar of the fire-gate, put it in his pocket.

He straightened up, turned round, faced Callaghan. His expression was benign.

He said: 'You're a strange fellow, Slim. An odd one. I've never been able to understand you very well; but I know your technique and I know that in nine cases out of ten that you handle you play it the shortest way off the cuff. You took a hell of a chance in the Vendayne case. You were damned lucky to get away with that. If you hadn't pulled it out of the bag we had a nice little charge waiting for you. And I know why you took the chance. You took a hell of a chance in that case because Audrey Vendayne was a beautiful woman and you like beautiful women.'

Callaghan grinned. He said: 'Who doesn't?'

'Everybody does,' said Gringall, 'but not to the extent that you do. Maybe one of these days it isn't going to be worth it.'

Callaghan sighed. He said evenly: 'Did they ever tell you about the brutal Cossacks. Well . . . they had nothing on you. Where's your rubber truncheon, you merciless copper? By the way, what about a drink before you go?'

Gringall sighed a little wearily. He said: 'All right. I'll have one for the road.'

Callaghan poured the drinks. He said: 'The trouble with you blue-inks is that you never believe anybody. Not even if they're telling the truth.'

Gringall put down his glass; picked up his hat. He said: 'All right, Mr George Washington. Thanks for the drink.' He went to the door.

Callaghan said: 'Maybe m a week or so you'll be talking to me through iron bars.' He grinned. 'So long, Gringall.'

When he heard the noise of Gringall's car starting up outside, Callaghan went to the telephone. He dialled the Dark Spinney number; waited. He grinned when he heard Patricia's voice.

'Listen, Madame "X",' said Callaghan. 'I'm in a tough spot and need some help. Where's your aunt?'

'Auntie's gone to Eastbourne,' said Patricia. 'She won't be back until after dinner tonight.'

'Good,' said Callaghan. 'Now listen carefully. Chief Detective-Inspector Gringall is on his way to Dark Spinney. He's just left here. He wants to talk to your aunt. When he gets there see that you're around. Tell him that she's gone off to see a sick friend – anything you like – and that she won't be back until tomorrow night, or the morning after. I want to gain a little time. Understand?'

'I've got it, Slim,' said Patricia. 'D'you think he'll believe it?'

'We've got to chance it,' said Callaghan. 'Even if he doesn't believe it what can he do? He won't sit on the doorstep and wait for her.'

'Very well,' said Patricia. 'I'll make it sound *good*. What else?'

'Where's Corinne?' asked Callaghan.

'She's in her room,' said Patricia. 'She's got a headache – a *real* one.'

'Go and tell her that she's wanted on the telephone,' said Callaghan. 'Tell her that Vones of Eastbourne want to speak to her.'

'O.K.,' said Patricia. 'Hold on.'

Callaghan waited. After a while Corinne's voice came on the line.

He said: 'Corinne . . . this is Slim. I haven't much time to talk to you now. I've got to see you. Some time tonight. Tell me where. I've some information that you ought to know about.'

'Yes?' There was a pause. Then: 'D'you know the Crumbles – just past Pevensey Bay? There's a place called the Officer's House. A place with four chimneys at the end of the old Coastguard Cottages.'

'I know,' said Callaghan. He grinned. 'A nice sort of place,' he said. 'It's where a man named Mahon murdered a woman some years ago.'

'That's right,' said Corinne. 'Well, keep on the path that runs past that house. It runs straight down to the sea. You'll find a motor-boat moored in on to the beach. It's called *Mayfly*. I'll be waiting there for you – at ten o'clock.' Her voice lifted a little. 'I'll take you for a nice ride on the sea,' said Corinne.

'I'll be there,' said Callaghan. 'The *Mayfly* moored in line with the Officer's House at ten o'clock. Now go back to your room and stay there. Gringall's coming around and you don't want to see him.'

'I certainly do not,' said Corinne. '*Au revoir*, Slim . . .' There was a pause . . . '*dear* Slim.'

'So long,' said Callaghan. He hung up.

He stood for a moment looking at the telephone. Then he poured himself out another drink, drank it in one gulp, lit a cigarette.

By and large, he thought, Gringall was right. For years he'd been skating on thin ice. Some time it was going to crack, and then it wasn't going to be so good.

This time the ice was *very* thin.

Callaghan sat at the steering-wheel of his car outside the Two Friars. Life, he thought, rather resembled a difficult bridge problem. The sort of thing one saw displayed in a newspaper with the caption: 'What does North do?' Callaghan wondered what the hell 'North', in the shape of Mr Callaghan, was going to do.

He lit a cigarette, began to cough, came to the conclusion that he was smoking too much. He started the car, began to drive towards Herstmonceux.

It was seven-thirty when he arrived at the R.A.F. Convalescent Hospital. He wondered whether he was going to be lucky.

The Matron was characteristic of the rather nice, sensible and not unattractive, person that one finds as a matron in such places. Her hair was turning grey; her face, pleasant and frank.

Callaghan adopted the expression of innocence which he used when telling some of his better sort of lies.

He said: 'Matron . . . I'm going to put my cards on the table. My name's Callaghan. I'm a private detective, and I'm investigating a little matter which – if you'll excuse me – I won't go into. I wonder if you'd be prepared to help?'

She looked at him. She thought she liked Callaghan; that he looked honest. She said: 'I will if I can. What is it?'

Callaghan said: 'You remember a Miss Corinne Alardyse who used to work here. I believe during the latter part of the war?'

She nodded. 'I remember her very well,' she said. 'She was a V.A.D. A rather beautiful girl; a girl of very distinct personality.'

'Right,' said Callaghan. 'And perhaps you remember a Mr Donelly – Lucien Donelly. He was an R.A.F. Officer who came here for post-hospital treatment. I think these two were rather friendly, weren't they?'

'Oh, yes,' said the Matron. She smiled reminiscently.

'We were all rather interested in them. We all thought that they were rather in love until . . .'

'Until what?' asked Callaghan.

She hesitated. Then she said: 'Well, of course, Mr Donelly was a *very* nice and attractive man; he had delightful manners too and he was *very* good looking. We all thought that something might come of it and then there was the car smash. You see, Mr Donelly had a car and used to drive it rather recklessly. One day he took Corinne Alardyse into Brighton; they were going to a matinee. Well . . . the suggestion was that he took a little too much to drink at lunch – quite an understandable thing in a man whose nerves had been rather shaken in the war. Anyhow, he ran into another car. It was a bad smash and the Brighton police decided to take action for dangerous driving. They came over here and made inquiries and talked to Corinne. She had to admit that Mr Donelly wasn't absolutely himself. She *had* to admit this because other people had seen him too and thought he was a little intoxicated. Well . . . eventually the police decided to call her as evidence and I remember that she was very upset about it. I thought, in fact, that she was unduly worried; that she was taking the thing much too seriously.'

Callaghan said: 'That's easily understood if she was fond of Donelly.'

'Possibly, but not to the extent she indicated. However,' the Matron went on, 'eventually she decided to go to Brighton and see the police officer in charge of the case and tell him that she didn't want to give evidence. She went and came back much happier. Inspector Manston – who was in charge of the case – had decided that they wouldn't call her as evidence, and they didn't. She was very relieved.'

'I see,' said Callaghan. 'And then?'

The Matron smiled. 'That was the end of the romance,' she said. 'After that Corinne seemed to change her point of view about Mr Donelly. I think she realized that there was a side to his nature that she didn't like. They were very cool to each other, and soon after she left. Mr Donelly is still in the neighbourhood, I believe. He runs a club near Rottingdean. I'm afraid that's all I can tell you, Mr Callaghan.'

Callaghan got up. He said: 'Thank you, Matron. I'm afraid this information doesn't help a lot, but you've done your best.'

Outside, sitting in the Lagonda, he thought: In for a penny, in for a pound. He was in bad with Gringall. Gringall was on his tail all right. Gringall believed that he, Callaghan, had switched the evidence; had moved the handkerchief, wiped the pistol and generally queered the pitch. And this time Gringall was going to get tough. Eventually, he would talk to Miss Wymering, who would deny that she had touched or moved anything, and then . . .

Callaghan sighed. Then it wasn't going to be so good. Gringall would move, and Mr Callaghan of Callaghan Investigations would be well and truly in the cart.

So why not go the whole hog?

Callaghan put his foot on the gas; the Lagonda shot forward. He brought her down to a steady fifty. He was in Brighton soon after eight o'clock.

Inspector Manston had gone off duty, but Callaghan found him at his house and wasted no time.

'My name's Callaghan,' he said. 'I'm a private detective. I was doing a job for the Alardyse family when Colonel Stenhurst's body was found. Possibly you've heard of me?'

Manston indicated a chair. He produced a box of cigarettes. When they were lit, he said: 'Yes, I've heard of you. Mr Gringall, who's down here on that case, mentioned you. What can I do?'

Callaghan said: 'I'm trying my best to give Mr Gringall a hand. We're old friends. Actually I've been able to put him wise to one or two things that matter in the case. Well . . there's one little point he asked me to clear up. I think you can do it.'

Mansion nodded. 'If I can,' he said.

Callaghan said: 'Maybe you'll remember a dangerous driving case. An officer called Lucien Donelly. He was a little high and ran into another car. Miss Corinne Alardyse – who was then a V.A.D. at the Herstmonceux Convalescent Home – was in the car. You wanted her as evidence and subpoenaed her. However, you withdrew the subpoena after she'd been over here to see you. I take it you decided not to call her because she told you she was married to Donelly and that it wasn't ethical for you to ask a wife to give evidence against her husband?'

Manston said: 'That's right. That's perfectly correct.' He smiled. 'Now I wonder how you knew that,' he said. 'Unless she told you, of course. And anyhow, I don't see what it's got to do with the Stenhurst business.'

Callaghan got up. 'Only a very remote connection,' he said. 'But Gringall asked me to check up on it. Thanks for your help.'

They shook hands. Callaghan went away.

Outside, he turned the car back towards Alfriston. He drove fast, the wind burning his cigarette quickly. He was grinning.

So that was that. Corinne was married to Donelly. And Donelly had written the anonymous note to the Colonel and afterwards sent a copy to Gringall.

So that was that!

Callaghan parked the car in the Two Friars garage; went to his sitting-room; began to walk up and down. Nothing added up, he thought. Nothing at all. Which was possibly as well, because when things didn't add up it was only because one little thing was wrong. One little piece missing.

He began to think about Viola Alardyse. He had told her that he would stop Donelly – if it had been Donelly who had written the anonymous letter – from doing anything else. Well . . . Donelly had sent the letter, and Callaghan hadn't stopped him doing something else. Donelly had sent the second letter to Gringall.

He thought some more about Viola Alardyse. Gringall had said that he was always getting in bad because of trying to help some woman who happened to be good looking. That was just nonsense. If a good-looking woman formed the basis of most of Callaghan's cases, it was because things happened to beautiful women. Things didn't happen to women with faces like the back of a cab and legs like drain pipes.

And what good had he done Viola? None at all. If she had been in bad when the job started she was in a damned sight worse now.

He sighed. The road to hell was paved with good intentions.

He shrugged his shoulders.

He was pouring a drink when the telephone jangled. It was Effie Thompson.

She said: 'Mr Callaghan, Nikolls has just brought in the copies of the reports he's got from Mr Aynesworth about Rupert Sharpham. He's bringing them down tomorrow morning. They're the usual service reports and flying records of an R.A.F. Officer. Very long and mostly routine. I've extracted the main headings and wondered if you'd like to have them right away.'

Callaghan said: 'Good girl. Let me have it.'

She said: 'The records are mainly flying reports, medicals and general service reports. Sharpham seems to have been a good officer. He was wounded twice before he crashed. Once early in 1942 he was hit in the shoulder by a tracer bullet and again at the end of the year when he was wounded in the right hand. His little finger was amputated and he had to stop flying for six months. At this time he was Flight Lieutenant. He was promoted Squadron Leader in 1943. Have you got all that?'

'I've got it,' said Callaghan. 'Go on.'

'Mr Nikolls said that this was the operative point you wanted,' said Effie. 'When Sharpham was shot down and crashed in Italy in 1944 he was flying an Army reconnaissance plane. He had a co-pilot. The co-pilot was Flight Lieutenant Lucien Donelly. Sharpham was only slightly injured, but Donelly was badly smashed up. His right arm was broken and his jaw and nose. His eyes were affected and it was thought that he might go blind. However, it seems that there was a good surgeon in the prison camp who was able to patch him up. When he was fairly well, he and Sharpham planned a break. They escaped from the camp but had to pass through a battle zone, and Sharpham was killed by a shell. Donelly got through to the British lines. He was in a bad state, but eventually recovered. He was evacuated to England and after treatment was sent to the R.A.F Convalescent Home at Herstmonceux. Mr Nikolls says that he considers that these are the main facts that you want. He proposes to bring the complete *dossier* down in the morning.'

Callaghan said: 'O. K. Tell him he needn't hurry. I've got what I wanted. Have you heard from Friquet yet, in Cape Town?'

'No,' said Effie. 'I spoke to him on the telephone and he promised to get busy and put a call through directly he'd got something.'

'All right,' said Callaghan. 'Let me have it as soon as you get it. So long, Effie.'

He hung up.

So that was that. That was the story. The jig-saw puzzle was beginning to straighten itself out.

He looked at his watch. It was half-past nine. He remembered Corinne. Corinne, who would be waiting at the Crumbles beach at ten o'clock.

Callaghan poured a drink. One of these days, he told himself, he would definitely begin to cut down on whisky. One of these days.

He put on an overcoat and cap. He went down to the car.

He started the engine. He began to think about Corinne.

CHAPTER SEVEN
A RIDE WITH CORINNE

IT WAS just after ten o'clock when Callaghan stopped the Lagonda two hundred and fifty yards away from the New Inn at Pevensey Bay on the Eastbourne Road. He parked the car on the side of the road; began to walk along the gravel path that led past the row of old Coastguard Cottages towards the sea. It was a lovely night. The Crumbles – a long desolate waste pitted here and there with a solitary cottage – looked peaceful, almost romantic, in the moonlight. Thirty yards ahead of him was the 'Officer's House' – the end house of the row of Coastguard Cottages – the house with four chimneys. It stood – a bleak, desolate and deserted shell – almost proclaiming its sinister association.

Callaghan remembered the case. It was here that Patrick Mahon – the good-looking, well set-up Irishman – had murdered a woman; had cut her up; burned the body. Weeks afterwards, a child playing in the shingle in front of the house had found a human hand, and then the wheels of the law had begun to turn. Their turning had ended at the scaffold.

He passed the house, continued along the path on its long journey towards the sea. Minutes passed before he saw the figure of Corinne sitting on the bows of a dinghy pulled up on the beach.

Beyond, moored on a long painter, he could see the shape of the motor-boat.

She got up as he approached her; came towards him. She was wearing slacks, a silk muffler and a duffle coat. A georgette scarf bound her dark hair. In the moonlight she looked quite lovely.

She put out her hand. She said: 'Slim, you are a *sweet*. It's so good of you to take all this trouble.'

He grinned at her. He said: 'I'm glad to be of assistance. Anyway, you're a customer. You're paying for it.'

She said: 'You mustn't talk like that.' She looked towards the sea. She said: 'Shall we go for a ride? It's a lovely night.'

Callaghan said: 'Why not?' She got into the dinghy. He pushed it off; jumped easily into the bows. She picked up an oar; sculled the few yards between the shore and the launch. They went aboard. Callaghan tied the dinghy to the stern.

She started the motor. They headed towards the open sea. The launch was a long slim craft – all engine.

'Does this belong to you?' Callaghan asked.

She shook her head. She said: 'No, this belongs to Lucien Donelly – my boyfriend.' She smiled at him. 'I persuaded him to buy it. I love the sea. He doesn't. But once on a time I used to get him to come out in the boat. Now I seem to use it mostly on my own.'

Callaghan asked: 'You prefer being alone?'

She said: 'I wonder.' Now they were passing through the line of breakers a quarter of a mile off the shore. She handled the launch expertly.

Callaghan said: 'You're pretty good with this boat. Isn't she too narrow for the sea? She looks like a river craft to me.'

'She's very fast,' said Corinne. 'You've got to handle her carefully. She'll turn over very easily. Let me show you.' She swung the wheel, brought the boat broadside on to the incoming tide. The *Mayfly* quivered for a moment; heeled over to an angle of about thirty-five degrees. Corinne swung the wheel again. The boat righted.

'You see, she's rather like a woman,' she said. 'You've got to handle her gently, otherwise she gets annoyed.' She laughed at him.

Callaghan produced his cigarette case. He said: 'Would you like to smoke?'

She said: 'No thanks. You have one. Tell me, Slim, did you find out anything about the letter?' Her voice was casual.

Callaghan said: 'Yes. I found out about the letter. Your guess was right. Donelly wrote it.'

There was a pause. Corinne made a little hissing noise. He thought it sounded like an angry snake: 'The louse . . . the fearful swine!'

'Are you surprised?' said Callaghan.

There was another pause; then she said: 'No, I don't think I am – not really. I've changed my mind; I will have a cigarette.'

He moved towards her; gave her a cigarette; cupped his lighter in his hand; lit it. The breeze had freshened. The launch rolled in the swell. The sea, quiet near the shore, was angrier here.

There was silence. It seemed that a long time went by before she spoke again. Then: 'You know, Slim, I expect you understand quite a lot about men and women?'

He shrugged his shoulders. He said: 'I don't think anybody does. Every man and every woman is a separate case to be considered on its own merits. But why?'

She said: 'I wonder if you can understand about Lucien Donelly and me – how I could be keen on a man that I detest.'

'Somebody once said that love was akin to hate,' said Callaghan.

Her voice was soft. She said: 'Yes, that's exactly what I mean. A man and a woman who hate each other yet can't escape from each other.' She went on: 'I suppose it would sound ridiculous if I said that I'm still crazy about Donelly in spite of everything?'

Callaghan said: 'Well, you had to be crazy about him – otherwise you wouldn't have married him.'

'My God, so you know that!' She laughed – a harsh little laugh. She said: 'Slim, you're not a bad detective. How did you find out?'

'I went to the Convalescent Home at Herstmonceux,' said Callaghan. 'I talked to the Matron. She told me about the car smash you had with Donelly when you were a V.A.D. there; how the police subpoenaed you to give evidence and suddenly withdrew the subpoena. I guessed that you told them that you were his wife.

A wife can't give evidence against her husband. They had to withdraw the subpoena.'

She said: 'You're very clever, aren't you, Slim? But *clever*. You really are. And so you found out that I married Donelly. No one knows but he and I and the Registrar where we were married, and the policeman I told about it. And why should *he* tell anyone? If I turned the boat over now you'd be drowned and the secret would be safe.'

Callaghan grinned at her. She was smiling. Sitting in the stern sheets, leaning back, one hand on the brass steering-wheel, he thought she looked like a female devil.

He said: 'The chances are that you'd be drowned. I'm a good swimmer. But if I couldn't make it I'd take damned good care you went down with me. You've made enough trouble.'

'Have I?' she said. '*Really*. Have I? We'll see. Now tell me something else, Slim. *Why* did he write that letter? How do you know that it was he who sent it?'

Callaghan lit a fresh cigarette. 'I got a sample of the type on the machine in his office. We got at his secretary – the girl who works for him there. The defects in the anonymous letter matched those in the sample. Take it from me he sent it all right.'

She said: 'Yes, but why?'

Callaghan said: 'That's what intrigued me at first. I couldn't understand. Now I think I'm beginning to understand.'

She said impatiently: 'Well . . . tell me.'

'Work it out for yourself,' said Callaghan. 'I take it the story is this: You met Donelly when he was a patient at the Convalescent Home. You fell for him. Why not? He's the type of man that any woman could fall for – charming, well mannered, delightful. All right, he knew all about Viola having married Sharpham in 1939. I'll tell you how he knew. Lucien Donelly was co-pilot to Sharpham. They were shot down together. They were in a prisoner-of-war camp together in Italy. Whilst they were there Sharpham got a letter from Viola telling him the story of the Will; telling him that because he'd married her she would have no money. He told Donelly. After Donelly had recovered, more or less, from his wounds, Sharpham and he decided to make a break. They got away from the camp, but by this time there was fighting in Italy. They had to pass through the battle zone, Sharpham won it. He was killed by a shell. Well, you can think the rest of it out for yourself, can't you?'

She said slowly: 'Yes, I can see.'

'It's easy to work out,' said Callaghan. 'Here was Donelly sitting on some information that meant money. He didn't come down to Herstmonceux Convalescent Home by accident. He *asked* to be sent there. He wanted to see what was going on at Dark Spinney. Well, he found out. He found that Viola, in spite of her marriage to Sharpham, was mistress of Dark Spinney and that she had inherited her mother's money. By this time he'd met you. He went for you in quite a big way. Why shouldn't he? First of all, you're a beautiful woman, and secondly he intended to use you as a permanent meal ticket. A clever fellow, Donelly. And nearly as bad as you are. You're a hell of a pair.'

She laughed sibilantly. She said: 'I think you're right . . . what a wicked pair we are!'

Callaghan went on: 'You fell for Donelly. When he proposed marriage to you, you liked the idea. Here was the first man, in spite of all your experience and *affaires*, that you had ever really fallen for. So you married him, and when you were married to him he told you the story. Now he'd got you. What good would it do *you* if Viola were dispossessed? What good would it do *you* if the truth came out? *You* wouldn't inherit because you also had broken the conditions of the Will in marrying Donelly. How he must have laughed at you.'

Again he heard the little hissing noise. She said: 'How right you are. *How* he laughed!'

Callaghan drew on his cigarette. He said: 'Well, it was easy, wasn't it? He told you the next move in the game – the idea of blackmailing Viola. That was a tough break for her, because she hadn't wanted the money. She had told her aunt the whole truth, but Miss Wymering talked her into going on with it because Sharpham was dead; because she'd never morally been married to him, even if legally she was his wife when the Will was read. So you went to Viola and told her that you had met a man called Donelly who knew the truth. You talked her into paying and she went on paying.'

'That's right,' said Corinne almost casually. 'It's a pretty filthy sort of story, isn't it?'

Callaghan said evenly: 'It's not so good. I wonder why you did it?'

'I really don't know,' she said. She paused, as if considering the matter, then: 'I suppose there were lots of reasons. First of all there was Donelly. I was mad about him.' She laughed. 'The joke is I still am. I'm still crazy about him and I *hate* him. The other thing was Viola. There's something about her that infuriates me,' said Corinne harshly. 'Oh, I know what it is. It's because she's better than I am; because she's decent and straight and good. All the time this has been going on I ought to have felt an utter bitch. She's given me things – money, cars, anything I wanted, so that I shouldn't think I'd been done out of anything.' She shrugged her shoulders. 'It only made me feel worse,' she said. 'I'm the sort of person who'd really *like* a good horsewhipping.' She laughed bitterly. 'The only person to understand that side of my nature has been my husband, and he's an expert at mental horse-whipping.'

'All right,' said Callaghan. 'This is all very well, but what's Donelly trying to do? What's the idea? He's sent another anonymous letter – a copy of the first one.'

'No!' said Corinne. '*Isn't* he wonderful? Have you ever met anything like it? He's got the most *lovely* nerve. But *lovely.* He's the sort of person who liked pulling off butterflies' wings. He's the complete and utter louse. The very *end* of everything. Tell me . . . who has he sent this letter to – not Aunt Honoria? Or was it to John Galashiels – the lawyer?'

Callaghan said: 'Neither. He sent this one to Chief Detective-Inspector Gringall of Scotland Yard, who is investigating your stepfather's death. Gringall told me so himself.'

She said: 'Slim, Donelly's idea is obvious. I told him a little while ago that Viola was getting fed up with the situation. Donelly has wanted more and more money. He's fearfully extravagant – a spendthrift. He hasn't even made money out of the Mardene Club. He just likes to have it. It gives him a sense of power. He meets women there – attractive women.' She laughed again. 'I don't delude myself that I'm the only one in his life,' she said bitterly. 'But I understand. If I were a man I'd be like that too.'

Callaghan threw his cigarette stub into the sea. He lit another one. He said: 'I've never met anyone who makes me feel quite so sick as you do. What a beastly little sadist you really are.'

She laughed bitterly. She said: 'Am I, Slim darling? How amusing! Hold on, we're going about.' She turned the launch in a wide circle. As the boat came almost broadside on, the spray shot over both of them. Corinne revved up the motor. The launch sped back towards the shore.

She said casually: 'I suppose he'd realized that Viola had pretty well had it. She was fed up with the whole thing. He's a pretty good psychologist, is my dear Lucien. He knew that if Viola got to breaking point she'd stop it. So he had to think of something else. He knew I was the sort of person who *must* have money too. Well, he's got me where he wants me. I'm his wife. If Viola were dispossessed, the estate would automatically come to me; that is unless somebody discovered I was married to Donelly. And who would there be to worry about that? No one, except members of the family and Galashiels, even knows the terms of the Will. Donelly knew that I should have said nothing; that I should have taken what was coming to me, and he knew that he'd have it – most of it. A nice, *nice* man!'

There was silence. Looking ahead, Callaghan could see the long stretch of shingle; the few houses and shacks.

Corinne cut the engine. The *Mayfly* floated placidly towards the shore. After a while she said: 'You might throw out that hook. We'll stop here. Come over and sit by me, Slim. I want to talk to you.'

Callaghan said: 'All right. I'll try anything once.' He threw the anchor overboard, moved towards the stern where she sat. She put her hand over his.

She said: 'Slim, I want you to do something for me. This is from the heart. I mean this. It's a good thing. I wonder if you'll do it. It's something I want done – that only you can do.'

Callaghan asked: 'What's that? If I can do it I will. Strangely enough, I believe for once you're speaking the truth.'

She said: 'I want you to thrash Donelly just once. I want you to go to Mardene and find him in that den of his and thrash him. If you do that I'll do something for you – something you'll like very much.'

'Yes,' said Callaghan. 'And what's that?'

'She said: 'I won't tell you now, but I promise you it'll be good. I can't do it unless you beat up Donelly. That must be done. If you do that, you won't lose anything.' She looked at him sideways. 'Nor will Viola,' she said. There was a pause. 'You're keen on Viola, aren't you? You're the sort of man who would be.'

Callaghan said: 'Am I? I wouldn't know. Callaghan Investigations never thinks that way about its customers.'

She smiled at him. She said: 'Like hell it doesn't. But you'll do it for me, won't you, Slim? After all, I am a client. I paid you seventy-five pounds. Well . . . is it a deal?'

Callaghan grinned. 'I'd forgotten about the seventy-five pounds,' he said. He was thinking that the situation was damned funny. He felt sure that Corinne had paid him with seventy-five pounds that she had stolen from the money for which Donelly had blackmailed Viola. Anyhow, it was Viola's money.

He said: 'I don't like Donelly. He's made a lot of trouble for me. I'm in a little bit of a jam myself with the police. He's responsible for that too. Maybe I'll get out of it, but at the present moment it looks as if I won't. All right, Corinne, I'll go and see him tomorrow night. We'll have a showdown.'

She squeezed his hand. She said: 'Thanks, Slim . . . thank you. That's fine. I promise you you won't regret it.'

Callaghan said: 'Let's go.' He hauled up the dinghy.

The morning sunshine came through the window of Callaghan's sitting-room at the Two Friars, illuminated the patterned carpet, threw a shadow across the big face of Windermere Nikolls, who sat, a whisky glass in his hand, in the corner by the window.

Nikolls said: 'So it don't look so good . . . hey? It looks like as if this time we've had it? Me . . . I am certainly not surprised. I always sorta thought that one of these days we was goin' to run inta one lovely who would put the old Indian sign on the firm, and it looks like we have done it in a very big way. So what happens now?'

Callaghan, slumped in the big armchair, his feet on the mantelpiece, an unlit cigarette hanging from the corner of his mouth, shrugged his shoulders.

'The form is going to be something like this,' he said. 'That is unless something turns up and I don't see why it should. I stalled Gringall yesterday. Patricia told him that Miss Wymering was away visiting a sick friend or something like that; but that was only a stall. He'll contact her today or tomorrow. If he's in a hurry he'll find her today.'

'An' he gives her the works,' said Nikolls, finishing his whisky.

'He gives her the works,' said Callaghan. 'She tells him that she was not responsible for interfering with *any* of the evidence; that *she* didn't move any handkerchief or mess about with the revolver. Then Gringall knows it *had* to be me.'

Nikolls nodded. 'So then he gets himself a warrant under the Police Act and knocks you off,' he said. 'Just to show there's no ill feeling.'

Callaghan shook his head. 'No,' he said, 'he won't do that. Gringall's a damned sight too clever. If he charges me he knows I'll keep my mouth shut and he can't make me talk. Not until he gets me into the witness-box.'

'O.K.,' said Nikolls. 'Well, what the hell *is* he going to do?'

'He's going to make a bargain with me,' said Callaghan. 'He knows goddam well, at this moment, that I moved the handkerchief and cleaned the pistol and all the rest of it. He *knows* that. Directly the Wymering woman denies doing it he can *prove* it. Gringall is going to do nothing to me if I tell him *why* I did those things. And if I tell him *why*, I also tell him, in effect, that I thought there was a hell of a good chance of our client, Viola Alardyse, being charged with the Colonel's murder; I tell him in effect that I considered there was ample *obvious* motive for her doing so. That's all he wants. He'll have enough to advise the Coroner on the adjourned inquest and then it's up to the Coroner's jury.'

Nikolls said: 'It don't look so good for our client. It don't look so good if you tell him that, but . . .'

Callaghan asked: 'But what?'

Nikolls grinned. 'You *won't* tell him,' he said. 'You always was a sucker for a lovely. You'll keep your trap shut and take the rap rather than shoot your mouth an' put the Viola piece in bad. I know you.'

Callaghan said: 'Why not? Viola Alardyse is our client. You can't let a client down.'

'Jeez . . .' said Nikolls. 'Am I hearin' right? When I think of some of the stunts you've pulled on clients. . . .' He sighed. 'Maybe it's worth it,' he said, 'if she's payin' enough dough.'

Callaghan grinned. 'She hasn't paid anything,' he said. 'The only money we've had on this job comes from Corinne.'

Nikolls shrugged his shoulders. He poured two more drinks, gave one to Callaghan. He said: 'It looks like we're workin' for everybody. Nobody gets any dough an' you probably finish up in the can. Ain't life good!'

'It could be worse,' said Callaghan. He drank the whisky. 'Do you know where that girlfriend of yours is – Donelly's secretary?'

'Yeah,' said Nikolls. 'I got her address. She oughta be at home right now.'

'All right,' said Callaghan. 'Get into that car of yours and go and find her. Take her out to lunch; find out if you can what Donelly's movements are today – *all* day – especially tonight. Find out what time he's going to arrive at the Club. Get everything you can.'

Nikolls got up. He put his empty glass on the table; fumbled in his pocket for a cigarette. He said: 'O.K., Slim. I'll be seein' you. If she's got anythin' extra I'll come through. If not I'll be back later maybe.'

He went out.

Callaghan lit his cigarette. He began to think about Corinne. An original, a unique type was Corinne, he thought; a luscious, alluring, devilish and sadistic piece. She and Donelly would make a couple of rattlesnakes seem sweet natured by comparison. Donelly was just a heel and Corinne was a woman who could lie like Ananias and still make you believe – for the moment – that she was speaking the truth. He remembered what she had told him at their meeting at the Crown Inn. He could hear her charming, low, inviting voice mouthing soft lies . . . she'd never heard that Viola had been married . . . '*I thought that whatever happened I must do my best to save Viola*' . . . '*I want you to find out who the writer was so that we can stop him from hurting Viola; so that she can be safe . . .*'

Callaghan grinned. So that was that. And then last night. . . . A hell of a woman, thought Callaghan.

She'd admitted everything without so much as turning a hair. Admitted that she was married to Donelly; that she hated Donelly even although she couldn't get away from him; that she hated Viola. Callaghan wondered if her main trouble was not that she hated herself.

He began to think about Corinne and Donelly. A fine pair. A super pair of blackmailers. A man who could pick a type like Corinne; know that she was safe; that he had found a kindred soul; talk or charm her into marrying him, and then, having roped her like a steer, turned her into a blackmailer – a woman who was prepared to blackmail her own sister. . . . Not that Corinne hadn't had all the makings in the first place.

Now Callaghan understood. He understood why Honoria Wymering had talked Viola into keeping silent about her marriage. Aunt Honoria had got a pretty good idea of Corinne. She knew what would happen if Corinne had come into the money and Dark Spinney. Callaghan thought that Aunt Honoria had been dead right. But where had it got her . . . and Viola?

Callaghan began to think about the night before; about his trip with Corinne. His nice 'ride on the sea'. He could visualize her, in the stern of the *Mayfly*, her hand on the steering-wheel, her immense eyes looking straight ahead; an almost demure, innocent expression on her face. He remembered how her laughter had changed in tone and timbre when she had been talking of Donelly – the harsh, low, hateful laughter – when she had admitted that she hated him, loathed him, but couldn't get away from him. A sweet pair; a delightful husband and wife.

And now she wanted him beaten up. If Callaghan would only beat him up. . . . He thought he could understand that. Dominated by Donelly, the idea of someone inflicting physical hurt on him appealed to her. Some of the sadism which she had vented on Viola was now to be switched to Donelly. And afterwards . . . Callaghan grinned cynically. Afterwards she would probably commiserate with him whilst she laughed inside. . . .

A sweet woman!

Callaghan thought she was amazing. Yet last night there had been a ring of truth somewhere in the atmosphere. She had not denied or tried to duck the truth when it was thrown at her. But she had wanted something 'from the heart'. If Callaghan would only beat up Donelly that would be good. It would be a good thing. It would be a good thing for everyone.

What the hell had she meant by that one?

Callaghan shrugged his shoulders. He took his feet off the mantelpiece; threw his cigarette stub into the grate; walked to the window. He thought that there were times when thinking did little good; got you nowhere; mainly because there was nothing to think about. Nothing made sense.

The telephone rang. Callaghan strode quickly across the room; picked up the receiver. It was Effie Thompson.

'Good morning, Mr Callaghan,' she said. Her voice was prim. 'I hope you had a good night.'

'Very good night, thank you, Effie,' said Callaghan. 'What about you?'

'It was hardly good,' said Effie. 'Seeing that I slept in the office all night in the big chair in your room just in case the John Friquet call came through.'

'Good girl,' said Callaghan. 'By the way, when I get back you might remind me to talk to you about a rise some time. I think you deserve it – that is, if I'm not in jail.'

She said: 'I've heard that one about the rise before. I'm not even thinking about it. By the way, Mr Callaghan, what do you mean . . . "if you're not in jail"?'

Callaghan said: 'You never know these days.'

'So it's like *that*?' said Effie. Her voice was troubled.

Callaghan said: 'It could be. Well, what's the trouble?'

She said: 'John Friquet came through this morning. I'd have got you before, but there's been a delay on the line. Rupert Sharpham, who used to work as a dancing instructor at the Rosehill Dance Hall, is your man all right. Friquet gave me a physical description, and if you check up with the R.A.F. medicals in the Sharpham *dossier* Nikolls brought down you'll see it's the same man. There's a strawberry birthmark under the left arm and several other distinctive features.'

Callaghan said: 'Right. So it's the same man. Go ahead, Effie.'

'Sharpham is wanted by the Cape Town Police, the British Rhodesian Police, and on two charges by the Pietermaritzburg Police,' said Effie. 'He was married early in 1938 to Ernestine Rasslaer at Bond Road Registrar's Office, Cape Town, and deserted her later that year. There is one child by the marriage. The wife is still alive and is working on a farm in Hermanos, Cape Province. The wife had an order for maintenance and a committal order for contempt in the Cape Town Court. She has been trying to find Sharpham ever since he disappeared. Friquet says that this is all he has up to date. He's trying for more.'

Callaghan grinned. 'Cable him not to worry,' he said. 'That's quite good enough for me. When you cable, ask him to send me a certified copy of the duplicate certificate in the Registrar's Book. I'd like that as soon as possible – by air mail.'

'Very well,' said Effie. 'I suppose you wouldn't know when you'll be back. There's a lot of correspondence. Miss Vendayne's been through once or twice. . . .'

'I can't help that,' said Callaghan. 'I'm stuck here for a day or so. I hope to be back soon. Play everything along until I arrive.'

'Very well,' said Effie. 'And good luck, Mr Callaghan. *Please* keep out of jail if possible.'

'Thanks,' said Callaghan. 'I'll try to.'

He hung up. He stood looking at the telephone for a moment. He said: 'Well . . . I'll be damned!' He went to the cupboard, found the whisky bottle, put the neck into his mouth and took a long swig. He lit a cigarette.

There was a knock at the door. He thought: This is Gringall. This is where the trouble starts. He was wrong. It was Patricia.

She stood enframed in the doorway, a charming picture in a red and brown flecked tweed coat and skirt, shining brown brogues and a brown felt hat with a red ribbon pulled demurely over one eye.

Callaghan said: 'Come in, Patricia. What's new?'

'I've got the numbers of the banknotes, Slim,' said Patricia. She produced a piece of paper from her jacket pocket. 'Here they are. They weren't at all suspicious at the Bank. They thought it quite normal.'

Callaghan put the paper in his pocket. He said: 'Thanks, Patricia. You're a great help. Would you like a cigarette?'

'Yes, please,' said Patricia. 'I would. How is everything, Slim?'

'Not fearfully good in one way,' said Callaghan. 'That is, speaking personally. I'm expecting a little trouble from Mr Gringall.' He gave her a cigarette; lit it.

He went on: 'Where's Aunt Honoria?'

Patricia said: 'She'll be back in about half an hour's time. She's been shopping. And Mr Gringall will be waiting for her. He's been through on the telephone twice this morning. I'm afraid that there's nothing to be done about it. Is it *very* bad, Slim?'

'Not at all bad,' said Callaghan. He smiled at her. 'Just inconvenient. By the way, where's Viola?'

'She's at home,' said Patricia. 'Did you want to talk to her?'

'I shall,' said Callaghan. 'When you get back, ask her to meet me by the gate in the wood. You know the place. Ask her to be there at three o'clock this afternoon. Without fail.'

'Very well,' said Patricia. She got up; stubbed out her cigarette in the ashtray. She said: 'I'll be on my way. Don't do anything that's at all dangerous, will you, Slim. You know I'm really *rather* fond of you.'

Callaghan said: 'That's fine. I'll be very careful.'

She flashed him a smile from the doorway. She said: 'I think you're a hell of a man, Slim. I think you've *got* something.'

Callaghan grinned. 'Me too . . .' he said. 'The trouble is I'm not quite certain what it is. So long, Patricia.'

She went away.

Callaghan took the piece of paper that Patricia had brought from his pocket. He took out his note-case. He extracted from it the banknotes that Corinne had given him at the Crown Inn. He looked at the numbers. They were the same!

Callaghan smiled. Corinne had not only twisted her own sister; she'd even twisted Donelly. Callaghan imagined that the banknotes lying on the table were part of the last pay-off from Viola. The probability was that Corinne had not even handed them over to Donelly. She'd kept them. That is why she had told Viola that Donelly was pressing for more money.

Callaghan put the piece of paper and the banknotes back into his pocket. He put on his hat. He went downstairs to the garage; started the car. He drove slowly away from Alfriston along the lonely road past Pevensey Bay. He reviewed the events of the last three or four days. The pieces were beginning to fit into the jig-saw puzzle. Vaguely, the picture was beginning to shape itself.

At five minutes to three Callaghan parked his car on the far side of the small wood that fringed the hillside between Dark Spinney and the main road to Eastbourne. He walked along the bridle-path round the hill past the green-gated Dark Spinney wall, up through the wood.

Viola Alardyse was waiting by the gate. The sunshine illumin-ated the open field. It flecked her pale hair with golden shadows. She was wearing a grey Oxford flannel frock. A light camel-hair coat hung over her shoulders. Callaghan thought: A hell of a woman. Whatever it is I think it's been worth it.

As he approached her she smiled. She said: 'Good afternoon. You don't look unhappy, but then you never do. You're rather like a smiling oasis in a rather gloomy desert.'

Callaghan said: 'That's the first time I've been called an oasis, but I accept the compliment at its face value.' He went on: 'I've got some shocks for you – some shocks and maybe a bit of good news. I want you to know what the position is just in case I should have to depart suddenly.'

She raised her eyebrows. He thought he had never seen such lovely eyes. Their translucence was almost dazzling.

She said: 'But you're not going away? I shouldn't like that.'

Callaghan said: 'No?' He was thinking to himself that his only reason for making a quick exit would be Chief Detective-Inspector Gringall. He said: 'Tell me why you wouldn't like that.'

She turned her head away; looked over the gate across the open field to the woods on the other side. She said slowly: 'I don't really know. I've been unhappy for a long time – fearfully unhappy for the last five or six days. Strangely enough – and I don't know what my reason is for saying this – the one bright spot in my mind seems to be associated with you.'

Callaghan grinned. 'So I'm not only an oasis in the desert, but I'm a bright spot in your mind. I'm beginning to think that you don't hate me as much as you used to.'

She looked away. She said: 'I don't hate you.'

Callaghan said: 'Prepare yourself for a shock. The idea that you were ever Mrs Rupert Sharpham is entirely wrong. You never were. The idea that you broke the conditions of your mother's Will is also wrong. You never broke them. You are rightfully the mistress of Dark Spinney and all that that means. And how do you like that?'

She looked at him in amazement. She said: 'But what does this mean? This is ridiculous. It can't be true.'

Callaghan said: 'It is true. There's one very good thing about this. It was awfully lucky for you that war started when it did, and that Sharpham went into the R.A.F.; otherwise you might have lived together as man and wife. You wouldn't have liked that.'

She said: 'Listen, I'm fearfully anxious and curious about all this. What does it mean?'

Callaghan said: 'In 1938 Rupert Sharpham was employed as a dance instructor at a place called the Rosehill Dance Hall in Cape Town. Early that year he married a woman called Ernestine Rasslaer. She's been looking for him ever since. There is one child by the marriage. She's working on a farm in Hermanos, Cape Province. That means to say that his marriage with you in 1939 in Kensington was bigamous. It doesn't exist. No man can marry two women.'

She said: 'My God!' She leaned against the gate. For a moment Callaghan thought she was going to faint. He was glad when she decided not to. She said quietly: 'But this is wonderful . . . *wonderful!*'

'It's not too bad,' said Callaghan. 'It settles all sorts of points.'

She asked: 'What's to be done about this? Something must be done. Are you certain?'

'Quite certain,' said Callaghan. 'I got the complete R.A.F. records on Sharpham yesterday, including all his medicals. I had a physical description from my Cape Town Agent John Friquet. The Sharpham of the Rosehill Dance Hall in Cape Town and the Sharpham you married and who went into the R.A.F. are the same man. I've asked Friquet as a matter of form to send a duplicate copy of the marriage certificate by air mail. When we get that we'll get the Kensington record cancelled. Anyhow, you're still Miss Alardyse.'

She said: 'I think you're rather a wonderful person.'

Callaghan thought of Gringall. He said, his tongue in his cheek: 'One or two people *might* think differently.'

She looked at him intently. Her eyes were shining. She said: 'I don't care what anyone thinks. *I* shall always think of you as a rather wonderful person . . . always.'

Callaghan said: 'That's very nice. Now let's come to the bad part. This isn't going to be so good.'

Her face was serious. She said: 'Is there more trouble?'

'Yes and no,' said Callaghan. 'There's not more trouble for you. It's Corinne. Corinne, I'm afraid to tell you, although she's a client of mine, isn't a very nice person.'

She said: 'Oh!' There was a pause, then: 'I didn't know that she was a client of yours.'

Callaghan said cheerfully: 'Of course you didn't. There was no need for you to know. But when people want to consult me I always let them. Corinne was very keen to find out who'd written that anonymous letter. She had an idea but she wasn't certain. She had an idea that Donelly at the Mardene Club had written it. She wanted me to check on it. She gave me seventy-five pounds to do that.'

Viola said: 'Yes? And then?'

'I think I ought to tell you,' said Callaghan, 'that the seventy-five pounds she gave me was part of the money she got from you not very long ago to pay to Donelly. She even twisted you – her own sister. How much money did you pay?'

She said in a low voice: 'Four hundred pounds.'

Callaghan said: 'The probability is she kept a hundred. Anyhow, the seventy-five pounds she gave me was part of that money. I checked up the notes with your bank. I've been assisted by Patricia. A good little girl that.'

Viola said: 'Patricia's a darling. So she's been helping you?'

Callaghan nodded.

She said: 'It seems that when you're not working for the Alardyse family they're working for you.' She laughed. 'I wonder which of us *isn't* your client.'

Callaghan said: 'I have broad shoulders and I like a lot of clients.' He went on: 'The worst is yet to come. Corinne is married. She's married to Donelly. She's been married to him for some time.'

Viola leaned against the gate. She looked unutterably shocked. Her face was white. She said: 'You mean . . .'

Callaghan said: 'I mean just that. Here is the story: Rupert Sharpham – the man you believed was your husband – and Lucien Donelly were friends together in the R.A.F. They were flying together when the plane was shot down. They crashed. Donelly was fairly badly injured. Sharpham got away with it. They were taken by the Italians and put into a prisoner-of-war camp. Well, under such conditions men talk to each other. They couldn't have been in that camp very long when Sharpham received your letter – the letter you wrote to him which told him that as a result of your marriage to him you would lose your inheritance except the three hundred and fifty a year. He told Donelly this. The one thing he omitted to tell Donelly was that he was already married to the woman in South Africa. Some time after this Sharpham and Donelly planned to escape. Sharpham was killed in the process. Donelly came back to England in possession of a very nice little piece of information. He had to have further medical treatment, and I have no doubt that he wangled that he was sent to the Convalescent Home at Herst-monceux. You understand so far?' asked Callaghan.

She nodded. 'I understand perfectly,' she said.

Callaghan went on: 'Then he had another bit of luck. He met Corinne, who was working there as a V.A.D. You can imagine the rest. This Donelly is pure poison. He's a charming, delightful, fascinating and attractive scoundrel – a really bad hat.' Callaghan smiled at her. 'In point of fact he's very nearly as bad as Corinne. I think it was rather natural that they should fall for each other. They did. But Donelly wasn't taking any chances. Once he was married to her the rest was easy. So they got married. When and where I don't know, but I know they were. After the marriage, when Donelly had had a chance of seeing how much Corinne disliked you, he told her the story and they began to blackmail you. It was a joint affair. Don't believe for one moment that Corinne was just a go-between. She was in it up to the hilt, and she liked it. Then, as time went on, his demands got bigger, but I take it that by this time Corinne had begun to twist Donelly. She was sticking to part of the money before she handed it over. Donelly became dissatisfied. He began to distrust her and wondered what was going on. What could he do? There was one very simple and easy way in which he could protect himself. He took it.'

She asked: 'What was that? What could he do?'

Callaghan said: 'Isn't it obvious? He wrote that anonymous letter to your stepfather. He knew what the result of that letter would be. Your stepfather would have to take action. You would be forced to renounce your rights in the estate and those rights would go to Corinne. Realize that nobody, with the exception of one or two people who weren't even interested, knew that she was married to Donelly. Then Donelly had her where he wanted her. At any moment he could give her away in the same way as he thought he was giving you away. In other words, he intended to become a sleeping partner for life in the Dark Spinney estate. Altogether,' said Callaghan, 'not a bad scheme. But it just didn't work out.'

She said: 'All this sounds almost incredible.'

Callaghan nodded. 'The truth always does sound like that,' he said. 'But that's how it is. It clears up one or two points, but we're not out of the wood yet.'

She said: 'I think you've been wonderful. How I hate myself for having disliked you at first.'

Callaghan grinned. 'I don't mind being disliked at first. I think that's rather nice. Somebody said that hatred was akin to love.' He lit a cigarette. He said: 'I've got to go.'

She asked: 'What are you going to do now? I want to know. Tell me what is the next thing?'

Callaghan grinned. He said: 'The next thing, I think, is for me to keep out of the way of Chief Detective-Inspector Gringall. He's not particularly fond of me at the moment and I'd hate anything to happen to me which would prevent me carrying out this investigation to its logical conclusion.'

She said: 'Slim, what do you mean? What have you done?'

'Nothing very much,' said Callaghan. 'But you know English policemen have a very old-fashioned idea against having evidence interfered with, red herrings being drawn all over the place and general obstruction from private detectives. They don't like it. Do you blame them? I don't.' He went on cheerfully: 'You know, this isn't the first time I've been up against Gringall – not by a long way. There have been other cases – other little businesses – and he's got a good memory.'

She said: 'I see. So it's like that?'

'It's just like that,' said Callaghan. 'The other thing is that Gringall's rather annoyed with this case. He can't get anywhere. He's a very good policeman, too. I don't know what the country would do without policemen like Gringall. However,' he went on, 'I've got an idea that unless I'm very lucky it might be a good thing for me to keep out of his way for a bit. But don't worry, I shall be in the neighbourhood.'

She nodded. She said: 'I understand. Is there anything I can do? Will you keep in touch with me? I'd hate not to hear from you.'

'Don't worry,' said Callaghan. 'I shall be in the neighbourhood. In the meantime, *au revoir*.'

She held out her hand. She said: '*Au revoir* for the moment. I shall be thinking about you.' She smiled. 'God bless you, Mr Callaghan.'

Callaghan laughed at her. He said: 'If you talk like that I shall burst into tears.'

He went away. She stood leaning against the white gate, watching him as he threaded his way between the trees. She wondered if he would look back.

She was disappointed when he did not.

Nikolls was sitting in the bar parlour of the Two Friars when Callaghan went in. He got up, walked to the bar; ordered a double whisky and soda; brought it back to Callaghan.

'Me . . . I go for the country,' said Nikolls. 'They got more whisky here than you get in London an' the air tastes good. You can drink a helluva lot more. I reckon I'm a child of nature – a hick.'

Callaghan said: 'All you need is straw in your hair.'

'Yeah,' said Nikolls. 'Maybe I'll have that in a minute, too. Me . . . I'm worried on account of a dream I had last night. A lousy dream it was. I dreamt that they threw you in the can. Maybe it don't mean a thing; maybe it was the lobster . . . if you get me?'

Callaghan said: 'I hope it was the lobster and not a presentiment that's going to come off. Did you get a line on Donelly?'

'Yeah,' said Nikolls. 'There's a big night on tonight at the Mardene – an extension. They go on until midnight. The babe reckons that Donelly won't show up until eleven o'clock. She's got an idea he's goin' into Brighton. But she reckons he'll be back by eleven so's to be there when the joint closes. Then he does the cash an' checks the doings generally, an' goes to bed. That's what she *thinks*.'

Callaghan nodded. He drank the whisky. He said: 'I suppose you've got a date with her tonight?'

'Yeah,' said Nikolls. 'Sort of . . . if you get me. If there's nothin' doin'.'

'There won't be anything doing,' said Callaghan. 'Nothing that matters. But be around tomorrow morning. There might be something then. Come and see me at ten o'clock.'

'O.K.,' said Nikolls. 'I'll be along.' He went away.

Callaghan lit a cigarette. He left the bar, walked slowly along the passage, up the stairs to his sitting-room. In his mind there was a definite idea that something was going to break . . . *something*. His brain was vague with all the possible implications of the word.

He opened the door of the sitting-room. Gringall was standing in front of the fireplace, smoking his short pipe. The pipe was hanging from the front of his mouth; his hands were in his pockets. He seemed deep in thought.

Here it is, said Callaghan to himself. This is where the fun starts. He wondered just how tough Gringall was going to be.

Gringall said: 'Hallo, Slim. I've been waiting for you. I thought you'd be back fairly soon. I s'pose you wouldn't have a drink?'

Callaghan thought: What's the idea . . . what goes on? What's he trying this time? He said: 'Of course.' He went to the cupboard, produced the bottle, a syphon, tumbler. He began to mix the drinks.

Gringall said: 'I feel I almost owe you an apology, Slim.' He took the glass that Callaghan held out, drank with satisfaction.

'And what do you have to apologize to me for?' Callaghan asked.

Gringall knocked out his pipe on the grate. He put it on the mantelpiece behind him to cool down. He said: 'You know. You know perfectly well that I thought you were lying about not having interfered with the Colonel's body and the evidence. You knew damned well that I was going to get a denial from Miss Wymering and then get tough with you. I practically told you so.'

Callaghan said: 'I know you did, but I don't have to take everything you say seriously.' He thought: What the *hell* goes on?

Gringall drank some more whisky. 'I take it,' he said, 'that you had a pretty good idea that it was Patricia Alardyse who took the handkerchief and generally messed about with things. I suppose you guessed that?'

Callaghan grinned. He thought: Patricia, you *pearl*! What a girl! He said: 'I don't go in for guessing. How did *you* find out?'

Gringall said: 'If I'd thought about it sufficiently, I should have considered it a possibility before today. You see, quite naturally, I've gone into the characters of most of the members of the family. Well, Patricia, it seems, is rather given to being theatrical. She's a great film fan and seems to spend most of her time giving bad imitations of her favourite stars. She's got an overdeveloped sense of the dramatic. It's just the sort of thing she *would* do. Just stupid, silly *theatre*.'

Callaghan nodded. 'Did she admit it?' he asked.

'She did,' said Gringall, 'and she was damned scared too, I can tell you. I went there today and had a long talk with Miss Wymering. I talked about her going out to have a look at the body. She said she hadn't moved or touched anything; that she was terribly shocked and wanted to get away as soon as possible. She had the vaguest idea of what anything looked like. All she could remember was the horror she had of seeing her brother-in-law lying there like that.'

'Of course,' said Callaghan. 'It must have been a hell of a shock for the old girl.'

Gringall finished his whisky, put the glass down on the table. He picked up his pipe, began to refill it.

He said: 'I told her that *somebody* had messed about with things, and that that somebody must have had a reason for doing so. I told her that the only two people who had seen the body since the time that Sallins discovered it were herself and you; that if she hadn't done it you *must* have.'

Gringall grinned apologetically. 'I was wrong of course,' he said, 'but I think I was entitled to think that. I've known you tamper with evidence before now just because it suited your book. However,' he went on, 'she said she didn't see why *you* should have been interested in moving anything. I told her that *that* wasn't the point. The point was that if she *hadn't* you had; that as she'd denied doing anything irregular I was going to take a tough line with you about it.'

'I see,' said Callaghan. 'And then what?'

Gringall laughed. 'Then the door opened,' he said, 'and the minx Patricia, as white as a sheet, and giving a bad imitation of Theda Bara in the old film days, made a heavy entrance. She'd been listening to my conversation with her aunt at the keyhole, and she was scared *stiff*. She stammered and stuttered and eventually admitted that she'd moved a handkerchief that was by the Colonel's body. It was one of her own handkerchiefs with her initials on it. She'd lent it to her stepfather a week before to clean his glasses with when the laundry had failed to arrive. Also she remembered having handled the pistol when the Colonel was showing it to her some weeks ago. Her great fear was that with her fingerprints on the pistol – the little idiot hadn't realized that someone else's fingerprints *must* have been superimposed over *hers* – and her handkerchief near the body, she might be suspected. So she wiped off the pistol and grabbed the handkerchief and beat it. She was too scared to tell anyone, but when she heard me talking to her aunt about it she came to the conclusion that open confession was the best thing. I gave her a lecture and that's that. But it makes everything very difficult.'

Callaghan said: 'Yes . . . it would. You're practically back where you started.'

Gringall nodded. 'Ye-es . . .' he said. 'Perhaps and perhaps not. By the way, you might tell me something. I don't mind your using my name in a good cause if it *was* a good cause. What was the big idea in telling Manston of the Brighton Police that you were doing a job for *me* when you were making inquiries about Corinne Alardyse?'

Callaghan said seriously: 'I thought it would help. I had to find out about that. It worked. Corinne Alardyse has been married to a man called Donelly, who runs the Mardene Club near Rottingdean, for some considerable time. Donelly is the person who sent the anonymous letter to the Colonel in the first place and the copy of it to you afterwards.'

'You've been a busy little bee, haven't you?' said Gringall. 'I knew that Corinne Alardyse was married – Manston had already told me that when I was checking on the family. That's why he was rather surprised when you appeared and began asking questions in *my* name. He telephoned me immediately you'd gone. But how did you know about the letter?'

'The typewriter at Donelly's place,' said Callaghan. 'We checked on the letter. We got at Donelly's typist. Incidentally, Corinne was fairly certain from the start that he'd done it. She wanted to be quite certain.'

Gringall said: 'So you've been working for *her* as well. You do get around, don't you?'

Callaghan grinned. 'You're telling me,' he said. 'I didn't *have* to work for her; I thought it might be useful. I'm not very keen on her. Donelly's a damned bad type and she's worse.'

'She could be, very easily,' said Gringall. 'She was the person, I take it, who cut the telephone line the night before Stenhurst was murdered?'

Callaghan said: 'She *said* she'd cut it.'

'I wonder why she had to do that?' asked Gringall.

Callaghan shrugged his shoulders. 'The idea was that she'd overheard the Colonel talking to my office. He said he wanted to see me urgently; that he'd had a letter which was obviously worrying him. Nikolls told him he could get me later at a club. The idea was that she didn't want him to get me later at a club or anywhere else; that she wanted time to think.'

'In other words, that she wanted to find out what was in the letter,' said Gringall.

'Right,' said Callaghan. 'That's *her* story.'

Gringall said: 'And you don't believe it?'

'No,' said Callaghan, 'I don't believe it – or any part of it.'

'Why not?' asked Gringall. 'It seems reasonable.'

'Nuts,' said Callaghan. He grinned at Gringall. 'Work it out for yourself. Here she is, in the hallway, listening on the hall telephone to her stepfather talking to my office. She hears that he's received this letter. This letter which is so urgent and important and odd that Stenhurst has to start telephoning private detectives after office hours. How could she reasonably expect to gain time by cutting the telephone line? If Stenhurst wanted to come through and the line was cut he'd go out and find another telephone. Damn it, that is *exactly what he did.* His second call to me – the one I didn't get – was from the call-box on the Hangover-Alfriston road. And that's that.'

'All right,' said Gringall. 'Supposing that that *is* that. There's still the letter. She might have thought that the old man wouldn't go out and telephone. She might have thought that if she could gain a little time she might get her hands on that letter and find out what it was all about before the trouble started.'

'Nuts,' said Callaghan once again. 'Whatever old Stenhurst was, nobody has ever accused him of being a fool. You don't mean to tell me that Stenhurst was going to leave this urgent and important letter – the anonymous letter with a bunch of dynamite inside it – the information that Viola Alardyse was married – lying about the place so that she could pick it up. You don't really think she thought *that* . . . do you?'

'No,' said Gringall. 'Not now you put it like that I don't. But she might have had *some* idea that she could get a look at that letter somehow . . . you never know.'

'All right,' said Callaghan. 'You never know. Let's leave that point for the moment. The thing I'm concentrating on is the cut telephone line. She *says* she cut it. She *says* that because it suits her to say that.'

Gringall said: 'The line *was* cut. The telephone people in Alfriston told me so. It was a clean cut. Someone had to cut it.'

'Of course,' said Callaghan. 'Of course someone had to cut it. That's obvious. And it's obvious who *did* cut it.'

Gringall said: 'I'm beginning to think that for a private dick you're not so bad. Sometimes' – he grinned at Callaghan – 'sometimes I think you've got brains.'

'Somebody has to have some brains,' said Callaghan sourly. 'And anyway there are times when a private dick is in a better position than a policeman. He can do all sorts of things that a police officer *can't* do. There are no Judges' Rules for him. He can cajole, bribe, threaten, do what the hell he likes. All he has to think about is how near the wind he's sailing, and whether he can keep outside the jug and inside the law.'

'A nice little speech,' said Gringall. He relit his pipe. 'And I accept the implied compliment to the police in the spirit in which it is meant.' He grinned at Callaghan. 'Now,' he went on, 'tell me something. Who *did* cut the telephone line and why? And how do *you* know?'

Callaghan said: 'For crying out loud! Didn't you tell me?'

'What the devil *are* you talking about,' said Gringall. He put his pipe down on the table. He stood frowning at Callaghan.

Callaghan laughed. 'Listen, sleuth,' he said. 'Wasn't it you who told me that when the Colonel made his second call – the call that we know was made from the call-box on the Hangover-Alfriston Road – wasn't it you who told me that the girl at the exchange overheard the conversation; that she was able to tell you what was said? Well . . . that tells us something. It tells us that the call-box is connected *by the exchange* to the caller. But what about the telephone at Dark Spinney? The telephone there is a dialling telephone. If the Colonel was prepared to make his first call from Dark Spinney; if he was prepared to talk about the letter and wanting to see me urgently and all that from the house, why in the name of all that's holy does he have to go out and walk a quarter of a mile to make the second call which was, in effect, much less private than the first one?'

Gringall said: 'You tell *me*.'

'Because he *knew* the telephone line was cut,' said Callaghan. 'For the very simple reason that *he had cut it himself!*'

Gringall whistled through his teeth. 'You're beginning to be *very* interesting,' he said. 'Tell me some more.'

'All right,' said Callaghan. 'I will. And I'm not charging anything either! When the Colonel made his first telephone call to me, from his study, Corinne Alardyse was listening on the phone connection in the hall. She hears what Stenhurst wanted to see me about. She wants to gain time *to stop me getting any telephone call from the Colonel.* Her idea is to telephone through to Donelly and get him to fix it somehow. She goes out to do this. She intends to telephone from the call-box. And then she remembers something. She remembers that the call-box is a non-dialling one – that the call goes through the exchange. She knows damned well that there's precious little telephone business in this part of the country at night; that the girl at the exchange may hear the call – as she heard the Colonel's second call – and remember. So she goes back to the house, sneaks into the hall and telephones Donelly from there and then – '

Gringall said: 'I've got it. The Colonel listened to *her* call.'

'Right,' said Callaghan. 'He heard the tinkle that a connected telephone invariably makes when the other extension is being used. He picked up the receiver and heard her telling Donelly that he'd got to do something. He heard Donelly tell her that he *would* do something; that he would call her back and tell her what the position was. Do you get that?'

'I get it,' said Gringall.

'Corinne thought that Stenhurst was in bed and asleep. She stuck around waiting for the call from Donelly. But Stenhurst was *very* angry. He wasn't sweet tempered at any time and now he was *mad.* He thought like hell she would get a call from Donelly! He cut the main telephone connection; walked out the back way and made his second call from the call-box. Well, I didn't get that call,' said Callaghan, 'and for a damned good reason. Donelly had got cracking all right. When that call came for me at the Night Light Club I was out cold. Somebody had slipped me a Mickey Finn.'

Gringall said: 'I see. It just shows the sort of thing that happens to you private dicks.'

'I know,' said Callaghan. 'You policemen have a much better, sweeter and quieter existence.'

'All this brings us to the day after,' said Gringall equably. 'The day of the murder. I suppose you know who did *that* too!'

Callaghan nodded. 'I'm pretty certain,' he said. 'But I'm not talking. And it's no good you riding me or trying to be tough.'

Gringall said: 'I'm not saying a word. I'm just a listener in this act.'

'Like hell you are,' said Callaghan. 'But I'll tell you something, Jigger. This case is at boiling-point. You know that no crook ever commits a major crime without getting into a hell of a mess afterwards. The more they try to get out of it the deeper they get in.

'This business has come to a crisis,' Callaghan went on. 'The crux of the whole job is just around the corner. I've always followed my nose and my nose tells me that something is going to happen within the next twelve or twenty-four hours that is going to blow the whole works sky-high. All you have to do is to sit down and wait.'

'All right,' said Gringall. 'I just have to sit down and wait. What makes you think it's all over bar the shouting, Slim?'

Callaghan said: 'When thieves fall out honest men sometimes come into their own. There's a lot of trouble brewing in this part of the world. I can feel the atmosphere closing in. Be patient, Gringall. You've waited so long and it would be damned silly to spoil things by throwing a spanner in the works.'

Gringall put his pipe in his pocket; picked up his hat. 'I'm not throwing any spanner in any works,' he said. 'I'm going over to Brighton to see my old aunt. I haven't seen her for years. Perhaps I'll see you tomorrow. Then we'll talk officially.'

Callaghan grinned. He said: 'Yes, I'll see you tomorrow . . . I *hope*.'

CHAPTER EIGHT
MADAME NEMESIS

CALLAGHAN sat at the end table of the almost deserted bar at the Royal Suffolk Hotel in Brighton. He finished his seventh double whisky and soda, pondered on the stupidity of heavy drinking, walked to the bar, ordered another double Haig, carried the glass back to the table.

He was depressed.

He decided that he was just a little high. Not high enough to be pleased or excited or verbose or any of the other things that go with being really high, but just depressed. Actually, thought Callaghan, he hadn't anything *not* to be depressed about.

He drank some of the whisky; lit a cigarette. One of these fine days, he thought, he was going to cut down on whisky and cigarettes. First of all he'd save a hell of a lot of money in the course of a year, and secondly he'd get rid of that morning cough that was beginning to trouble him again. He thought it would be a good thing to have some cases where you didn't feel you had to drink in order to maintain your point of view. He thought it would be very good to have cases like that. He thought too that it would be damned improbable if he ever got any. Those nice easy sort of jobs seldom came the way of Callaghan Investigations.

He concluded that he was indulging in a little alcoholic self-pity. Something would have to be done about that. He finished the whisky, got himself another one. That was nine, he thought; he'd have one more and by that time the bar would be closing. After that he'd get on with it.

He began to think about Gringall. Gringall was going to be tough in a minute – damned tough. Callaghan was not deluding himself on that point. Never for one moment had he fallen for the idea that Gringall believed that Patricia had moved the handkerchief, or otherwise disturbed the body of her ex-stepfather. Gringall knew better. He would have checked on the whereabouts of everybody at the time of the discovery of the Colonel's body. He would have known that Patricia wasn't even around; that after Miss Wymering had seen the body she had locked the door of the pagoda and nobody had entered the place until the police had arrived. When Gringall said originally that if Aunt Honoria hadn't messed about with things then it *had* to be Callaghan, he was talking sense. He knew it and he knew that Callaghan knew it.

But he was playing it this way, pretending that he had accepted Patricia's very helpful story, because he wanted to give Callaghan a little more time. Just in case he could still pull something out of the bag.

And Gringall was right. His attitude was that it was Callaghan who had gummed up the works in the first place. It was Callaghan who had supplied the red herrings which had adequately prevented the police from even having a chance of doing their job properly. That was all right with Gringall. Provided Callaghan paid the bill by producing the equivalent of that which he had destroyed. Gringall wanted evidence. *Real* evidence. If he didn't get it, Callaghan was going to be for the high jump. Of that there was no doubt.

He began to think about Corinne. Corinne was a very nasty piece of work. Her mind was wicked enough to be chaotic. She had all the mental versatility of an amateur sadist. She was one of those people who 'advanced in all directions', working towards an end and not caring a hoot in hell what happened to other people *en route*. Not even Mr Callaghan. Certainly not Mr Callaghan. . . .

Corinne was definitely a throw-back. Callaghan began to think about Viola. He came to the conclusion that he was *for* Viola in any event. He liked the way she walked, her voice, everything about her. She had that supreme quality of *being* something rather special; that quality rare in women; that odd something that you couldn't describe but which hit you like a steam hammer. Viola was like that and Miss Wymering was charming and well bred and decent and Patricia was young and straight and a good sport. Patricia would make a damned nice woman one of these fine days, thought Callaghan. But Corinne . . . Corinne was the end. The utter end of all things.

The bar-tender looked at Callaghan. There was no one else in the bar. He said: 'I'm closing up in three minutes' time. Would you like one for the road?'

Callaghan got up. He said: 'Why not?' He went to the bar, put down his glass, watched it being refilled, drank the whisky in one gulp. He said to the bar-tender: 'Is there a telephone?' He put a pound note on the counter.

The man said: 'There's a box down the corridor.'

'Thanks,' said Callaghan. 'You can keep the change.'

He went out of the bar, along the corridor into the callbox. He dialled the number of the Mardene Club. His strap-watch told him it was just eleven o'clock.

A voice came on the line. It said: 'Yes . . .?' It was a peculiar voice, high pitched, incisive, oddly sibilant, Callaghan thought it sounded like the voice of a pansy.

He said: 'Is Mr Donelly there? I'd like to talk to him.'

'He's not here,' said the voice. 'Hell be here at twelve o'clock. But he won't see anyone then, and I doubt if he'll even talk to you on the telephone. The Club closes at twelve.'

Callaghan said: 'Maybe. But he'll talk to me and like it. My name's Callaghan. You might tell him. I'll call through again.'

'Very well,' said the voice. It sniggered. 'Fearfully thrusting, aren't you?' it said. 'Awfully he-man and all that sort of thing.'

'Why not?' said Callaghan. 'Don't you like it?'

He hung up.

Outside the night air was cool and refreshing. The moon was full and a breeze came from the sea. Callaghan walked round to the Pavilion where he had parked the car. He got into the driving seat, lit a cigarette. He sat there for a quarter of an hour smoking. Then he started the engine, let in the gear, moved slowly away towards the Eastbourne Road.

The clock of Hangover church struck twelve. Callaghan, who had stopped the Lagonda on the grass verge just before he came to the call-box on the Hangover-Alfriston road, got out of the car, threw his cigarette end away, and went into the call-box. He put the two pennies in the box, gave the operator the number of the Mardene Club. She had a nice voice. He wondered if it was the same girl – the girl who had listened to Stenhurst's conversation with the Night Light Club. Callaghan thought that this telephone-box, a red kiosk on a lonely country road, might well be considered historic in a small way.

The same high-pitched incisive voice answered him. It said: 'Hallo, would that be the charming Mr Callaghan?'

Callaghan said: 'It would. Is Donelly there? Tell him I want to speak to him.'

'All right,' said the voice. 'But you wouldn't be rough about it, would you?'

Callaghan waited. A minute passed. Donelly came on the line.

He said: 'Hallo, Callaghan. It's nice to hear from you again. How are you? I like talking to old friends.'

Callaghan said: 'I'm glad about that. I want to talk to you.' His voice was pleasant.

Donelly said: 'Well, actually I wanted to go to bed. I've had a hard day today, but if it's important . . . Anyhow I'd like to see you. Come round and have a drink.'

Callaghan said: 'Thanks. It is important in a way. I've got some money for you.'

Donelly said: 'No!'

Callaghan could visualize him smiling. 'Now I wonder what money that would be.'

Callaghan said: 'I'll tell you. It's some money Corinne forgot to give you the last time. It's seventy-five pounds that somehow got stuck in her hand-bag.'

Donelly laughed – a carefree laugh – the laugh of a man who had nothing on his mind. He said: 'Well, if that doesn't beat cock-fighting. So the little so-and-so held out on me?'

Callaghan said: 'Yes. But not really. She's repented as you can see.'

Donelly said: 'You know, there are moments when Miss Corinne Alardyse is an extremely wise girl, as well as being a beautiful one. When shall I expect you?'

Callaghan said: 'I'll tread on the gas. I'll be with you in about twenty minutes.'

'All right,' said Donelly. 'I'll be here.'

Callaghan hung up. He came out of the box. The slow drive to Alfriston had cleared his head. He felt rather like a prize-fighter entering the ring on his toes. He thought: This is it. This is where it goes one way or the other. He got into the car.

On the road he pushed the accelerator down to the floor-boards. The Lagonda sped towards Rottingdean.

It was twelve-thirty when Callaghan drove the car into the shadow of the bushes on the dirt road leading past the Mardene Club carriage-drive. He locked the car, walked along the road, turned into the carriage-drive. His hands were in his pockets. He was relaxed, almost cheerful. He walked slowly up the steps, rang the bell under the pillared portico. He waited. A minute passed and a light went on in the hall. The door opened.

George, his broad face smiling, stood framed in the doorway. He said: 'Well . . . well . . . if it ain't that pip, Mr Callaghan. How're you going, Sir?' He grinned at Callaghan cynically.

Callaghan said: 'I'm going very well. Where's Donelly?'

'He's waiting for you,' said George. 'Come this way, Mr Callaghan. Welcome to our happy home.' He grinned again, re-closed the front door, locked it, bolted it. Then he led the way down the passage.

Callaghan followed him into Donelly's room. Donelly was sitting behind his desk. He was smoking a cigar. He wore a black velvet double-breasted smoking-jacket. His shirt and collar were of white silk, his evening bow of black watered silk. Leaning up against the wall beside the fireplace was a young man. He was a tall, broad-shouldered, white-faced young man. His eyes were rather close together. His lips looked as if they had been painted. His face wore a peculiar smirk.

Callaghan said: 'Good evening, Donelly.'

Donelly said: 'Good evening, Callaghan. I'm glad to see you. This is my assistant – Mr Eustace Villet. We call him Eustace for short.'

Callaghan said: 'I suppose he's the sissy who spoke to me on the telephone.' He said to Villet: 'Eustace, you must learn to be polite when you're talking to people, otherwise one of these fine days you're going to get hurt.'

Eustace said, in the same incisive high-pitched voice: 'Really! I wonder who's going to hurt me'

Callaghan said: 'I will probably. I'd take you apart now for tuppence.'

Eustace put his hand in his pocket, produced two pennies.

Donelly said: 'Now, Eustace, don't lose your temper. The trouble is you get so worked up about everything.'

Eustace said in a bitter voice: 'I hate his damned guts. Who does he think he is?'

Callaghan lit a cigarette.

'George,' said Donelly, 'don't stand about there doing nothing. Get some drinks.' He grinned at Callaghan. 'The Mardene Club always looks after its guests,' he said.

Callaghan thought there was something ominous in the words. He moved a little to the right so that he stood in front of the fireplace. George served the drinks.

There was a pause; then Donelly said: 'What's the trouble, Callaghan?'

Callaghan drank half his whisky. It was a strong long drink. He put the glass on the mantelpiece behind him. He said: 'Look, I don't think we ought to waste any words. We all know what we're talking about – at least you and I do, Donelly. The last time I was over here I told you I was a friend of Corinne Alardyse's; that I was doing a job for her. I pointed out to you that I was a friend of hers even if she didn't know it. Well, I imagine she knows it now.'

Donelly said: 'Yes? All this is very interesting.'

'It could be,' said Callaghan. He brought out his wallet, extracted the fifteen five-pound notes. He walked across the room, laid them on the desk in front of Donelly. He said: 'There's the seventy-five pounds your wife took you for on the last pay-off. I think there ought to be honour amongst thieves.'

Donelly laughed. His laughter was almost happy. Callaghan thought: This man is tough. He's got a hell of a nerve.

Donelly said: 'So you know we're married?'

Callaghan said: 'I know a hell of a lot of things. I think you're a lousy pair. You've got one redeeming feature – you're damned clever.'

Donelly spread his hands. He put his half-smoked cigar down, took a drink. He put the cigar back in his mouth, inhaled with pleasure.

He said: 'Coming from you that's rather a compliment. I don't think we've been unclever.'

Callaghan said: 'You haven't been. Most of my life I've been dealing with crooks. They usually slip up some place. As far as I can see you haven't. You've got it all in the bag. The unfortunate thing is that Corinne has slipped a little.'

Donelly shrugged his shoulders. 'Women get that way,' he said. 'You see the trouble with them, Callaghan, is that they haven't got our sense of logic.'

Callaghan said: 'You're telling me.' He grinned. 'No one in their right mind could accuse Corinne of being logical,' he said.

There was a silence; then: 'Well, thank you for the seventy-five pounds,' said Donelly. 'I think that was rather nice of Corinne to send it back to me.' He smiled. 'You're certain she did send it back, aren't you? You're certain that you're not just cashing in these few chips for some reason best known to yourself?'

Callaghan said: 'Actually you're right. I am. She didn't send that money back. She paid it to me to find out who wrote the anonymous letter to Stenhurst. This was before the copy of that letter had been sent to Gringall. I found out, but I came to the conclusion that I didn't want the money.'

Donelly said: 'I think that's very altruistic of you. May I ask why you don't want it? You're not in business for your health, are you?'

Callaghan said: 'No, I'm not in business for my health, but that money stinks a little too much for me.'

Donelly said: 'Dear . . . dear . . . money never stinks. It's a very nice thing. You can always buy something with it.'

Callaghan said: 'I'll take a shade of odds with you that you're not going to buy anything with it for long.'

'No?' said Donelly. He leaned back in his chair. 'You tell me why not.'

Callaghan said: 'Your best bet is that you're married to Corinne. If anybody suggested that you've been blackmailing Viola Alardyse for a long time you'd deny it. You'd say you knew nothing about it. You'd say that you've received sums of money from time to time from your wife, and of course a wife is quite entitled to give her husband money. You'd say you knew perfectly well that that money came from Viola Alardyse and you knew what it was. It was part of the money which Viola was giving to Corinne because she felt she'd done her out of her inheritance. Right?'

'Right,' said Donelly.

Callaghan went on: 'You wouldn't of course tell anybody that you, having discovered in Italy from Sharpham that he was married to Viola, came down in Herstmonceux for the purpose of finding out what the position was down here, and deliberately went out to marry Corinne Alardyse so that you could blackmail Viola through her. You wouldn't tell anybody that?'

Donelly laughed. 'Of course I wouldn't,' he said. 'It isn't true. Your first explanation is the right one.'

'That would be fine,' said Callaghan. 'That would be good for you if Corinne were to hold up that story, but it wouldn't be good for you if she threw it down.'

Eustace, leaning up against the wall, moved a little. He said in his peculiar voice: 'Oh, this is awfully boring. I'm fearfully impatient with all this.'

Donelly looked at him sideways. He said: 'Why don't you keep your mouth shut, Eustace? When I want you to talk I'll ask you.'

Eustace relaxed against the wall. George at the far end of the room stood leaning against the sideboard, his large hands folded in front of him. Donelly drank a little more whisky. His smile was almost permanent.

He said: 'Do you think she's going to throw it down?'

Callaghan said: 'I don't think. I know she will.' He thought to himself: I wonder how good this bluff is. I wonder if it's going to get you anywhere.

Donelly got up. He came round to the front of the desk, sat on the edge of it. He put his cigar in the ashtray. He said: 'You know, the trouble with you is, Callaghan, you're trying to bluff and you don't know what you're bluffing on. In other words, you're a man who's got two or three pieces of a jig-saw puzzle and you're missing the other two and you're trying to kid me you've got them.'

Callaghan said casually: 'That remains to be seen.'

'All right,' said Donelly, 'that remains to be seen, but I'm going to tell you something about my beloved wife. I know that she spends quite a lot of her time disliking me just a little. The rest of the time she spends being quite crazy about me – quite a lot. You're never going to get her to do anything that's going to hurt me. You're never going to get her to say anything that's going to hurt me. I'm sitting right on top of this job at the moment, and you know it. I don't give a damn what Corinne's done. I don't care what Miss Viola Alardyse says.' He grinned. 'Or should I call her Mrs Sharpham?' he said. 'Whatever anybody may do or may say, no one can do anything to me. I've got myself rather well covered. I think you're in a difficult spot, Callaghan, and you know it.'

Callaghan said: 'Yes? Aren't you forgetting one thing?'

Donelly asked: 'Such as what?'

'Such as the murder of Colonel Stenhurst,' said Callaghan evenly.

Donelly shrugged his shoulders. 'I'm not even interested,' he said. 'Incidentally, I think old Stenhurst committed suicide. That seems to be the idea in these parts. In any event whether he committed suicide or whether he was murdered, I don't even care. Why should I?' He looked at Eustace. He said: 'You know, Eustace, in a minute I believe he'll be accusing me of having murdered my ex-stepfather-in-law.'

Eustace looked at Callaghan. He said: 'The poor damned fool . . . the stupid cheap private dick.' He spat the words out.

Callaghan said, almost nonchalantly: 'One of these fine days, Eustace, I'm going to get around to you.'

Donelly said: 'Don't let's have any threats. We've talked very happily up to now. Why spoil the atmosphere?'

Callaghan said: 'Quite.'

Donelly picked up his cigar. He began to smoke again. He inhaled two or three times with obvious satisfaction. Then he said: 'I don't know why you've brought this Stenhurst death into this, Callaghan. As I told you I'm not even interested. On the day that Stenhurst died or was killed, whichever way you like to have it, I spent the whole day at Brighton, and there are about thirty people can testify to that fact. You're not by any chance suggesting that I killed him, are you?'

Callaghan said: 'No, but his death is going to make things very tough for you.'

'Really,' said Donelly. 'Because of what?'

Callaghan said: 'Because of Corinne.'

Donelly got off the edge of the desk. He threw his cigar into the empty fire-grate behind Callaghan. He said: 'Listen, I'm beginning to be bored with you. I've met your type of person before. You're a small-time dick trying to stick your nose into other people's business and make yourself a few pounds. I suppose you even thought you'd have a chance of blackmailing me. You come over here and you try to bluff me about what my wife is going to do. Corinne is going to do this . . . Corinne is going to say that. She'll never do anything that'll hurt me. She couldn't.'

Callaghan said: 'You think so?'

'I don't think so, I know it,' said Donelly. 'Listen to me, Callaghan. I know Corinne better than you do. I know what she's made of. I know what she's like. Her main trouble,' he went on with a smirk, 'is a certain sadism of which I'll give you an example in a moment. You will remember that in her last conversation with you she suggested that you might come over here and beat me up. She said it might be a good thing if you did. In other words,' Donelly went on, 'she gave you to understand that if you came over here and gave me a damn good hiding she might even talk to you about something that mattered.'

Callaghan said nothing.

'Instead of which,' Donelly continued, 'she telephoned through to me tonight and told me exactly what she'd said to you; suggested that you might be fool enough even to try to do this thing just because you are a stupid fool. And then,' said Donelly, 'she asked me, as a special favour to her, to lay something on for you. She asked me to fix things so that when you got here you should get the biggest beating up you've ever had in your lousy life. She asked that, and by God we're going to deal with you in a really *big* way. When these boys have finished with you, your own mother won't know you. You'll make a nice strip to stick on the wall. Then perhaps, when you get over it, *if* you get over it, you'll think before you stick your god-damned nose into *my* business.'

He went back to his seat behind the desk. Eustace began to rub his hands together.

Callaghan picked up his glass from the mantelpiece. He said: 'Listen, Donelly. . . .' There was almost a note of entreaty in his voice. 'Maybe,' he said, 'I've been a bit stupid over this. At the same time, there's no reason why we shouldn't . . .'

He threw the half-glass of almost neat whisky straight into Eustace's face. Eustace let out a yelp. He put his hands to his eyes. The sound had hardly died before Callaghan picked up the inkstand from Donelly's desk, slung it across the room at George. George ducked; the stand hit the wall with a crash. George, a smile on his face, his head down, came charging for Callaghan like a bull. Callaghan stepped back. As George came within striking distance he brought up his foot. It took the big man in the stomach. George gave a yelp; fell sideways on the carpet. At the same moment Eustace, mouthing obscenities, came for Callaghan.

Callaghan gave before Eustace's charge; he threw himself backwards. As he hit the floor he jerked his knee up. Eustace carried on to Callaghan by his own speed and weight, caught the knee in his stomach but not before he had sent a smashing right-hander to Callaghan's mouth. Callaghan swung his left, hit the other man on the side of the head. As Eustace fell sideways, Callaghan got to his knees and George, rising slowly to his feet, began to advance, as Eustace, lying on his side, kicked Callaghan in the face.

Callaghan got up. He spat out a back tooth. His lips, upper and lower, were cut and bleeding; a stream of blood ran down his chin on to his tie. Eustace rolled away out of reach; began to get up. He stood, holding on to the mantelpiece, getting his breath.

Callaghan said: 'Tired . . . Sissy?' He turned away to meet George.

Donelly had picked up a fresh cigar. He was still smiling. He leaned back in his chair. He said: 'Take it easy, George. There's a lot of time and mind that *judo* stuff. Use your feet.'

George began to circle Callaghan. Callaghan moved backwards and sideways. He was beginning to regain his breath. He said to George: 'Talking of *judo* how do you like this one?'

He put out his right hand; bent double. His expression and attitude denoted a frontal attack on George. George stood back and waited for it. Callaghan turned suddenly, presented his back to George; struck Eustace, who was still holding on to the mantelpiece, across the jaw with the *judo* 'block' cut effected with the edge of the hand. There was a crack. Eustace shrieked in a high falsetto, put up his hand to a dislocated jaw. Tears began to run down his face. Callaghan spun round as George came in, kicked out backwards with his left leg, caught Eustace below the right knee. Eustace changed his falsetto to a low moan, fell into the fireplace; lay there drooling.

Donelly said: 'Let's hear from you, George.' The tone of his voice had altered. He sounded a little worried.

Callaghan said: 'Come on, George.' He spat out another – a second – loose back tooth. He squared up to George in the approved method of the boxing-ring.

George fell for it. He made a feint with his left; put up his right; then, suddenly, lashed out with his right foot. The kick was high, aimed at Callaghan's stomach.

Callaghan was waiting for it. He jumped backwards, caught George's foot, twisted it, toe and heel; threw his opponent. George fell backwards. Callaghan jumped sideways, then forwards. Now he was behind George's head. As the fallen man turned over and got to his knees, Callaghan slashed a terrific upper cut to his jaw. George went out cold, just as Eustace, using his last remaining strength, threw one of the heavy fire-dogs in the fire-place at Callaghan.

The brass fire-dog hit Callaghan on the side of the neck. He fall backwards, turned over on to his face, tried to get to his feet. At the third attempt he managed to get on to his knees.

Donelly pushed his chair backwards. He said: 'You're not bad, Callaghan. Not at all bad. Now I'm going to finish you off . . . and *how*!'

Callaghan got to his feet. He presented an extraordinary picture. His right eye was closed and surrounded by a dark patch. His neck was cut and swollen. The front of his shirt collar, tie and waistcoat were covered with blood from his cut and bleeding mouth.

He began to play for time. As Donelly came round the desk, Callaghan circled backwards round the room. As he passed George and Eustace, he carefully stepped on their prone bodies, putting all his weight on them, squeezing the air out of them.

Donelly came after him. He was cool and fresh. He said: 'What can you do? Why don't you take what's coming to you? You haven't a dog's chance. You're almost out *now* you fool. . . .'

Callaghan swallowed. His hands dropped. He groaned with pain, moved in front of the desk, fell forward, his head down, to his knees. Donelly grinned. He stepped in, his fist clenched. As he moved forward, Callaghan flung his body towards him, caught him behind the knees, pulled, and as Donelly's knees gave, pushed with all his weight. Donelly, resisting the movement, was easy prey. As he put his weight forward, Callaghan suddenly *pulled*. He smashed his head into the other man's stomach, and as Donelly, the wind knocked out of him, fell forward, Callaghan caught him on his shoulder, threw him backwards. Donelly hit the desk, fell sideways. One side of his face was badly cut by the edge of the desk. He stood, swaying a little, half-dazed.

Callaghan got to his feet. He stood in the middle of the room, looking at Donelly. He was breathing hard. George lay motionless on the floor to the left of Callaghan. Eustace, half-lying in the fire-place, his legs stretched out on to the rug, began to move. He was muttering to himself in an odd voice, swearing and whining alternatively.

Callaghan backed to the sideboard. He picked up a decanter; flung it at Eustace. The decanter hit Eustace in the face with a soft thud. It bounced against the grate, smashed into fragments.

Now Callaghan was breathing more easily, but his neck had stiffened. He could hardly move his head. His sight was limited to the vision of one eye, half-closed.

He said, through swollen, bloody lips: 'Well . . . Donelly, what are we waiting for?'

He moved forward. Donelly, recovered from his fall, advanced to meet him. Callaghan fell quickly to the floor, caught Donelly's legs in the *judo* scissor-grip, threw him sideways. Donelly fell on to Eustace. Callaghan rolled over towards Donelly. He threw a right hook towards Donelly's jaw, missed. Before he could recover himself Donelly was on him, his hands on his throat, squeezing with all his strength.

Callaghan pressed Donelly's right hand away. The room was going dark. Donelly was throttling him with his left hand. Almost unconscious, Callaghan forced Donelly's right hand to his mouth, bit with everything he had. His teeth, biting across the fingers, met at the bone. Donelly's grip loosened for a moment. Callaghan brought up his knee, flung himself sideways, taking Donelly with him. As their bodies moved, he brought up his elbow, smashed it into Donelly's face.

Donelly lay still on the floor.

Callaghan struggled to his knees. The room was going round. It became light and dark alternately. He shook his head like a prize-fighter who has taken a knock-out punch and is trying to beat the count. The room began to revolve more slowly. He got to his feet, staggered to the sideboard, fell against it. He found the whisky bottle, pushed the neck between his broken lips and drank.

He turned; stood, half-feinting, supported by the sideboard.

Eustace lay quite still in the fire-place. George, one palm flat on the floor, was trying to acquire sufficient *morale* to move. Donelly was lying flat on his back, his legs outstretched – unconscious.

Callaghan turned slowly. His neck was stiff as a board. He ached in every limb, in every muscle. He picked up the whisky bottle and took another swig. He dropped the bottle on the floor. It smashed. He watched the whisky soak into the carpet.

He moved slowly forward, husbanding his strength, moving with care. George now on his hands and knees, weaved backwards and forwards, trying to clear his vision, to concentrate on the difficult business of getting to his feet.

Callaghan muttered: 'Let me help you . . . pal.' He knelt down carefully by George's side. He steadied himself by placing his left hand on the floor. He swung his right; smashed it into George's face. The punch made a noise like a mallet striking soft wood. George toppled over slowly.

Callaghan got up. He moved over to Donelly. He stood looking at him. He saw something on the floor. He looked at it for a long time. Then, although the process hurt him, he began to grin. He mouthed through lips that were twice their usual size: 'Well, I'll be damned!'

He picked the thing up from the floor; put it into his pocket. He began to move towards the door, dragging one leg behind him. In the doorway he turned and looked at the three recumbent figures. He grinned again. He went out.

It took him a long time to open the main door at the Mardene Club. When it was opened, he pitched forward, slithered down the steps, began to lurch unsteadily down the carriage-drive. The night air, filling his lungs, hit his stomach on top of the whisky. He was half-cut, half-unconscious. He negotiated his way precariously down the carriage-way. Once he fell against a tree, bruising his ribs; once he fell into a ditch concealed by the overgrown rhododendron bushes that fringed the drive. It seemed a long time before he arrived at the entrance gates; turned left; staggered towards the spot where he had left the car.

Inside, underneath the aches and pains, the drumming in his head, the burning pain of his left ankle, the throbbing in his neck and the continuous waves of nausea that assailed him, there was a peculiar sense of elation. He struggled to concentrate on this feeling, to make it the basis of a clear series of thoughts.

Sometimes you got a break. Sometimes. . . . Well, he had a break now. Definitely a piece of luck. Only one thing could have told him . . . one thing . . . and that thing had happened.

He fell against the side of the Lagonda, straightened up, put his hands on the top of the car to steady himself, drew great breaths of the night air into his lungs. His mind became clearer with each minute. After a while he sat down on the running-board of the car, on the near side, in the shadows; then he put his head between his knees for a few minutes. He sat up, leaned his head against the side of the car; began to think.

He grinned. If he felt bad, Donelly, George and Eustace must be feeling a damned sight worse. The thought brought a great deal of comfort to Callaghan. It acted as a tonic. He began to be more interested in life.

A shadow crossed the road. A swift, silent shadow. It sat down on the running-board beside him. It said: 'Slim . . . Slim . . . . what have they done to you, my poor, *poor* sweet.'

It was Corinne.

Callaghan looked at her sideways. It was necessary for him to look sideways because his left eye was entirely closed. He tried to grin but the process was too much for his cut and bruised lips. He said: 'You so-and-so. You utter and complete bitch!'

Corinne said: 'I know . . . I know . . . but it isn't true, Slim. It isn't true. It *had* to be like this. It had to be. . . .'

Callaghan muttered: 'Like hell. . . .' The words died away.

She said: 'I told you it would be good. You'll see.' She got up, put her hands under Callaghan's shoulders, half-pulled, half-pushed him away from the door. She opened the door, helped him into the passenger seat. She went over his pockets, found the car key. She walked round the car, slipped into the driving-seat. She said softly: 'You'll see, my sweet . . . you'll *see*. Just be patient.'

Callaghan was cursing under his breath.

She started the car. She swung on to the main road to Rotting-dean; then turned left towards Eastbourne. She was driving fast. She stopped the car on the Pevensey Road, a quarter of a mile from the Coastguard Cottages. She parked it in the shadow of the bushes on the left of the road. She walked round the back of the car, opened the door, slipped the car key into Callaghan's pocket.

'Come on, Slim,' she said. 'I'm going to get you right. I've a cottage here. Trust me . . . just *once* more.'

Callaghan managed a grin this time. He said: 'I'll try anything once; twice if I like it. I'll try this twice and I *don't* like it!'

He got out of the car. His neck and limbs were stiff. Each movement sent a dozen pains shooting through him. She put her arm through his. They began to walk up the path that led towards the sea; turned right towards the small, isolated cottage.

It was three o'clock when Callaghan opened his eyes. He turned his head with difficulty; closed his eyes again; tried to concentrate on what had happened. He remembered. He looked at Corinne.

She sat in a big armchair watching him. There was a spirit stove with a coffee-pot on it, on the table at her elbow. She poured out the strong black coffee, added two heaped teaspoonfuls of sugar, brought the cup to him. Callaghan took the cup in a shaky hand; began to drink the coffee. She went back to her chair.

He finished the coffee. He swung his legs off the bed, sat looking at her. He saw his torn and bloodstained jacket, tie, collar and waistcoat on the chair in the corner of the room.

He said: 'Well . . .?'

She smiled at him. Her smile was slow and languorous. She was at ease. She said: 'Listen, Slim, it *had* to be like this. He didn't trust me. He'd suspected me ever since you went there and said that you were a friend of mine even if I didn't know it. He thought I was employing you. I had to do something to *make* him trust me again. I *had* to. It was in a good cause. You understand? So I telephoned and told him you were coming. I asked him to beat you up. I told him I wanted you *hurt*; that I loathed you; that I loved him and couldn't bear him to think ill of me. Well . . . he fell for it. He'll trust me again now. Everything will be all right. He'll do what I want.'

Callaghan said thickly: 'You dear little thing. You little *sweetheart*.'

She said: 'I know you hate me. . . .'

Callaghan grinned. It was easier now. He said: 'Hate isn't the word. Tell me, you lovely thing, what was all this in aid of? What's the big idea?'

'You'll see, Slim,' she whispered. 'You'll see.' She came close to him, knelt down by his side, looked into his face.

Callaghan was still grinning. 'What a god-damned fool you are,' he said. 'I wish I could tell you how I pity you. . . .'

She drew away. She snarled: 'Pity me! What for? I don't need your pity. . . .'

Callaghan said: 'You need everybody's pity. You're just a prize idiot who's been taken left, right and centre. You haven't enough brains to come in out of the rain. Your boyfriend had you taped, hog-tied and fixed since the first time he saw you. How he must have laughed when he *pretended* to marry you!'

She looked at him with wide eyes. She said: 'What do you mean – pretended! Are you mad? Donelly *did* marry me. Once he loved me. Once. . . .'

'Nuts,' said Callaghan. 'He never loved you. If he ever loved anyone it was your sister Viola. . . .'

She made a hissing noise. She said in a low tense voice: 'What do you mean by that, you fool . . . you poor, stupid fool? What do you mean?'

Callaghan looked at her out of his one good eye. The expression on his face, due to the closed and bruised eye, was grotesque. It seemed that he was leering at her. He said, almost casually: 'He never loved anyone in his life. He couldn't. He's not made that way. But if he ever got even near the process the person who made him feel that way was Viola. *Not you.* There was a chance that he might have felt something for her.' He grinned. 'My bet is that Viola was his original love.'

'A silly stupid lie,' said Corinne. 'He never met Viola. He's never even talked to her. Donelly loved me once. . . .'

'Nuts,' said Callaghan. '*He isn't even Donelly. He's Sharpham – Viola's husband. It was Donelly who died in Italy.*'

She said in a whisper: 'Oh, my God . . .! You're making this up. It isn't true. It can't be true. . . .'

Callaghan said: 'Has Donelly – this man you *think* is Donelly – has he got a strawberry birthmark under the left arm?'

She nodded.

Callaghan said: 'He's Sharpham. He's Rupert Sharpham . . . Viola's husband. Listen. . . .'

He looked at her. Her eyes were blazing. She looked anywhere but at him. She looked like an insane creature.

Callaghan went on: 'He's Sharpham. He just reversed everything. When he and Donelly were shot down in Italy it was *Sharpham* who was smashed up – *Sharpham* who had his jaw and nose broken; *Sharpham* whose face was remade by the Italian surgeon in the prison camp.

'Then he got the letter from Viola telling him that because she had married him she'd lost her money. You can bet that pleased him. But he kept the information to himself. Then, when he was better, he and Donelly planned to escape. It was Donelly who was killed. He was killed by a shell, smashed up, unrecognizable – I've read the R.A.F. reports.

'Don't you see it was *easy* for him. He took Donelly's papers and identification and came back to England as Donelly. The report of Sharpham's death, the method of his death, *everything* came from him. The situation was made for him and he took it.

'He got away with it. No one recognized him. No one could. He came back as Donelly. He came down to Herstmonceux because it was near Dark Spinney. He wanted to see if there was anything doing. *And he found you*! What a bit of luck for him. He found you – you poor, besotted little fool. He laid for you and you fell for it. You, who had had a dozen *affaires*; who were experienced in love. You had to marry *him*. You just *had* to marry him. And you married Sharpham – Viola's husband. And I'm still laughing.'

She said in a low, hoarse voice: 'I don't believe it. *I don't believe it.*'

'All right,' said Callaghan. 'Listen to this. Sharpham was hit twice before the crash in Italy. Once in the shoulder, the second time the little finger of his right hand was shot off. Tonight when Donelly was trying to throttle me I bit into his hand. His little finger came off in my mouth. I found it afterwards on the carpet. *It's made of rubber.* Have a look at it.'

He got up, lurched over to his coat, fumbled in the pocket. He produced the thing he had found on the carpet at the Mardene Club. He showed it to her.

'Sharpham's little finger,' he said. 'The thing he's been wrapping you around for a long time. I'm sorry I can't leave it with you as a souvenir.'

He began to put on his waistcoat and coat. The process was difficult. It took time.

She sat down on the bed. She was very pale. She looked straight in front of her. After a while she said: 'Go away. . . . Please go away. . . .' Her voice was a low monotone.

Callaghan picked up his stained collar and tie. He thrust them into his jacket pocket. At the door he turned and looked at her.

He said: 'Good night, Corinne. It's not so good, is it, sweet? This is where the bill comes in.'

He went out.

She sat on the bed looking straight in front of her. After what seemed a long time she got up. She walked into the living-room, took a bottle of whisky from a cupboard, poured out a drink, drank it. Her hand was steady.

She went to the telephone, dialled a number. She waited. Then she said: 'Lucien? My darling, darling, *darling*. How I love you. I was waiting at the top of the drive tonight. I wanted to see him go by. He was smashed up and broken and *hurt*. I loved it. He could hardly get into his car, and when he drove it away it was lurching all over the road just like he was . . .'

She listened. Then: 'Darling . . . I *must* see you. And it's such a lovely night. Have a drink and then come and meet me. Ill be waiting for you at the boat . . . we'll go for a ride on the sea, my sweet. I've so much to tell you . . . so many things. . . . Yes, I know it's late; but afterwards we can go back to the cottage and sleep and sleep. I've got to talk to you . . . for your own sake as well as mine. . . . Yes . . . in an hour . . . I'll be waiting for you at the *Mayfly*.'

She hung up the receiver. She drank a little more of the whisky. She began to laugh. She stood in the middle of the room, laughing. She laughed until she began to cry.

When she had done with crying she went into the tiny bathroom and bathed her face. She came back to the living-room, and sat down at the desk in the corner. She began to think. She began to think of all sorts of stupid, silly and childish things. She remembered *nice* things that had happened a long, long time ago.

But you did a thing, and then other things happened, and it went on and on, and you had to do other things to try and put the first things right. But you didn't put anything right. You got deeper and deeper into a morass. A horrible morass. Only the sea was clean . . . only the sea. . . .

She took paper and pen and began to write. She wrote for a few minutes, read what she had written, addressed an envelope. She looked at her watch. She realized she must hurry.

She put the notepaper into the envelope, sealed it. She went out to the lean-to garage beside the cottage, started up the little car, drove it on to the road. She turned towards Alfriston.

Callaghan stopped the Lagonda outside the Two Friars. He got out unsteadily, found his key, opened the side door, walked shakily up to his sitting-room. He opened the door. Nikolls was sitting in the big chair. He was reading *How to be a Master of Women*. He looked up and saw Callaghan.

He said: 'Jeez. . . . Have you had it! Oh boy . . .!'

Callaghan said: 'Yes. . . . I walked into a door.' He took the rubber finger from his pocket, threw it on the table.

He said: 'Put that somewhere safe. Believe it or not, we've got some evidence. That's it.'

He took out his cigarette case; opened it. Then he dropped the case, crashed against the table; slithered down on to the floor.

Nikolls got up. He said: 'Well now . . . ain't that a pip?'

He went into the bedroom for the cold water jug.

CHAPTER NINE
CURTAIN

Callaghan was standing in front of the fire-place smoking a cigarette. His eye was bandaged and there was a wide strip of sticking-plaster across his lower lip. One side of his face was swollen; an immense bruise stretched from his right ear downwards towards the neck. But he was not unhappy.

Nikolls came in. He said: 'Gringall left Eastbourne at eleven o'clock. He oughta be here by now.' He fumbled in his pocket, produced a Lucky Strike, struck a match artistically on the seat of his trousers, lit the cigarette. He inhaled with pleasure.

'I'm feelin' sorta faint again,' he said. 'That before-lunch feelin'. I reckon we oughta have a drink. Anyway, we got somethin' to celebrate.'

Callaghan said: 'I suppose we have. There's a new bottle in the cupboard.'

Nikolls got out the whisky, a syphon and glasses. He mixed the drinks. He said: 'I wonder what Corinne's gonna do. That one's in a spot all right. I reckon she don't feel so good.'

'I know what she'll do,' said Callaghan. 'She doesn't scare easily.'

Nikolls sighed. He said: 'This is a helluva case. We get leg-work an' beatin's up an' no dough. The only dough we got outa this business was from Corinne an' you haveta give that back to Donelly or whatever that punk's name is. So we get sweet nothin'. I reckon we're philanthropists. We're good. As well, you mighta got thrown in the can. It ain't ethical. Nothin's right.' He finished his whisky.

Callaghan said: 'Go over to the Mardene and see if your girl-friend's there. Tell her she needn't worry about her boss getting annoyed if you go over the place. Have a look in the safe. She'll probably know what the combination is. See if you can find anything to tie the ends up.'

'O.K.,' said Nikolls. 'But that's mayhem, hey? Supposin' Donelly gets funny.'

Callaghan said: 'How the hell can Donelly get funny? Get going, Windy.'

Nikolls looked at the bottle regretfully. He sighed once more. He went away.

Callaghan mixed another drink. He stood, the tumbler in his hand, looking through the window at the sunlit sky.

The door opened. Gringall came in. He said: 'Good morning, Slim. What's happened? You look as if you've been run over by a tank.'

Callaghan grinned. He said: 'You ought to see the other fellow – the *three* other fellows. Have a drink?'

'No thanks,' said Gringall. He produced his pipe, began to fill it. He said: 'This morning, about an hour and a half ago, the bodies of Corinne Alardyse and the man Lucien Donelly were washed up a couple of miles east of the Crumbles. Does that make any sense to you?'

Callaghan nodded. 'Plenty,' he said. 'She was married to Donelly – you knew that; but she didn't know until I told her last night that the marriage wasn't legal. Donelly isn't Donelly. He's Rupert Sharpham, who married Viola Alardyse in '39. I didn't bother to tell her that the Viola marriage was illegal too. Sharpham had a wife and child in South Africa. She's still trying to find him. He married Corinne so as to get a stranglehold on her so that he could blackmail Viola with impunity. I hope the body isn't knocked about. I want to get a good identification.'

Gringall said: 'The bodies are all right. Swollen – but not too badly. You've been a busy little bee, haven't you?'

Callaghan said: 'You're telling me. This time Callaghan Investigations have got all the kicks and no ha'pence. Besides taking a chance on a police prosecution.'

'Meaning that it *was* you who messed about with the Colonel,' said Gringall. 'I knew that Patricia was only fronting for you.'

Callaghan nodded. 'I'm glad I did it,' he said. 'It worked out all right. And you've got all the evidence you want. Corinne Alardyse wrote me a letter last night. She must have driven over here and pushed it through the letter-box soon after I left her.'

Gringall said: 'What about Stenhurst?'

'She killed him,' said Callaghan. 'Personally, I think she was a border-line case – if not the *real* thing. The night Stenhurst telephoned my office he overheard her talking to Donelly on the hall telephone. And the Colonel wasn't half such a fool as they thought he was. He'd been making inquiries about Donelly and the Mardene Club for some time. That's what the trouble was about at dinner that night. He knew that Corinne was married to Donelly. When he read the anonymous letter saying that Viola was also married, the old boy got *very* annoyed. You can imagine?'

Gringall nodded. 'He would be,' he said.

'My guess is the next day Corinne got a look at that anonymous letter. She probably sneaked into the Colonel's room and read it. Immediately she got the idea that Donelly had sent it. She was dead right. She got very angry with Donelly. She intended to force a confession out of him that he had sent the letter. You can imagine the sort of pair they were. She loathed him but was attracted to him. She couldn't escape from Donelly although she hated his guts.

'That afternoon she went to the Colonel's room again and got his revolver. She loaded it and went over to talk hard sense to Donelly. She was furious with him, and probably intended to threaten him with the gun. But Donelly wasn't at the Mardene Club. He was over at Brighton with friends and she couldn't talk to him. She drove back to Dark Spinney in the early evening. She had the gun in her hand-bag. She came in through that green door in the estate wall. I imagine that as she entered the garden she saw the Colonel walking along the upper path. He'd been waiting to have a showdown with her. He took her into the pagoda and got very tough with her. He showed her the anonymous letter; told her that he'd overheard her talking to Donelly – or Sharpham, whichever you like – the night before. He wanted an explanation. And he was probably damned tough.

'I imagine that Corinne told him to go to hell. Then he played his trump card. He told her that he knew she was married to Donelly. Well . . . that didn't suit her a bit. That spoiled everything for her.

It meant that they couldn't go on taking Viola for money. Can't you imagine that pretty little scene in the pagoda?'

'Yes,' said Gringall. 'It must have been *good*!'

'I bet it was,' said Callaghan. 'Then she remembered the gun in her hand-bag. She pulled it out and let the Colonel have it, and that was that. Then she remembered something else. She remembered that when the Colonel had been showing them the gun some weeks before, they'd all handled it. It might easily be that Viola had handled it last; that Corinne would remember that her fingerprints would be the top ones on the gun. And it might easily be that she also remembered that she'd had gloves on all the afternoon from the time she took the gun from the old boy's room, before she went out looking for Donelly, to the moment when she'd killed him.

'That suited her very well. She dropped the gun, left a handkerchief of Viola's half underneath the body, slipped out of the garden and drove off back to Eastbourne or somewhere by the back road. And no one saw her. She got away with it. Having stopped Stenhurst's mouth, and knowing that it *looked* – having regard to the anonymous letter – that *Viola* had all the motive in the world for knocking off Stenhurst, she felt all right about that. But now she was concentrating on Donelly. She wanted to get proof that he'd sent the anonymous letter. If it *was* he, she knew exactly what he was playing for. She didn't like that. So she gave me seventy-five pounds to find out. She thought you could buy anything with seventy-five pounds.'

Gringall grinned: 'But not Mr Callaghan?' he asked.

'Not this time,' said Callaghan. 'And not for seventy-five pounds. When Callaghan Investigations goes in for funny business it wants *real* money.'

He lit a fresh cigarette. 'She admits killing Stenhurst in her letter. She admits everything that we know. It wasn't a bad letter, having regard to the fact that she must have been hopping mad when she wrote it. She must have telephoned Donelly after I left her. She knew he'd fall for her line because she'd sold me out and warned him that I was going over there to get rough with him. She had to make him feel that he'd got her where he wanted her once more so that she could get him into that boat and turn it over when they were well out to sea. She was pretty good with that boat. She gave *me* a demonstration not so long ago.'

Gringall said: 'You *do* get around, don't you?'

Callaghan grinned at him. 'We don't start anything we don't finish,' he said. 'I've put her letter in an envelope, with Sharpham's rubber little finger – he got his own shot off – and a few notes I've made. There it is on a plate. And there's no charge.'

Gringall said: 'I think I'll have that drink now.' He went on, as Callaghan poured out the drink: 'You'll have to stay over for the inquest next Thursday, Slim. You're a witness. There'll be a legal point as to whether she was of "unsound mind" when she turned the boat over. The Stenhurst killing will be "wilful murder" against her.' He picked up the envelope; drank the whisky. He said: 'Well . . . I'll be on my way. So long.'

Callaghan said: 'So long. . . .'

Gringall went out.

The telephone rang. It was Effie Thompson. She said: 'Mr Callaghan, Miss Audrey Vendayne's been through again. She says Devonshire is looking too lovely, and would you care to go down there this weekend or next weekend.'

Callaghan said: 'Next weekend maybe. I can't go this week. I've got an inquest on Thursday.'

'You sound awfully funny,' said Effie. 'As if you've got something in your mouth.'

Callaghan said: 'I'm glad you think it *sounds* funny. I'm one side tooth and two back teeth short. Call through to Miss Vendayne and tell her I'll telephone her at the end of the week.'

'Very well,' said Effie.

Callaghan hung up. He went to the window; stood, looking out on the peaceful sunlit street below.

The Coroner said to the Jury: 'Gentlemen, I am very sorry that you've been kept so long over this unfortunate case. Before I discharge you I wish to say that I have been asked by Chief Detective-Inspector Gringall of Scotland Yard to thank Mr Rupert O'Brien Callaghan of Messrs Callaghan Investigations for the great assistance he has rendered to the Police in the investigation of the three deaths on which you have already brought in your verdicts. Gentlemen, you are discharged.'

Outside, in the sunshine, Callaghan saw Gringall. He said: 'Well . . . what are things coming to? When the Police start thanking Callaghan Investigations. What goes on?'

Gringall said: 'Eyewash, Slim . . . just eyewash. And let me give you a tip. You've got away with it again. But one of these fine days you're going to take one chance too many and you're going to get yourself in a hell of a mess.'

'No?' said Callaghan. 'Well . . . when I do I'll come and see you about it.' He grinned. 'Remember me to the Chief Commissioner,' he said.

Gringall shook his head sadly. He walked down the street. Callaghan went over to his car, started the engine, drove slowly away towards Alfriston.

The sun was bright and hot. Over the sea the gulls broke the silence of the countryside. Callaghan thought that by and large life could be a great deal worse.

In front of him, just past the junction of the Hangover-Alfriston road he could see the green door in the Dark Spinney wall. As he passed it the door opened. Viola and Patricia Alardyse came out.

He stopped the car. They came towards him. Patricia said: 'Good morning, Slim. Viola and I have been talking about you. I've told her that it's no good worrying about what *has* happened. The thing is to get as much happiness out of life as possible. I'm right, aren't I?'

Callaghan nodded. 'Absolutely,' he said. 'It's a sin to be unhappy on a day like this.'

Patricia went on: '*I've* got to walk to the village. I'll be seeing you, Slim. We thought – at least Viola thought – that you might like to stay down here for a bit and take a rest. We'd love to have you at Dark Spinney. I think it would be *terrific* fun. Viola thinks so too, but she doesn't like to say so. She's having one of her ultra-modest fits this morning.'

Viola said: 'Patricia, *how* can you say such things . . .?'

Patricia said: 'You'd be surprised! And I can say a lot more if necessary.'

She went off. She laughed at them over her shoulder.

Viola said: 'Will you stay, Slim . . . please! Well none of us ever be able to tell you how grateful we are. You've done so much. . . . Aunt Honoria says she'll never forgive you if you don't stay.'

'That would be terrible,' said Callaghan. '*Not* to be forgiven by Aunt Honoria. So I'll stay. Thank you very much. But I'll have to telephone my office. Get into the car – we'll do it from the call-box up the road.'

She got into the passenger-seat. Callaghan swung the car round. It disappeared round the bend of the road.

Patricia came out of the doorway where she had been hiding. She crossed the road, went through the green gate. Miss Wymering was coming towards her down the gravel path.

She asked: 'Is Mr Callaghan going to stay?'

'You bet,' said Patricia. 'He's just driven off with Viola.' She sighed. 'That girl doesn't know what's coming to her,' she said.

'Whatever *do* you mean?' asked Miss Wymering.

Patricia said primly: 'I mean that Viola's in a spot. When Slim first came down here she was *tough* with him. But *tough*. She was going to have him thrown out. Remember what she told us last night. And now look at her. Every time she looks at him her eyes shine like stars.'

Patricia sighed. 'That girl's for it,' she said. 'If he doesn't stop that car at the corner of the wood and extract some sort of payment on account he's not the man I take him for.'

'But,' said Miss Wymering, 'I don't know what you mean. Mr Galashiels has sent him a cheque for a thousand pounds. We passed it yesterday. It's to be an estate payment.'

Patricia said darkly: 'Come up for air, sweet. I wasn't talking about *money*.'

'Goodness,' said her aunt. 'Surely you're not suggesting that after *all* this trouble Viola is thinking about falling in love and marrying?'

'I'm not suggesting anything,' said Patricia. 'And you needn't worry about Viola getting married either.'

She began to walk towards the house.

She said: 'Didn't you ever hear a gramophone record called "Love 'em and Leave 'em Joe"?'

THE END

Lightning Source UK Ltd.
Milton Keynes UK
UKHW011258240222
399185UK00001B/75